Between

Cayenne Sirois

Book Cover by Marta Dec

Editing by: CSK Editing Services

979-8-9994510-1-9 paperback

Dedicated To:

All those who have a book idea but are waiting for something,
like a sign from the universe, that you should do it.

This is your sign.

Write the book.

Prologue

They say the moment of death happens quickly.

There's no pleasant drifting into the ether, applause as everything fades to black, a deceased family member beckoning you toward a bright and beautiful light.

There isn't time to calculate your net worthiness by adding and subtracting and dividing all the happy memories, sad moments, crippling anxiety, hopeless depression, intense love, deep hatred, accomplishments, and missteps to arrive at "well, it was worth it."

That's what they say.

But I can tell you differently.

Chapter One

"Don't forget, after running errands, I'll need you back at my place so we can go over the script for tomorrow. Also, please, please don't forget to ask for light ice. I hate when my drink gets watered down. Okay, thanks girl! See you soon! Enjoy your free morning!"

Hayley's voicemail played over my earbuds while I attempted a two-mile run. I say "attempted" because I'm not in any kind of shape, but I run to burn off aggravation.

Hayley had given me the morning "off" but just had to call—early so she didn't actually have to talk to me—to tell me how to do my job, which she *knew* annoyed the hell out of me. I was extremely competent and irreplaceable to her, and now I was annoyed which meant there was a good chance we'd get into an argument later on when I arrived for work.

Early in my life, my dad told me, "if you don't learn to argue, you'll never be heard in this world."

So I made sure I was always heard.

I grimaced as I went over the errands I had to run for Hayley: pick up a matcha latte, return sponsored items, retrieve her dog, Snickers, from doggie daycare, and do her grocery shopping. Being the personal assistant to a well-known influencer was supposed to have been a temporary gig but I had been doing it for years and it was boring as hell and wearing thin.

Hayley's pretentious attitude was especially irritating. She amassed a large social media following by sharing questionably relatable videos about dating, raw vegan meal preparation ideas, and daily gratitude yoga exercises. In most of her videos a camera was aimed ever so subtly at her ass. She was always sure to give her followers tips on how to build glute muscles like hers while I had her plastic surgeon's number saved on my phone so I could schedule her lifts and tucks.

My phone buzzed and I fished it out of my pocket to see a reminder for "M and H Collab filming!!!" shared with me by, guess who. I rolled my eyes as I pictured the "M" in that joint effort—a blue-eyed, well-tanned, midnight-haired man with a bright grin for his social media followers. Dimples and a signature mole below his right eye beckoned people to follow him on his music journey.

Miles Sharpe.

He was an extremely popular singer and musician and Hayley wanted to ride his coattails by having him do a cooking video with her while he was in town for his tour. She was critical of him—behind his back, not to his face of course—and had been ranting for weeks now about "having" to work with "such a loser". I felt a little smug when she railed because I had known he was a shallow and frivolous celebrity for a while. I mean, it was obvious with the charity work he did and how it always *somehow* got picked up by the media and shared in fawning posts that made him out like an altruistic god walking among us. Please. I'm sure he showed up at some kids' hospital, did a photo or two and then booked it out of there to go party. I saw right through his act and loathed the fact I had to waste hours of my time being around him and Hayley, even if I were getting paid to do so.

I groaned as I remembered yet another job listing my mom had sent me the other day, this one for a museum curator, a position I would love but absolutely didn't qualify for anymore despite my ten year-old history degree and interest in archaeology.

In college, I had been ecstatic to go to class each day and discover something new to me, but old to the world. The idea of resurfacing ancient memories, items, bones—*anything* from the past—excited me and a job that required hyperfocus, dexterity, organization, and cataloging skills. I wasn't great at really connecting with people, but talking to others about artifacts from another time was never a problem. In fact, some of my favorite memories were of attending my professors' office hours and marveling over translated tablets, discussing our favorite artworks throughout time, and theorizing about missing links in the historical record.

When I graduated my mom threw me a party. My father had stumbled in late, buzzed, and with some new girlfriend. All he said to me was, "congrats kid, you'll be a really smart person who works at a coffee shop." My chest still tightened with pain whenever I thought of that moment.

After graduation, I made some attempts at job applications, fumbled a few interviews with some local museums, and then ultimately gave up. Dad vocalizing my fear of never achieving what I desired put up a stumbling block in my brain that I just never seemed to get around. Mom constantly sending me job postings only reminded me of the failure my life was turning out to be.

During our weekly call two days ago my brother Aspen said, "Mom means well, don't let it get to you. It's not like she's always going to be there to give you a hard time."

I responded with, "Well, she could maybe start taking the unwanted energy she focuses on me and shift it towards you. I may not be the saint who spends time resuscitating the poor children of the world, but I still do things that...matter."

"I'm a pediatric doctor, stop playing dumb and making fun of me about it. She gives me plenty of grief for not being married, so you can stop whining and just deal with it like I do. Go be mad at Dad if you want to take your shit out on someone."

That struck a nerve, because he knew I cut Dad out of my life a couple years ago because I couldn't manage my unresolved anger at him for leaving Mom and us. Then Aspen asked me about the Miles and Hayley collaboration and—for the twelfth time, I swear—whether I could give him her number, especially now before Miles swooped in. I hung up on him.

I let out a long, audible sigh at my life, at my work situation, at myself. *Pathetic*.

Giving myself a mental shake, I tried to pull myself back into the moment of my run. I tried *not* to think about how every burning breath made me want to die and *really* tried to ignore the nagging cramp in my side. I looked down at my fitness watch and felt my shoulders slump. I was only three quarters of a mile in.

Shit.

I glanced at the crossing countdown at an upcoming intersection just as twin beads of sweat crawled over my brow and into my eyes, stinging and burning. I squinched my eyes, trying to soothe and clear them, then opened them just enough to blurrily see eight seconds left as I stepped off the curb into the crosswalk.

Before I could fully register what was happening, cold, hard metal smashed into my left arm, there was a sickening snap, and I sprawled to my right. My left foot was wedged underneath a car wheel. What the—

"FUCK!" I screamed as I fell to the right and hit the ground. Quickly, I pushed myself up into a half-stand using my right arm and leg. With my good arm, I latched onto the grill of the offending, and rather douchey, Jeep truck that had hit me. My left arm hung at my side, feeling like it had been cleaved in two.

A shrill and panicked "HEY!" escaped me. I could see the driver, bobbing his head up and down as he looked to his left to make a right turn and I could feel the vibrations of drums, base, and guttural vocals through the truck's hood under my hand.

For fucks sake, the guy was absolutely blasting metal music.

I heard honking and looked to see some wide-eyed drivers half-opening their car doors, trying to decide if I needed any assistance.

I pounded my hand on the hood, about to scream to get the driver's attention, when the truck gunned forward again, the driver completely oblivious to what was happening. I wailed as my left foot was pulled deeper under the tire.

I fell backwards.

My useless arm burned.

A horn blared.

My temple cracked against the edge of the curb.

Sound ceased altogether.

There was pain, there was blackness.

Then there was nothing.

Chapter Two

I came to groggy awareness, my eyes fluttering open, as a scorching sensation declared squatting rights in my core. *God that hurt.* I thought I could hear a faint beeping, like an alarm of some type. *Mine? How long had that been going off? Was I going to be late for something?* Choking sobs echoed around me. I realized I was lying down so maybe I was dreaming? Trying to wake myself up and out of the dream, I squeezed my eyes shut, then opened them to see I was surrounded by an inky, purpleness...and a statue of a person stood in front of me. The statue was carved from white marble and had golden eyes and caramelized-looking veins snaking across its features. A wispy, deep indigo material pooled around the bottom of the statue and twirled up the length of its body and around its delicate forehead. I registered somewhere in the back of mind that it was the most perfect thing I had ever seen. I also registered it was breathing and that I wasn't asleep.

I was struck by a feeling of intense foreboding as a sly smile cracked through the statue's marble skin. It looked at me and whispered in a softly lilting voice, "someone always likes to sleep in."

I turned over and dry heaved. I was completely freaked out, but on the plus side, the scorching sensation inside of me had faded away by the time I stopped heaving.

After a few minutes I sat up and took better stock of my surroundings. I noticed ten people in my general vicinity, some sitting upright, others folded over, a few pacing but all suspended in the air and all looking panicked. I saw a child, likely less than ten years old, sitting cross-legged and twitching anxiously. My gaze lingered on the little boy, heart twisting at how vulnerable and alone he looked. I forced myself to look away when I noticed the tears welling in his eyes.

Turning my head in every direction all I could see was amethyst cloudiness stretching endlessly around me and the others. I looked down at the ground I was sitting on and saw there was nothing *there*. I felt the pressure of a surface against the back of my legs and under my hips, but it was as if I were floating in air.

I glanced again at the other people and realized they were being held up in the same way. *What was happening? Where were we?*

"Hello," the statue quietly addressed us. "Welcome. You have all found yourself in the Between, and I am here to see you to your next destination. Think of me as your guide between worlds, if you will, but know that you alone get to decide what happens next.

"Right now, your mortal body is in stasis—the terminology *coma* might be more familiar to you—in the Before. You, however, are in the Between, a midpoint between there and the After. To return to your body and life in the Before you must overcome some tribulations I have devised. If you are unable to complete the tribulations you will immediately take your eternal spot in the After. You may choose to forgo the tribulations and take your spot in the After now. If you choose to participate in the tribulations, you can decide at any time that you no longer wish to and move on to the After, while allowing your body to pass on peacefully in the mortal world.

"Understand me: if you succeed in overcoming all of the tribulations you will return to your mortal body in the Before, and you will have received a second chance at living your life." The statue paused for a respectful moment to let that information sink in. "Are there any questions?"

Silence held for a moment and I assumed we were all trying to process what the statue—I decided to call it Marble in my head—had just told us. And that the statue was alive. I could feel the ghost of bile inching up the back of my throat.

A deep voice sounded throughout the barren space. "Why are we here?"

"Fight!" I flinched as that startling demand echoed around me. I glanced at the others but they all had their attention turned to Marble, like they hadn't heard anything.

Marble cocked their head to the left, a weird smile on their face making my stomach churn. "Isn't it obvious? All mortals who are in stasis find themselves here. You are near death and if you want to return to life, you must earn the chance to do so. Oh, and if it was not, let me be perfectly clear: if and when you go to the After, your mortal body in the Before will die."

I stared, stunned at what they had just said. *I am effectively dead and in limbo? I exist in a stasis that will end in death unless I can make it through some tribulations? Why? Why was I here?*

Marble's honey gaze turned to me then and my strained nerves suddenly began to ease. I thought I could smell the scent of citrus drifting towards me and in my mind I saw a candle casting a warming light during a thunderstorm. I felt so calm I could have just closed my eyes and drifted away.

"Don't do this! Come back!" The voice from before broke around me and the warm serenity I had just experienced evaporated as intense pain coursed through my body for a few seconds. Wait, how could that be? I thought my body was...elsewhere. And how could I have thrown up if I didn't have a body anymore? I looked down and saw my arms and legs and shook them a little to confirm they were there. I looked at the statue, more confused than I had been two minutes ago.

Marble somehow seemed to understand my confusion, even though I hadn't voiced it aloud.

"Ah, yes, your body. As you will all have noticed, or will notice if you focus, you have corporeal form here in the Between. This form is separate from your mortal body in the Before but it too can cease to be."

Silence stretched. No one had anything to say to that little tidbit of information. Marble watched us, apparently perfectly ready to stand there forever until one of us said something.

"Tribulations?" I finally managed in a rasp.

"Yes, tribulations. Little sufferings to test your being. You see, the After is your true home and is ready to welcome you now. The After is also benevolent, however, and if you choose not to go there at this time it extends to all of you the opportunity to return to the Before and your mortal life until returning here one day."

"Okaay...and who are you?" I asked.

"Your guide between worlds."

"Yes, you said...but I mean, *what* are you?" I tried again.

Marble tilted their head to look me over. "I am an asset to the After."

"And what is the After?"

"The After is eternal rest."

I shook my head as I got to my feet. The fear and confusion that had threatened to overwhelm me started to give way to annoyance. Marble's replies didn't answer my questions. Were they an animated statue, or were they alive in some way? Were they saying the After was heaven? It seemed like it from how they described it but then why not just say that?

Marble seemed satisfied they had responded adequately, however, and now turned their gaze to each of the others in turn. Fearful expressions melted away when Marble's golden eyes rested on each person. "The After wants you to have a fair chance to return to the Before, if that is what you choose."

They stepped toward a woman who looked to be in her forties. Gaunt and bald, she had deep lines running along each side of her mouth, which seemed to be tightened in pain. As they pointed at her, the luxurious indigo material draping Marble flowed over their raised arm, covering what I assumed was their hand. It could have been a lobster claw for all I knew. Webbed frog foot. Monkey paw.

"What do you choose?" they asked.

"I want to go to the After," the woman whispered. "Please."

Marble's face broke into a bright smile. "The After welcomes you home...Melinda," they said as their hand—okay, so it was a hand—softly traced her cheekbone and a shimmering light seemed to emanate from within her.

Marble's eyes fixed on the radiant smile that spread across Melinda's face, even as the light broke through her skin.

"Thank you," she whispered tearfully. "Thank y—"

And then she was gone, only a glittery and sparkling wind left behind, which swirled in the purple air before winking out and disappearing.

Marble turned back to the rest of us. "Does anyone else choose to go to the After at this time?"

Four people moved to stand in front of them. A plump, white-haired man with distinct laugh lines quoting his eyes. A short woman with ebony skin, and mostly grey hair. Another individual, tall, with the fresh skin of youth but matted red hair and sad eyes. Last, a bronzed skin beauty who looked like she could only be thirty or so. One at a time, Marble gently laid a hand on each person and they too vanished on a shimmering breeze.

I shook with trepidation as the last two people disappeared. *They were so young*, yet ready to move on to the After. *Why?* Maybe they were sick in the mortal world and were tired of fighting to survive...Or had they somehow found Marble's elevator pitch of the After too enticing to pass up?

I asked myself what I wanted to do. I didn't feel peaceful acceptance coming over me, nothing that made me want to go on to my eternal reward in the After. But I couldn't think of anything that compelled me not to—no loved one, no friends, no unfulfilled duties I couldn't abandon. I tried to pull up the memory of someone that would be enough for me to say "no, thank you" but all that reached back to me was emptiness—and a vision of my head slamming into a curb.

"NO!" I shouted, clutching my temples as I fell to my knees and bent over, thoroughly startled and bewildered. Marble's swirling robe edged into view and I panicked. "Do *not* touch me," I yelled as I struggled to my feet.

Once again those golden eyes gazed back but neither warmth nor calm encompassed me this time. I glanced down to make sure their hands were folded in front of them and not reaching for me.

Marble smiled briefly as if to be reassuring, but I noticed one corner of their mouth fell ever so slightly as they looked at me.

"This experience is...jarring for some mortals. The After understands—"

"I don't give a *single* fuck about the After!"

Both corners of their mouth sloped sharply downwards and a crease appeared between their eyes.

"—that losing connection to your life in the Before can be..." they trailed off contemplatively. "Frightening to some."

"What do you mean by losing connection to our life in the Before?"

It was the speaker from earlier who had asked why we were here, the man with the deep voice. I looked over at him and noticed he had gleaming blue eyes.

Marble pivoted and gazed at the man serenely before delivering another shattering revelation. "As long as you remain here, in the Between, you will have no recollection of your personal memories, only your final moment of life before arriving here. You may still retain knowledge you acquired in the Before, but nothing more. As I said, you have corporeal form here but your being is now made up of whatever will you possess. Either the will to find peace or the will to fight,"—a brief glance at me—"the will to return."

So that deep void of nothingness in my brain was where recollections of loved ones and time spent with them were supposed to be. And Marble said that emptiness was merely *frightening*. A ghost story told around a campfire is frightening. The monster in the closet that needs to be chased away before a kid can sleep is frightening. A haunted house's cheap, quick scares are frightening. What Marble was talking about was grade-A *terrifying*. How was I supposed to decide what I wanted to do when I couldn't remember anything that would help me make a decision?

"And how do we know if what we return to is worth going through the tribulations?" the blue-eyed man asked.

"You do not, and will not, know," Marble replied.

"Hold on. We have to get through your tribulations just to maybe return to a life we don't know is good or bad?" I asked.

"Correct. You must choose what you will do here of your own free will, knowing you could return to suffering or happiness if you succeed in the tribulations."

"I need you!" That voice called to me again, this time with more desperation, and rattled around in my head.

"Fight. Don't do this. Come back. I need you."

Will. A choice. A decision. I didn't know if my life in the Before was something I wanted to return to, and I didn't know if there was someone to return to, but I did know one thing.

"I am not ready for the After. I want to fight," I said, my expression hardening with resolve.

"As do I," the blue-eyed man said.

"Back, I wanna go back," the little boy said in a voice full of despair.

He was joined in his choice by three others.

And so there were six of us who would fight for the chance to return, who would resist going to the After.

Chapter Three

Marble took in our solemn expressions and nodded. "As much as the After wishes for you to come home, they also understand. They only wish to nurture you to contentment, for you to be whole, but respect your autonomy to—"

I startled them as I snapped, "wonderful, let's get on with the little sufferings already."

A couple of the others gaped at me. Maybe in the Before I wasn't gifted with manners. Or patience, for that matter. Either way, I was growing tired of Marble's monologuing.

They eyed me with a tight smile plastered on their stone face, one of the caramel lines near their eyes bulging slightly. "If I may," they said, ever so politely, "I am your guide here; therefore, I need to be able to finish a statement in order to direct you to your next destination."

I looked down and toed the deep purple air beneath me, grumbling "in fewer words, preferably."

"If you could repeat that, I did not quite understand your meaning. Are you imply—"

"Hurry the f—"

"You, *shut up*," bit out the man with the blue eyes, looking pointedly at me. His tone was more civil as he turned toward Marble, "and you, continue on with your explanation of where our next destination takes us...Please."

I scowled in his direction while Marble glanced at me before turning away. I heard something like rocks being ground against each other and flinched when I realized it was them clearing their throat. "Right, thank you. Since you all have made your decisions, I will guide you to the next destination for the tribulations."

"What about the others? The ones who left?" asked the little boy cautiously. "Don't you have to help them first?"

Marble leaned down, placing their hands on their knees. The smile they bestowed on the boy seemed genuine and it illuminated the boy's face. "I am helping them. You may only see one of me, but that does not mean that only one of me exists right now. I am ushering them into the After's gentle care as we speak."

The boy's eyes widened, clearly confused by this concept. "Oh," he whispered.

Marble straightened up. "The next space I take you to is where you will reside for the duration of the tribulations. To tend to the mortal needs your bodily form will experience, a bag of basic necessities will be waiting for each of you.

"You will interact with beings that make their home in the Between. These beings will be a part of your tribulations, as will other things. You will know when you are about to encounter a tribulation."

"Is there a place we are trying to get to? I know returning to our body, yes...but a kind of destination maybe?" This came from a vibrant and youthful-looking woman with deep brown skin complemented by dark hair that tumbled, shiny and slightly wavy, down her back gracefully. She was short and petite, and her full cheeks gave a delicate roundness to her features. She was absolutely beautiful, captivating in a way that made it hard to want to look away.

"Simply across the Between," said Marble.

"How many tribulations are there?" a middle-aged man with a slightly soft belly, golden blond hair hanging slightly past his ears, asked. Stubble coated his chin, and his eyes were absolutely bloodshot, like someone had just ripped him out of a smoke-filled room.

"An unknown amount."

"To you or just to us?" I countered.

Marble swung their head in my direction. "There are more than two, but fewer than twenty."

"That's actually extremely unhelpful," I pointed out.

"I... am not able to give more specific details," they said in a way that made it seem like they were holding something back.

"It sounds like you wanted to add an *or else* to the end of that."

Eyes flashing with irritation, Marble said through gritted teeth, "The number of tribulations you encounter will depend on which direction you take in order to cross the Between. Your fate is not preordained. I cannot intervene when a tribulation has begun, I can only ensure the rules of each tribulation are observed according to how I set them. Any decisions you make are your own. The After does not permit me to share any more information than that."

"Then you mean, yes, there is an *or else*—as in, or 'else the After will have my head'."

"My head cannot be removed, mortal. Yours can."

"Sounds like threats aren't exclusive to the After," I retorted.

The man with blue eyes—I decided to call him B for those eyes—scrubbed a hand down his face and looked at me. "Why didn't you take them up on going to the After if you are so obviously interested in dying?"

I rolled my eyes. "I'm not looking to die, I'm just looking for better answers than this loquacious marble slab is offering."

"And poking the wasp's nest gets you the answers you want?"

"Well I'm not sure, B. Just like you, I can't remember anything that got me what I wanted," I quipped.

His eyebrows furrowed in puzzlement and he opened his mouth to reply when Marble cleared their throat again. I clenched my jaw at the horrible sound.

"Sintra, mortals," they interjected. "Please, call me Sintra and not"—a quick glare in my direction—"loquacious marble slab."

"Thank you for that information, Sintra. Is there anything else we should know?" B asked genuinely. I thought he sounded pitiful, trying to be polite.

"I have no other information to offer."

"Are you coming with us?" the boy asked quickly, shaking his leg nervously, his brown curls bouncing on his head.

"I may join you prior to the start, or at the completion, of each tribulation but I will not be with you the entire time." This was said with a sweet smile for the boy, who Sintra seemed to prefer. Or at least have less animosity toward.

I walked over to the boy and knelt in front of him so that my face eclipsed Sintra's. I awkwardly reached for one of his shoulders, thought better of it mid-reach, and dropped my arm to my side instead. "You'll have us."

His doe eyes met mine. "I will?"

My heart cracked a little at his vulnerability. "Sure," I said, taking his hand in mine without thinking, "until the end."

"Until the end," he whispered back, his eyes wet as he looked earnestly at me.

I gave him a slight, probably not too reassuring smile, and his soft, small hand a squeeze. I stood then and faced Sintra with the boy tucked behind me.

"Well, *Sintra*," I said, provocation coloring my tone, "why don't you go ahead and guide us to the next destination?"

"Yes, now to your next place in the Between. The After will be watching with immense interest in you all." Their honeycomb gaze didn't leave mine, but their smile turned sharp.

And everything went black.

Chapter Four

S harp, searing pain consumed me, so intense I felt nauseated. All around me was blackness and a loud crackling sound. The taste of burnt rubber spread throughout my mouth and its scent shoved its way into my nostrils.

I was convinced I had pushed Sintra over the edge and they were sending me to the After, regardless of my having chosen the tribulations. But the After was supposed to be peaceful, which this sure as hell wasn't.

Mercifully, the pain ceased and I became aware I was standing but doubled over with the effort of gulping as much air into my lungs as possible. I warily looked up at the five others to see how they'd survived the pain we'd just experienced.

Everyone else looked completely refreshed, as if they had just spent an entire day relaxing and rejuvenating. And shopping—they were all now wearing relatively thick, seemingly waterproof pants, a spandex shirt as a base layer, and a pair of boots, all in an uninteresting grey.

The group eyed me with concern.

I looked to Sintra, completely baffled as I gasped for air like I'd just finished a two-hundred meter sprint but they just smirked at me.

When I felt like I could breathe normally again, I pulled myself up, placed my hands on my hips, and discovered I was wearing the same outfit as everyone else. I shifted my neck to the left and right, making it pop a few times as I realized I was going to be the only one going into the tribulations unrested. *So I got the clothing but not rejuvenation, seems fair. Not.*

"Are you okay?" The little boy startled me, appearing at my side before I detected his movement.

I looked down and tried for a convincing smile. "Peachy."

He nodded a few times as he kept his wide gaze on me.

"Welcome to your next destination, mortals." Sintra's voice drew our attention. Once again, they were beaming at the boy, seeming absolutely delighted to be around him. Protective instinct surged through me and I placed my arm around the kid's shoulders quickly.

Sintra's smile pursed slightly before they glanced away. *Good.*

"Behind you are your bags. Be sure to keep them close to you throughout the tribulations." Sintra moved as though to leave.

"Food?" I said.

"In your bag you will find mortal sustenance. A bar in the bag can be eaten in small bites to last throughout the entirety of your tribulations. One bite equals one meal. I suggest using it sparingly," they threw over their shoulder to me.

"And what about water?" This came from a man with a shaved head and whose deep, rich complexion was complemented by dark brown eyes. He looked toned and limber, and he had a scar that slashed through one of his eyebrows.

"A canteen is in your bag. It will refill automatically once it has been fully drained. The After ensures your comfort during your tribulations." Sintra's gaze cut to mine quickly, as if daring me to respond.

I stared back with affected nonchalance.

"Which way do we go?" B asked.

"Across," Sintra gestured to the space before us.

Under a dull purple sky, a desolate wasteland stretched out around us as far as we could see. Yellowed shrubs poked through grey dirt that looked fine and powdery in some areas and coarse in others. A few bare and mangled trees, their trunks warped with other trunks winding counter clockwise around them, stood in the stale air.

No sun warmed the landscape. In fact, I realized as a shiver knocked through me, it was *freezing* here. The whole place had the appearance of harsh, dark winter but felt lonelier and more draining, as if the very air siphoned away energy.

"How do we know what we are looking for?" asked the man who had wanted to know about water. "Please, ignore that asshole,"—a point to me—"I want to know more. Where are the tribulations? Do we have to find them? Or do they find us? Is this a fight to the death or is more than one of us allowed to survive?"

I reared back, horrified. One of us was a *child*. Surely the After wouldn't condone fighting a child to death if it was as benevolent as Sintra said it was?

Sintra seemed amused by the questions. "Mortals, this is not about surviving each other's malintent, it is about surviving the tribulations and more than one of you may survive. I know you are frightened, but I have exhausted all the information I am able to give. Across is where you will go and the tribulations are along the way," they said with a comforting smile. "I suggest you stay together as a group, but however you decide to go through the tribulations is also your choice. I will see you soon. Be well, mortals."

Golden swirls appeared around them and they slowly began to fade away.

"Until next time," I said coolly with a little wave even though a sense of futility was starting to creep up my spine.

Sintra's tawny gaze fell on me and hardened.

"If you make it there, that is." And then they were gone completely, on a golden-flecked wind dancing towards the purple sky.

I felt a tug on the bottom of my shirt and looked down to see the little boy staring at me with a concerned expression.

"Now what do we do?" he asked me.

"I have no idea, kid," I said distractedly. What was Sintra's comment about making it supposed to mean?

I will be making it, I am determined, I said to myself. *The After will not win me easily.*

B walked over to where we stood and hugged the boy to his side with an arm around his shoulders. "We're all going to come up with a plan together, don't worry. No one will leave without you. Why don't we take a moment to explore the packs Sintra gave us?" Looking at me over the boy's head, he gave me a hard stare that clearly indicated I had messed up.

I bent over to look the boy in the eye. "Hey, uhm, I'm sorry. I'm here and I'm with you. I won't leave you." I straightened back up to see B watching me cautiously. "And it doesn't seem like this guy will either. So now you have friends here. What's your name?" I asked.

His face crumpled, and tears welled up and streaked down his delicate features. "I don't know."

Dumb. That was dumb. Of course none of us knew our names, or who we had been, what we had done, in the Before. All we remembered was our last moment and that was with minimal clarity. Although I felt certain I didn't work in childcare in the Before, because I was two for two in causing the boy distress.

"That's okay, I don't know mine either and I shouldn't have asked," I said, pulling him out of B's arms and wrapping him in mine. "It's okay." I wiped away a few tears from his face.

"What should I call you?" the boy asked me.

I thought for a second, my last moment flashing across my mind. Loud noises, screaming, drums, an ugly vehicle. "Eight," I said. "I remember a sign that had an eight on it, so that's what you can call me."

"Not *asshole*?" The man with the scar chimed in.

"You know, I was willing to let it go the first time, but seeing as you're continuing to make a point of calling me an asshole, perhaps you should find a new group to walk across purgatory playground with."

"Funny, but no," he sneered. "We stay together. That's what Sintra suggested we do."

"Then you can call me Eight and keep your other thoughts to yourself."

B spoke quickly in an obvious attempt to dissolve the tension between me and the other man. "Great, Eight it is. And Eight, you already called me B, so let's just say that's my name then." He nodded to me in agreement.

I looked at him and nodded back. Then I took a moment to fully *look* at him. He was actually quite handsome with a strong, clean jawline and hair so black that in this muted space it looked as if it absorbed light. His blue eyes, like glacier melt, stared back at me. I spotted a little brown dot under his right eye.

When I realized I had been holding my breath while taking in his beauty I coughed—so smooth—and looked away. I saw a little grin settle on his face in response.

"Harley," the guy with the scar said. "I remember a motorcycle with that name on it, Harley-Davidson, but just Harley will do."

"Rain," said the little boy. "I saw rain on the window from the bed I was in, when...when...it happened."

I gave him a reassuring smile and nodded. "Good, Rain, I like that." I didn't press him for any more information, though a thousand questions pelted my brain, wondering why this child was in the Between with us.

The other two shared their new names next. The beautiful woman couldn't recall much of her final moment except that the tile in the room she was in had delicate flowers painted on its surface. So, she asked us to call her Lily. The blond-haired man remembered being on a boat in the ocean when water had swallowed him whole. As he sank beneath the water's depths, he saw *The Poseidon* painted on the boat's stern.

"You're really going to make us call you Poseidon? You don't have any shorter ideas?" I asked flatly.

His mouth hung open and his eyes darted around, as if looking for words he couldn't find while avoiding my stare. "Well—"

"Don," I interrupted. "I'll settle for calling you Don."

"Fine," he grumbled quietly. "Don then."

"Great, so now that we have a way to refer to each other, let's take a look inside our bags," B said.

We all reached for the bag nearest to us, opening the grey, thick canvas-like material to see what was inside. As I crouched on the ground to go through mine, I wondered if it would have killed whoever was in charge around here to provide colorful, patterned bags for our use. The grey ground, the washed-out shrubs and trees, all of it was so depressing.

In my bag I found a jacket and a sleeping bag, both made out of lightweight puffy—and surprise, grey—material. There was also a book of waterproof matches, rope that made up a considerable amount of weight in the pack, a large first aid kit, a metal canteen with a cloth grip covering it, something wrapped in cloth, a watch, and a lantern that clicked open and shut. I stirred my hand around the lining again to see if I'd missed any smaller objects tucked into the material but there was nothing more.

I looked over to see Lily staring at the first aid kit in her hands. "It's a little unnerving that the first aid kits are so big, isn't it?" I said to her.

She turned to me and replied, "medical kit."

"What?"

"It's a medical kit, not just a first aid kit. A little on the small side, actually."

I peered at her. "How do you know the difference?"

She looked back at the box in her hand and shrugged, slightly bewildered, before she said, "I don't know. I just do."

Pondering that, I let my gaze drift down to see I held the mysterious cloth-wrapped item from the bag between my hands. "What do you suppose this is?"

Harley responded before Lily could. "I think it's the food." He had removed the cloth to uncover a bar that was scored in nice symmetrical little sections, similar to how a chocolate bar would be. It was iridescent white and gave off a surprisingly potent glow. I could see it casting white light against Harley's skin.

"Really? Are you sure? This doesn't look like it's edible," I said as I unwrapped my own bar.

"Well, having never been here before, no, I'm not certain, but there doesn't look to be anything else to eat around here, unless you have an appetite for dirt," Harley replied sarcastically.

"What do you think it tastes like?" Rain asked as he turned his glowing bar over in his hands to inspect the other side.

I looked at B who was sniffing his; his blue eyes took on an intense hue from the alleged food's glow. "Mine doesn't even have a smell."

Immediately, the other five of us lifted our bars to our noses and commenced sniffing.

It was indeed devoid of any distinct aroma. Well, it seemed possible times were about to get desperate enough to force me to eat anything with a modicum of nutrition, glowing and scentless as it may be.

I wrapped the light chocolate back up and placed it in my bag. I ran my hand down the straps of the canvas material. I lifted the bag up and down, testing the weight.

Sintra had said we had to get across this space, and I didn't see any vehicles in sight so it seemed likely we would be walking and I worried about rashes developing from the material rubbing against my shoulders.

Sighing, I slung the bag over my back and adjusted the fit to my liking.

I looked to Rain to see how he was fairing with his bag. He was poking around curiously in the medical kit, about to pull out a pair of curved scissors when I grabbed his forearm and said, "okay, let's just put this away for now. Do you think you can carry your bag?"

The boy looked decently nourished. He was thin, for sure, but like a normal boy of less than ten.

"I think so," he reassured me.

"Rain, if your bag gets too heavy, tell one of us and we can take some of your stuff," said B, while he struggled with the right strap of his bag.

"Need help?" Don asked B.

"That's okay, Don, I think I got it. I just needed to rethread the strap a little."

"Are you sure? He's probably wicked good at knots and ropes," I offered.

"And how would you know that?" Harley asked.

"He mentioned a boat, boats have lots of ropes, meaning lots of knot tying as a requirement. You know, two plus two equals four and whatnot," I said matter-of-factly.

"Maybe he was just a guest on a friend's boat when it went down."

I shrugged. "Maybe he's the captain and his knack for knot tying will be coming in handy and you'll have to admit you're wrong."

"Or maybe if you're right, I'll ask him to teach me a couple of tricks so I can tie you to a tree and leave you."

"Sounds like something someone willing to fight to the death would say, what a surprise."

"For the love of god, can the two of you stop arguing?" Lily asked, glaring between the both of us pointedly. "We have a child with us that acts more like an adult than either of you."

I snapped my mouth shut while Harley refocused his energy on his bag. Maybe I was a lawyer in the Before.

We started walking across the grim landscape. Grey ground, yellow shrubs, eerie trees, and purple sky. All of us except Don put on our grey puffy jackets for warmth. He found the cold air to be comfortable. I found that to be crazy.

As we walked the back of my neck prickled with awareness and I couldn't shake the feeling we were being watched. Even though Sintra wasn't around, it was like their golden eyes were glued to me with each step I took.

Trying to distract myself I'd often look back to check on Rain who seemed intent on trailing our little group. He kept his eyes trained to the ground most of the time, kicking rocks and churning up plumes of ashen dirt every now and then to pass the time. Occasionally I caught B's eyes and averted my own quickly each time it happened. I didn't mind looking at him because he was handsome, but I did mind him *seeing* me looking at him.

When we started out I had removed the watch from my bag, determined to figure out how time worked in this weird space. The time read 20:00 when I first looked at it and as we walked the minutes slowly counted down to 19:00. I assumed that meant an hour had passed, and further assumed that meant there were twenty-four hours in a day here. So perhaps when we got closer to 08:00 that meant it would be a good time to stop to sleep. Sintra did say we had to tend to our mortal needs while in the Between.

"Eight, do you know where we are going?" Rain asked behind me. I slowed my pace until he caught up to me.

"Uhm, not really to be honest. I think we're all just going where Sintra told us to."

"Why didn't they give us a map or something?"

"I don't know."

"Does Sintra want us to die?"

"You know, that's a very good question."

"Am I going to die?"

I stopped and looked down at Rain, noticing his tear-filled eyes. I gaped, my mouth opening and closing like a fish, lost at how to answer that. *Are we?*

B appeared on Rain's other side.

"You know what I do when I feel afraid?" he asked.

"What?" Rain's voice quivered as he shifted his attention to B.

"I thank my brain for the fear. I thank it for trying to warn me, trying to protect me. I thank my fear because it wants me to be alive. By having fear as my friend, I know that it will be there for me to make sure I don't miss anything, that I stay sharp, that I don't make mistakes, that I *live*." B opened his blue eyes wide and then softened his expression with a smile.

"You say thank you?"

"Yes, you should try it. I'll go first. Thank you, fear, for caring about me," he said lightly, then nodded at Rain. "Now you go."

"Thank you, fear, for caring about me."

"For protecting me," B said.

"For protecting me."

"For keeping me alive."

"For keeping me alive," Rain repeated, a grin cracking his face. "That does make me feel a little better."

B tousled Rain's curls and raised a puff of grey dust as a result.

"Just say that every time you feel afraid, okay?" B directed, dusting some dirt off Rain's shoulder.

Rain bobbed his head up and down enthusiastically.

We continued walking. Rain maintained his sluggish pace and drifted back behind the group, kicking a stray piece of gravel along with him. I turned to B. "That was...nice. I hadn't really thought about it like that."

B shrugged and turned his gaze my way while his hands held onto the straps of his bag as he walked. My stomach fluttered when he smiled at me, dimples peeking out. "I guess I hadn't really either, it just popped into my head. Pretty good though, I'm going to keep that in my pocket for myself."

I laughed, a little harshly with the dust coating my throat. "A real philosopher you are," I said and looked away from him. "Maybe you're a therapist or something in the Before."

"Huh, you might be onto something."

We fell silent. I pretended to act interested in Lily and Harley's conversation about whether it made sense for someone to be on guard duty when we stopped later to sleep.

"What do you think you were? You know, in the Before," B asked me.

I hesitated for a moment. "Promise not to laugh?"

"Absolutely not."

I sighed. "A lawyer."

He startled me with a deep and lively laugh and I felt heat creeping across my face.

"Hey!" I shoved him lightly with my shoulder. "I said *not* to laugh, not make fun of me over it."

He continued to chuckle, shaking his head slightly.

"Think I'm not smart enough or something?" I challenged.

"No, Eight, I think you're well-equipped to be a lawyer with that mouth of yours. I mean, you looked ready to kill Sintra for using a few too many words to describe the After."

I kicked a rock and said, "Sintra irks me."

"I don't think anyone noticed."

I gave him a playful glare and noticed he was still smiling. I wasn't sure how tall either of us were, but a good foot separated our heights. I traced my eyes over his high cheekbones, and found I had to resist the urge to run my fingers over them and feel what I just knew would be soft skin. He gazed back, both of us lost in thought before I turned away, trying to ignore the heat that settled on my cheeks.

After hours of walking, Lily announced from up ahead that it was 11:30. Turning to the rest of us, she walked backwards and asked, "is anyone up for stopping now?"

It was earlier than the 08:00 I had thought would be a good time to rest, but Rain jumped up and down vigorously in my periphery. "Please, I'm starving," he pleaded.

Chapter Five

We spread out on the dirt underneath one of the large twisted trees. There were no shadows or sunshine in the Between, only the expanse of the uncanny deep plum sky above us, but it was comforting to have the large branches of the tree looming over us protectively.

A couple yards away I noticed a small creek, no wider than fifteen feet across, cutting through the barren landscape. For a moment the area seemed almost peaceful, if I didn't think too hard about where I was.

After long hours of walking we were all ready for the brief, slightly plush, relief of resting on our sleeping bags. We all pulled out our light chocolate, looking anxiously at each other, no one wanting to be the first to commit to a bite.

Don trembled as he looked suspiciously at the bar in his hand. "Sintra said just a small bite…"

"A small bite equals one meal, if I remember correctly," Lily said. I had laid my sleeping bag next to Rain's and closer to the tree's trunk, while Don, Harley and B had arranged theirs ten feet away. Lily was the last one to choose her spot and she had plopped down right next to me after the men had laid out their bags. I had the feeling she preferred sleeping closer to a woman.

"That sounds about right," I confirmed absentmindedly.

I looked over at Rain who was attempting to break off a square of his bar. I was about to reach for it to prevent him from taking too much at once when I realized he was having no luck breaking a chunk off. *What?*

I looked down at mine and tried to remove a piece. To my utter shock, it wouldn't break—it wouldn't even bend.

"Wow, I think it's bulletproof," I said.

"Am I going to break a tooth if I bite into this?" Lily asked, giving hers a useless smack against her canteen.

Tipping his chin in her direction Harley said, "Only one way to find out."

She glared back at him, obviously not interested in his proposition.

"Fine," B said, "I will risk going to the After. If this does me in then I want Rain to have my jacket."

"Deal," Harley replied eagerly.

B brought the light-colored chocolate to his mouth. A whitish, blue glow colored his fingertips and face as it got closer. He pulled his lips back, exposing all his teeth as he took the smallest, most dramatic nibble of the bar he could. He made a show of chewing the tiny morsel slowly, moving his mouth side to side, then his jaw up and down, likely rubbing it against the roof of his mouth. His eyes narrowed in concentration the whole time.

We all watched intently and held our breath.

Suddenly, B dropped the bar into his lap and grabbed his throat and gasped. "I...I can't...can't...it's...water, now, pl-please...help!"

We all flew into action. Lily and I collided while trying to get up, then she grabbed her canteen and I reached for my bag to find the medical kit. I had no idea what could possibly be in a medical kit for being poisoned or choked to death by light chocolate but I was desperate for anything.

Harley slapped B roughly on the back as B continued to wheeze. Don simply sat, frozen in terror, doing nothing because he's Don and he's useless.

I rushed to B's side with the first aid kit just as Lily ran up to him with the canteen.

"Stop, hold on, Harley! Enough with the smacking or I can't get him any water," Lily panted. She looked like she wanted to slap Harley's hands away, but also like she was afraid to do so.

I placed a soothing hand on B's arm while he coughed and choked. He was curled forward, his body shaking with the effort to drag in air, and I was worried he was on the verge of convulsing. I slid my hand down his arm and held his hand comfortingly. *I'm watching this man's final moments*, I thought. *This small intimacy is appropriate.*

Harley stopped slapping B's back and instead pulled on his shoulders to straighten him up from his curled position. With a wary eye on Harley, Lily placed her hand under B's chin and tipped his head back. Just as she was about to pour water into his mouth, B opened his eyes wide and let his tongue loll out and to the side. He crossed his hands against his muscular chest and rasped, "death by Between food."

There was a beat of silence before Lily shouted, "you asshole!" and shoved him backwards.

B steadied himself quickly while giggling. Twin dimples framed his mouth as each giddy noise escaped him. I snatched my hand from his with an indignant huff.

"Seriously, not funny," said Harley as he shook his head and walked back to his sleeping bag. "I thought you were a dead man."

"Only as much as the rest of you are," B replied. "Anyway, I think the only reason it can't be broken off into pieces is so it doesn't get smashed in our bags, it's actually pretty soft when you bite into it." Looking skeptical, and a little exasperated by his antics, Harley, Don, and Lily all took hesitant bites of the light chocolate.

Rain leaned toward B and, with a little giggle of his own, whispered quietly, "I thought it was kinda funny."

B winked at him. "Eat up, it is pretty filling actually, a little does go a long way." He wrapped his light chocolate back up in the cloth and shoved it into his bag before standing to stretch his long limbs.

"Ridiculous," I muttered.

But a small, wry smile lifted my lips before I took a bite of my own bar.

At 09:00, I decided to go sit next to the creek and cool my feet in its water. I was exhausted and my feet ached from all the hours of walking. Blisters hadn't yet formed—the socks Sintra blessed us with were relatively thick—but I could feel the faint twinge of pain on the back of my heel and side of my big toe that foreshadowed what would happen in the next few days. I made a mental note to look closer at the medical kit to see if there was some type of blister remedy among its contents.

I walked over and sat on the creek's edge and took off my boots and socks, shoving the socks into the boots so I didn't misplace them accidentally. All thoughts of submerging my feet were discarded, though, when I looked closer at the water. The liquid was extremely dark, near black, and seemed thick somehow; it slid past me in oily tendrils. I assumed it was icy cold too as there wasn't any steam rising from where the surface met the chilly air. But that wasn't all that gave me pause. There was something else about the creek, something I couldn't put my finger on at the moment, that made me uneasy.

I looked away from it as I created a loop from some string I had found in my medical kit and used it to pull my long hair up into a bun at the nape of my neck. Fixing my hair had me contemplating my appearance. During the walk, I had been too preoccupied with thoughts about the tribulations and fussing over my watch to realize I had no idea what my face looked like.

Now I looked down at my body and saw well-filled curves and smooth beige skin. My arms were decorated with a large smattering of freckles. I examined my hands and saw that my nails were unpainted, my cuticles appeared slightly manicured, and no callouses roughened my palms or fingers. It appeared hard labor was not a part of my life in the Before.

I wanted to know what my face looked like but the dark water of the creek provided no reflection. I had my canteen with me and pulled the grip cover off but the metal wasn't polished enough to act as a mirror.

I sighed, unable to hide my disappointment.

Dirt and gravel crunched behind me as a pair of footsteps approached. I twisted and looked up to see B standing next to me.

"Come to join the fun?" I asked, lowering my canteen.

He sat down, leaving a respectful distance between us. Once he was comfortable, he casually hugged his knees to his chest.

"If you prefer to brood alone, I can leave."

"I feel like brooding *is* typically a solo activity."

He lifted a thick eyebrow at me. "I find that having a friend to brood with is always better than alone."

"And you remember this from all those memories you have to go off of?" I said.

He grinned and nodded toward my canteen. "I saw you peering at that intently. Were you trying to catch your reflection in it?"

"I was...I thought it would be nice to see if my face was familiar to me, that's all."

He turned to me then, his head cocked to the side. "Hmm, that is a predicament...An easy one to solve, though. Let me help you."

I scoffed, a little taken aback by the offer. "You're going to tell me what I look like?"

"Why not? You have something else you need to be doing right now?"

I laughed at that. "Okay, fine, I'll bite. Tell me, what do I look like, B?"

He sat up straight then, suddenly becoming serious while he scanned my face, appearing to critically take in every detail. I shifted nervously at his intense focus on me.

"You have freckles," he said after what felt like an eternity. "They start around your temples, go across your nose and end on the other side. You have a few on your forehead too. Your eyes are blue-green, your nose is pretty straight, so you probably never broke it in the Before." When he glanced down at my lips, my heart fluttered for a second. "Your lips are a dusty-rose color and relatively full." I blushed at this observation. He smiled softly, taking notice of the color change in my cheeks, but cut me some slack and didn't comment on it. "Your hair is auburn, leaning a little more towards brown than red. You have a rounded jawline."

I took a moment to try to create an image in my head from all of his observations.

"Dusty-rose lips, huh? You sure know your colors," I teased.

"Must be a special talent of mine."

"Must be...maybe you're a painter," I mused. "What about my eyelashes?" I asked, rubbing a couple of them between my thumb and index finger, trying to assess the length myself first.

"I'd say they look decently long and full."

"Any scars?"

"None."

"Birthmarks or moles?"

"Not one."

I hummed in contemplation. Before I could think too closely about the question, it was out of my mouth. "Is it nice? Like, my face, is it okay looking? Like Lily, do I...am I...?"

"Do you want to know if you're pretty, Eight?" B asked, keeping his gaze focused on my face.

My face heated, likely turning at least two shades redder than it had been a moment before.

"I...I... well..."

"You aren't pretty."

Before I could tell him how rude that was, he continued, "You aren't pretty, I'd say you're beautiful."

Butterflies coursed through me. I swallowed, not sure what to say in response. "Do you want...?" I offered pathetically.

He let out a low chuckle. "I know I'm handsome, Eight."

I snorted and instantly felt like doing so contradicted the idea that I was somehow beautiful. Maybe I lost some points in his book over that noise, but he grinned at me anyway.

"How could you *possibly* know that? Did you smuggle a mirror into the afterlife somehow?"

"I can just feel it, sometimes you just know."

"Wow, maybe you're a priest or something in the Before. Humility looks really good on you."

He shrugged nonchalantly but after a beat he asked, "okay, what do I look like?"

"Oh, now you want to know?"

"I tell you, you tell me. I think that's fair, Eight."

"Right." I turned my gaze to him fully. His blue eyes stared back as I searched his features. I was really putting on a show here considering I had scrutinized his beauty on multiple occasions during the hours we walked. I couldn't let him suspect that, though. The medkit wasn't extensive enough to help me piece his head back together if it exploded with ego.

"Your hair is dark, black, I mean. Like jet black, I don't think I see a single brunette strand. You have a square jawline, looks pretty cleanly shaven, though I'm sure you already know that based on feel. Uhm, a strong nose? I'm sorry, I'm not really sure how to describe a nose, but it's...nice."

I said, "oh and you have a mole, under your, uh, right eye," as I pointed to it like an idiot. Dear god, had I ever even spoken to a good-looking man in the Before? I was terrible at this. "Blue, by the way...that's the color of your eyes. Which is why I thought B was a fitting name. You know, B for blue."

"And here I was hoping it was B for breathtaking," he said with a wink.

"It was actually for bigheaded, because you do have a rather large head, probably so it can fit all that pride in there."

He smiled playfully. "I like it more knowing that you couldn't stop thinking about my eyes."

I scoffed and rolled my own in response, even though he was exactly right.

"But truly, thanks, Eight. I appreciate your help."

Sure." I turned back to the creek. "Can I ask you one more question?"

"What's that?"

"How old do I look? And please, do not give me that bullshit underestimate-by-a-decade. I genuinely want to know how old I look to you."

He thought for a moment. "I think late twenties, early thirties, if I had to guess."

A bit of dread returned to my stomach, momentarily chasing away the light feeling from this conversation. I was likely still so young, lost in the Between. Did I have a family? Siblings? A partner? Having absolutely no recollection of myself felt like torture.

"How old do I look to you? Same rules apply," B asked me.

"I think you're mid-to-late thirties," I said. I eyed his hair again. He definitely looked older than Lily, maybe slightly younger than Harley, but too sharp-featured and built to still be in his twenties. Even so, either he dyed his hair in the Before or he was lucky enough to have seen no greys reach his onyx locks.

He nodded appreciatively. "I can handle that."

"You can handle being just in your thirties and possibly dying?"

He looked down at his legs, now stretched out before him as he leaned back on his hands. "Yeah, I think so. I mean, look at Rain. He can't be older than eight to ten years old."

I looked back to the sleeping bags, where Rain was tucked inside his, sound asleep. My heart twisted at the thought of someone I likely eclipsed in age by two solid decades and a few extra years also being held in a coma somewhere in the Before.

"You're probably right, I just assumed he was less than ten, but nothing more specific. I must not have had a lot of interaction with kids in the Before."

"Well, if it's any consolation, you're really good with him," B offered.

"Thanks," I muttered. "I obviously don't have quite as much wisdom as you do to help him."

"I think just being there for him is enough."

I hoped that was true.

Before everyone settled in Harley, Don, B, Lily, and I talked about keeping watch during the night. We were all tired, but it seemed like a good idea to have someone awake given the strangeness of our circumstance. I took that night's watch and sat on my sleeping bag with my chin propped in my hand. While everyone else fell asleep, I stared vacantly at the sky. It was slightly darker now than it had been while we were walking—during what I thought of as daytime. There weren't any stars to look at and no moon to illuminate the features around me. All I could see was a deep purple above and a dark landscape crawling up the horizon to meet it.

I shifted to get comfortable and a tingly feeling crawled up my spine.

"Fight for us. Don't give up, please."

Startled, I straightened up abruptly. Had someone in the group said something? I looked around and saw that no one else was awake. Their sleeping bags gently rose up and down while their inhabitants slept deeply.

I gathered my sleeping bag up over my shoulders and tried to shake off the eerie feeling the voice left behind. I glanced at my watch—06:00. It was going to be a long night.

Chapter Six

When the group woke, a slightly lighter sky was visible, which I guessed meant it was morning. I'd lost track of time while I thought of the voice playing over in my head. When everyone started stirring, my watch read 23:00, confirming my theory that this place was based on a twenty-four hour clock like the Before.

We all sat or stood up and stretched as we brought the day into focus. One by one we wandered off to relieve our bodily needs, then returned to shake out our sleeping bags to remove some of the grey dust they'd picked up from being on the ground. Except for Lily—being possibly the smartest one in the group, she hung her sleeping bag on a branch and gave it a good beating with the rope from her bag. I made a mental note to remember that for next time.

I helped Rain situate his sleeping bag in his pack after giving it a couple of good shakes.

"Are you sure you're okay to carry all this today? You're not too sore from yesterday?" I yawned, helping him pull his backpack on.

"Yep, I'm okay," he responded.

At that moment, I wished I had half the resolve this kid seemed to possess.

"Hey, did you sleep okay?" B asked me with a grin.

"Yep, wonderful, best sleep I've had as far as I remember," I returned sarcastically.

With an angry frown Harley said, "Good to hear you slept peacefully. Glad we put you on watch then."

"It was a joke, Harvey," I said through gritted teeth.

"Harley," he stated.

"Whatever," I muttered, turning back to Rain. "You should eat before we start walking," I pointed to his bag where his light chocolate was stored. While he pulled it out and took a bite, I moved my foot around awkwardly in my boot, trying to see if I could find a better position that didn't rub the tender skin of my heel.

"Looks like Sintra was kind enough to include some moleskin in the medkit, if anyone has any blisters that need to be situated before we walk," Harley tried to announce subtly, not making eye contact with me when I turned to him, seeming to be preoccupied with digging around in his medical kit.

The thought of relief instantly brought out my good-side towards him. "Great idea."

Harley leveled a look of mock concern at me. "Did I just hear you agree with me?"

"It's about to get even weirder because now I'm going to ask you for help. Do you know how to use moleskin?"

He gave me the slightest smile. "Sure, Eight, grab your kit and meet me by the boulder over there." He gestured behind him.

"Will do. Hey, maybe you were a nurse or something in the Before," I tossed out on another yawn.

He looked at me like I had two heads. "What?"

"A nurse, like someone who fixes people from injuries and whatnot?"

"Yeah, I'm aware of what a nurse is."

"It just seemed like you might know something." I was trying to be conversational, but felt a little awkward doing so with Harley. It was easier with B for some reason. "You never know what knowledge has stuck."

"I just hadn't really given much thought to what I was before being here," he responded with a shrug.

I decided to take the risk of being vulnerable with Harley. "B and I were just considering it while we walked yesterday, so it's been on my mind. I can't help but be curious if anything feels familiar to me from the Before," I said.

He nodded and gave me a small, sad smile. It felt more personal than any interaction I'd had with him so far, like a newfound alliance was forming that erased some of our tension. "That's an interesting thought. Maybe we could all talk about it while we walk today."

I smiled hesitantly in return. "I'd like that."

Hours later, as we walked with the creek on our left, I wrapped my arms around myself and shivered. The air was cold and still all around us.

Rain continued his rock-kicking-game to pass the time. It must've been entertaining enough because he rarely spoke, although his brow furrowed and an irritated look passed over his features every now and again.

"Everything okay, Rain?" I asked him.

"Fine," he muttered.

"You seem a little off," I prodded, watching the piece of gravel he had just kicked tumble into a shrub.

"I'm okay, promise," he assured me.

Well, that was a closed door. B and Lily had turned their attention to our conversation and I looked at them, confused by Rain's refusal to engage. Lily shrugged in a silent *I don't know.*

B's square jaw tightened with slight concern. "Hey Rain, are you feeling tired or anything?"

"We already took a break, I'm fine," he said.

"What if I gave you a ride on my back for a while, or took some stuff from your pack to make it lighter?"

"I said I'm *fine*!" Rain snapped at B, looking both flustered and irritated.

Lily, B, and I looked at each other, slightly shocked by Rain's outburst.

B walked up to my side and put an arm around my shoulder. Bending down towards me so he had better access to my ear he whispered, "I'm going to hang back with him for a little bit. Maybe just keep him company in case he decides he wants to talk." I could feel the slight heat of his breath on me and this time the shiver that tingled down my spine wasn't from the cold.

I tilted my head slightly towards him, afraid to move any closer and risk my face accidentally touching his. "That's a good idea," I whispered back, as casually as I could.

He slid his arm off my shoulder but the feel of his touch lingered. I watched him walk back towards Rain. As I turned my head forward again, I caught sight of Lily looking at me with a knowing smirk.

I rolled my eyes and looked away from her.

"Has anything come back to you about your final moment?" I asked, trying to distract Lily from commenting on whatever she thought she saw in my face a moment before. When her face paled in response, I realized a little too late that was probably an extremely personal question to any of us.

"No," she said quickly, "no, nothing."

End of conversation, I guessed.

She surprised me though when she asked, "do you remember anything else about yours besides seeing the number eight?"

I looked around at the landscape in thought, taking a moment to watch the black water of the creek. It seemed to be our guide now, as it traced a path for us in the direction Sintra had pointed us in. The voices I kept hearing made me think my imagination was getting the better of me, but I would have sworn the creek seemed to be gradually expanding in width.

"I...do, a little bit," I admitted. "I remember cars honking around me and really loud, almost blowing your eardrums loud, metal music. I think I was going across a road or something when this idiot hit me with his vehicle." I vaguely recalled the image of a man behind the wheel but nothing about his appearance felt certain to me...perhaps he was blond? The only detail I could recall with confidence was that his gaze was set to the left while he bobbed his head to the rambunctious music. He hadn't even *seen* me there. He hadn't been aware that he literally held my death in the palms of his hands when they were gripped to his steering wheel. "I think my foot was trapped under the wheel of his truck and I fell and hit my head."

I wondered if the man even saw me fall or if he just ran over the rest of my leg before driving off. Or did he stop, get out his car, and panic at what he'd done? Was it a hit and run? Had anyone bothered to help me?

I had so many questions, but was sure that I'd never get any answers.

"The worst part was I think it was a Jeep truck that hit me."

"Why is that the worst part?" Lily asked, her brows furrowing.

"Have you not seen one? What an embarrassing way to die," I scowled.

Harley and Don had overheard our conversation and offered sympathetic expressions over my final moment.

"I'm pretty certain mine was a car accident too," Harley said. "Well, car versus motorcycle, which is why I remember seeing the Harley-Davidson logo on what I think must've been my bike. I remember I was making my way towards a traffic light and I heard the screech of tires to my right coming from the road perpendicular to me. Next minute I'm on the ground, but still awake. Someone walked up to me, asking me if I was okay. They told me not to move, but I was too shocked to listen to them, I could barely feel a single thing from the accident. They got closer and started tapping me, asking if I was conscious. I think my helmet was too dark and they couldn't see my face. They just kept doing a thumbs up and down.

Harley shook his head. "I forgot they told me not to move and I took the helmet off my head and turned to look at them when everything went black. That's the last memory I have."

"You were conscious though before everything went black?" I wondered if he had been bleeding but hadn't realized it. Maybe he'd lost too much blood.

Harley shrugged.

"Were you bleeding that you can remember?" I couldn't restrain my morbid curiosity.

Harley contemplated that for a moment. "No, I didn't feel or see any blood, but it was so fast...yet so slow...if that makes any sense. I can't remember all of the details that well."

I nodded in understanding.

"Dissection," Lily muttered.

Harley turned to her with surprise. "What?"

Lily cleared her throat. "Your carotid artery was likely torn from the accident and when you turned your head you caused it to tear more, most likely causing a stroke. Or a vertebrae was already broken and when you turned, you caused greater damage to your spinal cord. That's why they were telling you not to move, to prevent either situation."

Don, Harley and I gaped at Lily in silence. I had thought she was in her early twenties. Wow, my gauge had to be horribly wrong or she had someone in her life that had a deep understanding of anatomy.

She shrugged. "I know that I know that, but I don't know how I do."

"I thought you were like twenty, max."

She gave me a warm smile. "Who knows? I could be. I don't feel any wrinkles on my face or see any age marks on my arms and legs. It's weird not knowing what your face looks like."

"Well, it looks great from my view, just so you know," I offered her reassuringly.

Her laugh sounded almost like bells when it rang through the space. I wouldn't have been surprised if the grey ground cracked open and life spring forth, it made one feel that joyous to hear it. Her smile was bright and calming through the lilting sounds.

"You're not too hard on the eyes either, Eight," she replied kindly.

Okay, that was the second time someone had said that. I started to feel a little less concerned B had told me I was beautiful out of pity from seeing me peering longingly into a canteen.

Both Don and Harley rolled their eyes and looked away.

"Don, want to share with the class next?" I used a nice tone, knowing I had probably been pretty unfair in my earlier assessment of him as useless. Sometimes certain people just irritated me, it seemed. I couldn't quite figure out why, but my annoyance had mostly been aimed at either Sintra, Don, or Harley—though the latter I was starting to warm up to. This likely said something about me in the Before, but wondering about what it said was futile seeing as I had no idea who I was or how I'd acted toward others.

"The boat I was on," he swallowed, "didn't sink."

I waited, counting to ten, to see if he'd say more than that. He wasn't very conversational, but the least I could do was try to be more patient.

"Right, *The Poseidon*." I gave him an encouraging look.

He inhaled deeply. "I remember there were people around me. I don't recognize them when I try to remember, but they were running around the boat in a panic. I think bad weather was approaching. On the way to turn the boat around a metal rod fell and hit me, knocking me in the water."

I was shocked he hadn't met his final death then. Bad weather, getting hit by a pole of some sort, and then being knocked off a boat? If he was unconscious—in stasis, as Sintra had said—in the Before, it seemed obvious someone had attempted to rescue him while he was unconscious. Someone that was probably missing him.

Harley must have thought the same because he put a hand on Don's shoulder and gave it a quick pat before saying, "someone cared about you that day, man."

Don nodded while looking down at the ground.

I looked back at B and Rain. It appeared B's attempts to get Rain to talk more were in vain considering they trudged along in silence. The four of us slowed down so they could catch up. When they did, B walked up to my side, his upper arm brushing my shoulder.

"Do you remember anything about your final moment?" Harley asked him.

B pursed his lips and my attention lingered on them slightly longer than strictly necessary.

He sighed and darted a quick glance at me. "What I can remember about my moment is not *nearly* as interesting as any of yours."

"Don't worry, I don't think we're planning a first place trophy for most interesting death," I winked at him.

He laughed, his bright smile angled down at me. "Can't help that something in me always wants to be the winner."

"Huh, maybe later we can dissect what that says about you as a person."

"Looking forward to it," he teased, then the sharp lines of his face turned more serious. "I was eating at a restaurant, laughing with a couple people around me. I think I must've been a little buzzed because my vision was slightly hazy. I just remember putting some food in my mouth and I suddenly couldn't swallow. My lips and mouth felt so tingly and itchy." He grabbed at his face subconsciously. "I started wheezing, desperate to breathe, everyone around me started panicking and that's all I can remember."

"That's an allergic reaction, right, Lily?" Harley asked.

She narrowed her eyes. "Yes, but I don't think that takes any special training to figure out."

Harley pursed his lips, trying to hide his embarrassment.

"It feels kind of like an anti-climactic way to go," B retorted.

"Honestly, your performance last night says otherwise. You made it look truly top tier to die by food," I joked.

His eyes twinkled slightly in appreciation.

Silence fell upon us as a group again. Even though I desperately wanted to know what Rain could remember about his final moment in the Before, I could sense from his mood that prodding around that subject wasn't a good idea. Truly, wanting to know was selfish on my part. I just wanted to rail against the injustice of his being with us, which wouldn't help the situation in any way. He was alone, facing an unknown set of tribulations and had no recollection of any of those he loved. That was a troubling enough thought without knowing what led him to this moment.

We continued our solemn march, with only the occasional short break to relieve ourselves, snack on light chocolate, or catch our breath to break up the monotony. Eventually, Rain gave in and let B shift the heavy rope in his pack to B's. Luckily the moleskin Harley had applied to my heel and big toe was holding up marvelously well. I let myself for one moment feel thankful to Sintra for that gift in the medical kit, then let my default frosty bitter feelings towards them quickly return.

We had been walking for about fifteen minutes after a break when I heard a little gasp from Rain. He and I had been leading the group but when I turned to him I saw that he had stopped a few paces behind me. His face had gone pale and his eyes were staring ahead.

"What's the matter?" Behind him, Harley and B were making small conversation, while Don trailed behind them. Lily was furthest back, seeming preoccupied with her own thoughts.

Rain held a trembling hand close to his chest and pointed ahead of us.

I turned my head to see what he was gesturing to.

Then I reached back and pulled Rain behind me while I took in what appeared to be an animal of some sort about twenty feet away. I couldn't make out what it was at first, but it was digging a hollow at the base of a tree.

"Stop!" I tried my hardest to whisper aggressively to get the group's attention, but in my panic my voice rang out louder than I intended.

The creature heard me and stiffened, then emitted a primal growl. I could see now that it had patchy tufts of sparse grey fur hanging in uneven clumps on its grey skin. The beast turned to us menacing golden eyes stared back at me. Its mouth was open, exposing long, sharp canines that were darker than the rest of its teeth. It reminded me of a dog or a wolf, although its head was much larger than the rest of its body and it had a long snout from which mangled whiskers poked out in random directions. At the other end, the animal's tail was long and naked, like something you'd find on a giant rat.

Behind me B said, quietly, "back up slowly, Eight" and I heard him pulling Rain towards him. I did just that, walking backwards carefully to avoid making any sudden movements or noise, and joined the group.

"What is that?" Rain whispered.

"I...don't know," I admitted, my heart sending electrifying pulses across my body in warning.

"Is it a dog?" Harley asked.

"Maybe a wolf," B said.

"Or maybe it's neither and something completely *else*," Lily whispered.

None of us moved. I barely noticed Rain's quaking body tucked protectively behind B.

The creature took a few steps away from the tree and toward us, sniffing the air in our direction intently. I saw it had dark claws that were so long, they curled into the dirt as it pawed the ground after sniffing us. I had no idea what that meant, but my entire body was tense with apprehension.

"We should kill it," I heard Harley say in a low whisper hardened with grim resolve.

"Why would we antagonize it when it hasn't done anything?" I whispered back, unable to look away.

"Yet. Do you want to wait until we're on the defense? Wouldn't you rather take it by surprise?"

"It can *see* us, we aren't taking it by surprise," I hissed.

"That's true, why force a fight we don't have to?" B added.

"I agree," Lily said, her voice quieter than usual.

Don said nothing but I noticed him take small steps to get behind all of us, almost as if to use us as a shield.

"Do you think I'm here to protect *you*, Don? Get out from behind me and stop acting like a little bitch!" I seethed, turning to look him directly in the eyes.

"I..." he started, and I couldn't tell if he was more afraid of me or the wolf-like thing at that moment.

I scowled and looked him up and down for emphasis, making it clear I wasn't impressed by his behavior.

Harley made a gruff noise under his breath, ignoring my interaction with Don, still stuck on the thought of slaughtering the creature. "So you just want to wait, hope we can pass by it, then pray it doesn't come for you while you sleep, is that it?"

The animal's head shifted back and forth, almost as if it was listening to our conversation about its possible impending death.

"Sintra mentioned we'd feel the tribulations and I definitely feel afraid," I said quietly, "but maybe we can avoid it if we don't engage? They said something about the path we walk determining the number of tribulations we encounter, so maybe we can walk around it?"

"I don't think we can say fear is the only indication of a tribulation. This whole place inspires fear," Lily replied. "I think the smart move is to avoid it if we can."

The creature stepped closer, dark saliva dripping from its mouth. My stomach knotted when I realized the saliva was dark because it was mixed with blood.

"We need to walk to the right and get around it," I said quietly but firmly. I had no idea whose blood that belonged to and I wasn't overly eager to find out.

"Very...very...slowly...as one," B agreed.

Moving steadily, we all moved to the right, one step at a time, staying huddled as close together as we could. The animal growled a warning but didn't come after us. It just watched as we made a long loop to the right, not giving the creature our backs. It shifted to keep us in view and we froze in response, wondering if it was about to charge us. Never taking its golden eyes off us, it backed toward the hole it had been digging next to the tree and curled down next to another grey body. My breath caught in horror as I realized there were two of them, but then I almost laughed in relief. The first animal had been *guarding* the second one. It wasn't aggressive, it was just being protective.

My relief was short-lived, however, because in the next instant and with its eyes still trained on us, the first animal sunk its teeth into the neck of the one in the hollow, its throat bobbing with each gulp of blood it took. The creature being attacked didn't stir or protest. In fact, it didn't move at all.

It had already died.

"Don't look," I instructed Rain who was, thank god, still behind B.

"What the *fuck*," Harley's voice went up an octave.

I looked to B, who was shaking his head, his face having paled a little. "Let's keep moving. Quicker, while it's preoccupied."

We all walked backwards several feet, but when the creature didn't make any movements we turned and made our way away from it more quickly. We looked back to see if it had changed its mind and abandoned its meal, but it didn't come after us. So we continued walking, all of us more aware of our surroundings now and feeling the need to scan each tree we passed for any hollows where more creatures could be lurking.

I shivered, trying my hardest to erase the image of sharp teeth sinking into grey skin, sliding through the flesh like butter. It took hours for the tremor in my hands to reside.

When we felt we had put significant distance between us and the creature, we decided to stop for the day. All of us had had enough; dust coated our mouths with a sour tang, and our legs wobbled with exhaustion. We had gotten off easy today with only mental scars from what we had experienced. Harley said he was ready to trek along for an entire twenty-four hours longer, but we finally talked him into resting when we reminded him we needed to save our energy for tribulations.

We laid our beds out in a similar arrangement to the day prior, this time keeping our distance from the base of the trees after realizing what could possibly be making its home inside them. We all ate our single bite of light chocolate together as a group, even if it only took a minute to do so.

The creek curved around our makeshift campsite. I found having a moment next to it at the end of our long walk sort of well-earned, a distraction from the Between. Watching the creek's oily, molasses-thick waves dance slowly around each other gave my brain a few moments to relax. As I stared at it, I realized the creek had grown, its edges cutting out so widely at our resting point that I thought I'd have to retire the name "creek" and begin referring to it as a river. It remained slow moving, not vigorous, but growing in size nonetheless.

B and Rain spent a few hours playing a game they had made up. A few of us asked them questions about the rules while they played, but both of them refused to allow us in their circle. All we could see from the sidelines were boxes, triangles, diamonds and stars being drawn in the dirt. There would be a few playful shouts and jests at each other between rounds and then both would furiously rub their hands in the dirt, erasing an apparently completed game to start anew.

B and Rain were cute together and I found I enjoyed watching them. B seemed to liven up more around the boy, his smile always soft and patient. He spoke gently, always giving Rain appreciative nudges or generous laughs at his jokes. It was obvious Rain equally admired him.

The dismal feelings that had accompanied me since arriving in the Between lessened ever so slightly when I was around them.

Eventually they erased their last game of the night and took a seat on either side of me. Don and Harley sat on the trunk of a downed tree a few yards away from the campsite. Lily sat on the trunk too, but several feet down from the two men. They had spent some time collecting enough scattered shrubbery and fallen branches to start a small fire with their waterproof matches.

The heat of the fire would call to me before the night's end, but in this moment I felt warmth radiating through me as I sat between Rain and B. They continued teasing each other about their game as I wrapped an arm around Rain and he leaned into my side. I let my other arm brush against B's as we leaned slightly into each other.

We had no previous memories to go off of to get to know each other. We had no personal stories to fill the gaps of silence that stretched out between us at times. In the Before, it was likely we used shared experiences from the past, present predicaments, and future hopes to forge new relationships with others. What people did for work, what school people went to, the way they took their coffee, what they wanted from life in the next five years, and so on. We didn't exist in that pretense anymore. We only had the shared bond of survival and needing each other to achieve that.

That was the only thing I knew with any certainty at this point, that we all needed each other. If today with the wolf-like creature proved anything, it's that we were stronger in numbers.

B had his shoes and socks off and his legs stretched out alongside mine. Our feet were right up against the water at the river's edge. B dipped his foot slightly below the surface, opaque blackness sluggishly rolling around his toes.

"B, what the hell are you doing, get your foot out of there!" I cried, staring at his toes like they were about to snap off and fall into the depths below. I had no idea whether or not there was something lurking in the water's depths, but I didn't think it was wise to press our luck.

"I'm fine, Eight, just letting my feet soak because they're sore. Might do you some good too, I saw how your feet looked after taking your moleskin off."

I scowled at him. "Well if I knew you had such a fetish for feet I would've kept you waiting a little longer for a glimpse at them."

"I'll make sure not to tell you when I find something about you appealing then, just to make sure you don't try to hide it from me."

We caught each other's gaze then and my insides melted a little. He stared at my lips.

"What's a fetish?" Rain asked.

The moment between us was broken by Rain's curiosity and the snorts of laughter we tried to cover by coughing. The laughter was a balm to my soul after the day we had had.

"Uh, it just means you like something," I said. "A lot."

Whether or not Rain made it out of here and didn't remember a single thing about this experience, I wasn't going to be the one to explain the meaning of fetish to him.

We looked at the river again. I pulled off my socks and let my feet play in the water next to B's, deciding not to shy away from it. I attempted to let go of some of my anxiety from the day. The strange water unsettled me, but I couldn't deny the soothing effect of its coolness on my poor feet. They soaked for a few minutes before Rain's small feet joined ours. B began to push thick little waves towards us, challenging me to ineffectively splash him with the syrupy water using my foot, leading to a little water war. We were jovial with fake battle cries, drenched pant legs, and more laughter before we settled down again. Under the water, B traced his foot up the side of mine quickly then along the underside, his foot deep enough that Rain couldn't see what he was doing. I rested my head on top of Rain's with a contented smile as pleasant fuzziness coursed through me.

"I was sleeping, I think, in...the Before," Rain whispered. "The room I was in was dark, but there were little glowing things above me. I think they look like shooting stars. My bed was blue and it was raining. I just remember being scared and I still feel scared."

I brushed soothing lines on his cheek with my thumb.

"It's okay that you're scared," I reminded him.

"I don't want to be scared anymore though, it hurts," he whimpered.

"Do you remember what we tell fear?" B asked gently.

"Thank you...?"

"Yes, thank you, fear."

Rain nodded. "Thank you, fear."

That night B and I slept in our sleeping bags with Rain in his between us. Lily once again slept on my other side, away from Don and Harley.

I offered to take watch for a couple hours before waking up Harley, knowing I wouldn't be able to sleep, my mind stuck on a loop of apprehension. I was concerned another creature would appear to harvest my blood or that I'd hear another voice at any moment. I'd probably been awake for an hour when I felt a slight stirring to my right.

Jumping with fright, I turned my attention only to find Rain looking at me sleepily, a smile on his pale, soft face.

"Hey, Eight?"

"Yeah?" I whispered.

"I just want you to know that I have a fetish for you and B."

A shocked, choked laugh sputtered out of me. I tried my hardest to silence it with my hand, but I couldn't stop my shoulders shaking with uncontrolled giggles.

I opened my mouth to correct his use of the word but gave up when I met his earnest, hopeful, doe eyes. I decided to let it go and be happy he hadn't woken up with nightmares from our encounter earlier or from talking about his final moment.

I exhaled one final laugh and bopped his nose with my finger. "I like you a lot too, Rain."

His smile grew more assured before he turned over to sleep again and murmured, "sweet dreams, Eight."

"Sleep tight, Rain."

Chapter Seven

The next morning began like the previous day's start. We woke up, took turns finding a spot to use as a makeshift restroom and ate light chocolate before beginning our walk for the day. I began to wonder if the Between was testing our capacity to move through endless, flat terrain on sore feet. I didn't know what my hobbies were in the Before, but given how little I enjoyed walking already, I was willing to put a large sum of money down that I was not active in any hiking community.

Before we started out, Harley had been attentive to helping me wrap my now weeping blisters with moleskin, and Lily had inserted some gauze as an additional buffer between my sock and boot to help prevent friction. My feet were swollen and achy, made worse by the cramped space in my boots, but the pain of that was relatively mild compared to yesterday's pain of raw skin catching along my sock. I didn't feel like anyone else in the group struggled with their footwear quite like I did. Maybe this was another *gift* only to me from Sintra.

Several hours into our walk, probably around 18:00, the land around the river began to dip in a slight gradient. A few times I stumbled on small rocks. Once or twice B had to catch my elbow to steady me.

As we walked, I noticed the river continued to expand, up to at least two hundred yards across. The gummy water had dropped significantly until only black-stained silt remained, unmoved by any current. By 16:00, the slight incline we had noticed two hours before had resolved into a hill that blocked our view of the river.

I had Rain's pack strapped to my front as we walked. Rain was on B's back, his small legs wrapped around his waist and his arms draped over his shoulder. They were playing a game in which he attempted to find an item that B had picked out with only color as a clue. I would've thought the game would be over quickly, given our surroundings, but they were good at making the game's premise work.

"Is it that rock?" Rain asked, his pointer finger and eyes focused on a spot ahead and slightly to the left.

B shifted him slightly on his back. "Nope."

"What about that patch of dirt?"

"Not it."

Rain scowled. "How am I supposed to find the grey thing when everything here is grey?"

"It is actually quite cruel of you to pick out something grey, B," I chuckled.

"I'm not working with many colors here, unfortunately."

"He didn't say that it had to be on the ground," Harley said in a low, exasperated tone, clearly sick of the game they had been at for over an hour.

B threw up his hands with a shout. "Someone gets it!"

Both Rain and I groaned and rolled our eyes. "Your jacket," Rain said, a little grumpily. It was obvious that he was a little put off by B's loophole in the rules.

B wiggled his eyebrows at me since he couldn't see Rain on his back. "Good job! I was starting to think you weren't going to get that one. Okay, now your turn."

"This game sucks. Can you come up with a new one instead?" Rain pouted.

Before B could reply, something liquid hit me in the face. I reared back, slightly confused. I traced my finger against my forehead where a fat drop of something cold was making a line down my temple. When I looked at my hand, uncertainty gripped me as a black water droplet slipped off my finger.

"Do you guys feel—" Lily started.

"Rain," Don finished for her while dark rain began pelting down on us.

We all looked to Rain who ran one hand through his brown curls, lowered it in front of his face and then looked inquisitively at the black streaking down his palm.

"This doesn't look like my rain," he said softly, before wiping his hand on his pants.

I protected my eyes with my hands while I looked up at the sky. Not a single thing had changed about the atmosphere above us. The rain seemed to be falling from nowhere.

Dread settled in my stomach as the rain began to fall more steadily and took on an ominous quality.

"I-I don't feel right," I said, my voice meek with uncertainty.

B turned to me, his eyebrows furrowing. His hair was wet, though the color remained the same, immune to the inky black rain drops.

I looked at Rain, then to Don, and finally down at my own hair. The rain was pouring down now and it looked like the three of us had dunked our hair in a bucket of gritty black paint.

"What do you mean, Eight?" B's blue eyes searched mine.

"I feel...like something's looming over us...it's like I feel...*death*," I said, meeting his eyes. His strong handsome face was streaked with black lines of water. "Pulling at me, beckoning me."

He stared at me intently, as if trying to find something in my expression that would better explain what I meant.

I swallowed hard. "I think we need to go towards it."

"You want to—what?!" Harley's shocked face pulled my attention.

"I don't *want* to do anything!" I yelled defensively over the sound of the heavy rain. "I said we *need* to, idiot!" My fuse was suddenly short and my ability to regulate my emotions was non-existent at that moment.

"How about you go ahead, and just you, go wherever that feeling is taking you. If you don't come back then the rest of us can agree it's a bad idea to listen to a feeling that reminds you of death!" Harley slapped his hand to his forehead, rubbing streaks of inky black water around his skin.

I ground my teeth together, trying to breathe through the awful feeling threatening to overwhelm me, trying to hold back a scream.

"No," B said sternly.

"*No?*" Harley bristled.

"No, we go together, we are in this *together*."

"What happened to wanting to avoid the danger, B? Now you expect me to just walk towards it because you and Eight *say so*? That wasn't the case yesterday," he scoffed. "You just want to do whatever she says, is that it?" Harley jerked a thumb in my direction.

B responded through clenched teeth of his own. "I'm not just *agreeing* for the sake of it. I just happen to think it's the right thing to do to follow our instincts."

"And mine said to kill that thing yesterday, but you didn't! And now your instincts tell you to follow death? You're a fucking idiot!"

"How would you even have killed it?! We don't have any weapons!" B shouted, black water nearly rolling into the tight lines of his mouth.

A few tense moments passed, only the sound of rain hitting the ground around us breaking the silence, as B and Harley stared at each other in a silent battle for dominance.

Harley broke eye contact first. "Well, you can have fun going with her, then."

"What if...what if this is how we are summoned to the first tribulation," Lily said quietly, her long hair plastered to her face and neck. "Sintra did say we'd feel it when we were about to encounter a tribulation."

Don shook his head in response, black water flinging off the ends of his hair.

"Then I really think we don't follow this feeling," Harley quipped. "I didn't feel death yesterday when I was by that creature, I felt like I could take it."

"Moron," B hissed.

"I'm sorry, but even if I didn't *like* them, at least I listened to what Sintra said! We don't get out of here unless we *finish* a set of tribulations, not if we *run* from them," I bit at Harley, crossing my rain-slick arms across my chest. "And Lily is right, this feeling is not like how I felt when we saw that wolf-thing yesterday. I didn't feel like I needed to approach the creature, that the possibility of my survival depended on going towards it and winning. But this? *This* feels exactly like that."

Harley didn't even blink and though I felt like I was sitting at the bottom of an abyss, I tried to remind myself to have some sympathy.

Because the look on his face was complete and utter alarm at the idea of walking towards the unknown. Not being able to see, physically see, what we'd find and assess for weaknesses or possible advantages had him scared. But whatever we'd find, going toward it was unavoidable—because we were being summoned.

"We don't have a choice," I whispered, letting the defeat be heard in my tone.

Harley and I just looked at each other for a while, my sense of panic building.

A million thoughts seemed to cross his face as he studied me. Whatever he saw must have convinced him because after a little bit he just nodded, uncertain and angry but starting to seem determined. "Okay then, Eight. Lead us to death."

I moved forward as the group followed behind me, eventually hiking up the hill's slippery slope, through shrubs and then down towards the river on the other side. The last we had seen the river, it had been empty but now rainwater was accumulating in its bed. I was leading our group downhill, stepping carefully on the wet surface, when something caught my eye and I snarled.

Sintra.

Chapter Eight

"Well, well, look who washed up in the rain," I sneered as I reached the bottom of the hill.

"Mortal," Sintra greeted me simply.

My companions caught up and all came to my side in trepidation, shock written across their features. Sintra had said in our Between... *orientation...* that they would meet us at some point during the tribulations.

So we had indeed made it to our first.

"Welcome mortals, to your initial tribulation," they confirmed with a smile that didn't soothe or comfort but instead felt merciless and pointed, as it hid the secret of what was to befall us shortly.

The black rain had no effect on Sintra's skin; it just glanced off, leaving the marble pristine.

"What is it then? Let's get this over with, Sintra." Harley's determination was still present. I hoped if I looked at him long enough, that feeling would spread to my veins, course through me, as a type of antidote to my disquiet.

"Cross the river bed."

I narrowed my eyes.

"That's...it?" B asked, unsure.

"Yes."

"To where?" Lily asked as her fingers rubbed black rainwater from her eyes.

"Over there," Sintra said, turning to point through the downpour. Across the river, the landscape changed abruptly. The hill had blocked the view but now that we were on the other side of it we could see a forest of straight trees. Their crinkled brown leaves and enormous branches hung towards the ground in melancholy.

"What's the point then, cross this river and then what?" I asked bluntly.

"You get a key. You will get a key for each successful completion of a tribulation. The keys go to a door that takes many, one that will take you back to the Before if all are brought to it."

I hated that cryptic rock.

Sintra glanced between us all before settling a lingering gaze on Rain who was still perched on B's back. I noticed B shifted Rain slightly on his back, breaking Sintra's stare. *What the hell?*

"I look forward to reuniting with you all on the other side. Best of luck," they said before a shower of golden speckles pivoted through the rain towards the forest.

I looked out across the river bed, which had an inch of rainwater filling it now. Boulders of various sizes jutted up from the bottom, some as small as my fist, others twenty feet high. They were all different shapes; some were smooth from erosion and slicked by the rain, while others had jagged ridges carving their surfaces.

"This feels like a trick of some sort," I said, trying to assess what surprises could be lurking in our path across the river.

"Everything is a trick here," Harley stated bitterly.

Fair point.

B helped Rain slide off his back to stand beside him. "Well, we need a plan. We do this together, no separating from the group," B said, giving Harley a side glance before placing his hands on his hips while he analyzed the boulder-studded riverbed.

I handed Rain's pack back to him. "Keep this on you, okay? We don't know what's out there and you might need it to stay safe."

Rain nodded his understanding.

I tilted his face up with my hand, wiped some black rainwater off his cheeks, and stated firmly, "we are going to be okay."

He looked over to B, who smiled in agreement.

The rain continued and the river's level rose as we spent some time devising a plan to cross the mucky ground to where Sintra waited for us. The soupy surface of the upper river was beginning to make its way down towards us, helped along by the addition of rainwater. Lily and Don tested the mud to see how deep we'd likely sink during our walk across. Luckily, our boots kept us from going more than two inches below the mud's surface.

"We have rope," Lily reminded us. "We can tie them together and wrap it around ourselves to help stabilize us so we can't be as easily swept away by the water."

"That's not a bad idea," Harley approved.

We pulled the ropes from our bags to get started. All I could manage was a basic overhand knot, which I was thought might do if I tightened it well enough, but the rain and my shaking hands meant I wasn't as effective as I wanted to be.

"Hand me the ropes," Don instructed softly.

Without question we all piled them by the side of the river and watched as he immediately set to his task, working complicated knots between the lengths of ropes in front of him.

Even with the ropes swelling slightly from the rain, there was no doubt Don was a master at what he was doing. I suddenly appreciated having him in the group, *for once*. In that moment, I was glad that I was paired in the Between with someone who knew his way around a boat and related accoutrements.

I tilted my head slightly up at Harley, glancing at him under my eyelashes, and gave him a knowing wink.

"Don't," he warned, narrowing his eyes. The scar on his face flexed menacingly at me.

I smirked before turning back to watch Don.

Once his knots were finished we looped the ropes around ourselves and secured them at our waists. We tightened our packs as much as we could and then stepped into the riverbed. Harley and Lily led us, followed by Rain, then B, then me, and then Don at the end. Lily had asked to go with me rather than Harley, but couldn't refute B's logic that someone with more weight should be paired with someone lighter, for stability purposes in the rushing water.

After days of walking, moving through the thick mud of the riverbed was difficult and torturous. It felt like mere minutes before my calves burned, begging me to stop at the nearest rock for a break.

I knew without confirming it aloud that we were hurrying to the best of our ability. It hadn't been long since we started our crossing but the continuous rain meant the water was now shin-deep for me. I mentally kicked myself that we had taken so long talking and planning prior to starting the crossing. We'd only given the water more time to accumulate, not realizing it had been doing so at a fast rate. The tide wasn't strong enough to knock any of us over at its current depth, but it definitely made our progress slower. Especially as the upstream river water flowed into the bed and mixed with silt, making it feel like we were trying to walk through wet cornstarch; one moment the current felt completely liquid and the next it felt like we were pushing through gelatin.

I held my breath a couple of times as I watched Rain trudging ahead of B. The water was higher up on him considering his size and he struggled and tripped through the inky fluid. I looked back, seeing we had only covered fifty of the two hundred or so yards it would take to reach the far riverbank.

"Pick your feet up Rain!" I called to him, trying to sound as calm as possible.

"I-I can't," he cried, "it's too much!"

Before I could respond, B said something to Lily and Harley, who took a couple steps back. B used the slack in the rope to lift Rain onto his shoulders, keeping him well above the water line.

Fear shuddered through me as I watched B's height lessen a bit, knowing that he was sinking deeper into the mud with Rain's additional weight.

Our miserable slog continued and the rain's race towards the unearthly river picked up again so that we were waterlogged and shaking with cold. By the time the water was up to my waist, the current had become noticeably stronger and less predictable.

I tried to keep from crying out with anger over the seeming impossibility of this task. I was so tired, freezing, and wet. I swore to myself I would find a way to kill Sintra once this was over.

I was moving forward as quickly as I could but I kept feeling a nagging pull in my rope from behind me. Don had kept equal pace with me in the beginning, but as the water rose his pace had slowed significantly. Frustration simmered in my gut.

Scattered debris began swirling on the surface of the water. Fallen branches, thorny shrubs, and dirt scraped along my limbs and threatened to snag on my puffy grey jacket. I tried my best to do some rhythmic breathing to pace and calm myself but shallow pants of fear took over when a large tree trunk broke through the water's surface up river from us.

In an instant, the trunk was picking up speed in the increasingly swift current. I felt the premonition of its dark promise but before I could think of a way to avoid it or get any warning other than a strangled cry out of my mouth, it was on us.

The trunk rammed into the rope that connected B to Lily. He must have heard me or seen the trunk emerge just after I did because he latched on to a nearby rock to steady himself and Rain. He cried out as the rope squeezed painfully around his waist.

Harley and Lily weren't quite as equipped for the tree's sudden collision. They were caught off balance and cast a little ways down the river. The rope between them held, but the one connecting them to B wrapped around the sharp edge of another rock and was severed.

"No!" I screamed uselessly when I saw Harley and Lily being swept away. I wanted to go after them but I was barely able to keep myself upright. The water was now underneath my breasts and still rising.

I lurched forward, trying to get to B, while I held my arms up to keep my hands as far out of the cold water as possible. I forced myself to keep moving but stole a quick glance across the river to see how much progress we'd made.

We still weren't even halfway there. Our progress was so slow against the resistance of the muddy bed and current.

No. Please, no.

We were all going to die in our first tribulation because of a tree trunk.

Keep moving, keep moving, I chanted in my head. I was now swim-hopping through the water, trying to increase my forward momentum as much as I could. After a few steps of progress, I felt the rope around me grow taut and pull me to a stop.

White-hot panicked rage coursed through me as I whipped my head around.

"DON! KEEP YOUR GODDAMN LEGS MOVING OR I WILL FIND A WAY TO CUT THIS ROPE!"

Don stood motionless as the water pushed forcefully around him. His face was completely devoid of color and his body shook with rapid breaths. He was frozen in absolute terror.

His final moment before coming to the Between had taken place in water.

And he was—along with me—almost certainly about to drown in it again if he didn't keep going.

"Don!" I called over the rushing water, a plea filling my voice. Still struggling to stay upright, I grasped one of the river boulders as leverage to turn toward him.

"What's going on back there?!" B shouted. He had only just started moving past the rock that he had clung to when Lily and Harley were cut free.

"Fuc—" I stopped myself from placing an expletive before his name—"Don won't move!" I screamed back.

I forced myself through the water until Don was within arms reach.

"Don, we *have* to move or we die!" I shouted into his face.

"I-I can't!" His pupils were blown and his teeth were chattering from the cold and the fear that was threatening to swallow him whole.

"You're going to get me killed! Is that what you want?!"

"No, I..."

"THEN MOVE! NOW!" I screamed.

Don's hands flew up and he grabbed his hair as he began sobbing and hyperventilating. The fierce current pulled at him and he lurched a little to the side to grab onto a rock, grimacing, and his face streaked with tears.

I snapped.

Steadying myself as I let go of the rock I had been clinging to, I drew my hand across the left side of my body and I threw as much weight as I could into the backhand I landed on Don's stubbled cheek.

I could feel my face heating as pure rage contorted it.

"Move," I growled, "*or die.*"

Don held his cheek with one hand as it bloomed deep red. His other hand still held onto the rock that his body now draped across, driven there by the force of my blow. His eyes welled with tears as he looked at me in baffled betrayal.

We were in this together, but I wasn't a team player when it came to my survival. I couldn't let myself feel anything for Don at this moment. I needed to survive this tribulation. I needed to make it to safety on the other side of the river.

I looked behind me and saw that B had removed the rope tying him and Rain together, and lifted Rain onto a ledge on the side of what looked like an eleven-foot tall rock.

I sent B a silent thank you for ensuring Rain made it to safety. B scrambled up the rock behind Rain, and then lifted him even higher up to the flat top before using his long limbs to pull himself up with ease after Rain.

I turned back to Don, my nostrils flaring.

He was upright again at least. With his eyes locked on mine, he took a small step forward, then a second.

I turned and we were both finally moving forward again. *Thank fuck.*

We were uncoordinated, flopping across the water hurriedly. It was now over my shoulders and I ached inside and out as I tried to make it to B and Rain's protected area. The rope grew taught around my waist against the current and I realized if we made it to the rock, I wasn't going to be able to easily steady myself and lift the rope off and over my head.

The unrelenting rain struck against the water surface and into my eyes, blurring my vision. I tried to keep my chin above the surface, but oily waves slapped against my mouth, forcing me to taste the putrid currents. I coughed and spit, wanting to remove the foul taste as much as possible.

Don's weight on the rope between us pulled on my stomach to the point of nausea. I swallowed bile and tried not to vomit.

I made it to the rock where B and Rain huddled, and grabbed onto the ledge.

"Eight! Hurry!" Rain's voice was shrill with fear.

"Climb, Eight!" B instructed desperately.

My hand found a relatively stable jug on the rock and I managed to pull myself up so that my chest was half out of the water. As I did, I looked over to see Don was several feet behind me, hugging another rock and unable to navigate the rapids.

"You have to get to me, Don! You have to let go of that rock or we won't make it!" My heart pounded wildly in my chest. My knuckles were white with how hard I was holding on to my own boulder.

"I can't! I'll pull you down the river!" he cried back, his voice cracking with emotion.

"You have to! You can make it! I have a hold of the rock and all you have to do is get to me!" I shouted over my shoulder, black water slapping my face. My grip on the jug allowed me to resist some of the water's pull but my legs were still being battered.

With a sureness I hadn't heard before in his voice Don shouted, "no, Eight!"

Tears formed in my eyes; I was so tired and desperate to get out of the river that I was certain I had misheard him.

I looked back over my shoulder.

And froze in disbelief at what I saw.

Don had managed to pull himself high enough onto the rock he had been clinging to that he could scrape his body—and the rope between us—back and forth against its sharp edge.

"DON!" I screamed frantically. He looked up momentarily as he sealed his fate.

Our eyes didn't leave the other's as the rope frayed and broke, and I watched him let go of the rock and accept his death. I couldn't look away and tears carved a path down my dirty face as the river swallowed him whole.

Chapter Nine

"EIGHT!" B and Rain's anguished shouts of instructions to reach them came to me as if from a great distance. I couldn't take my eyes from the spot where Don had gone under. How easy it would be to just let go...let myself drift down the river to join him in his watery grave.

I could feel myself begin to accept the idea. My heart was hammering uncomfortably in my chest, and my mind was starting to drift. I wished more than anything that I had some happy memory to cling to. I wished I could think of a loved one from the Before, relive my favorite day, or think of the happiest place I'd ever been, anything to give me some semblance of peace in my final moment. I couldn't allow myself one final look at B or Rain, I couldn't let them see that I had given up. I wanted them to think it was an accident, that I hadn't meant to let myself be devoured by the greasy water, but that it'd just inevitably won its battle for my soul.

"We're losing her!"

A muffled and unfamiliar voice shouted in my head like the one that had called to me while I tried to sleep the first night. The one that had haunted me for the rest of the night and into the first few hours of the following day.

The part of me that had wondered where the voices came from before was numb. I didn't care what they meant for me anymore. I was vaguely aware that my heart suddenly felt like it was being crushed in my chest. I was disconnected from the pain of it, though, as I became increasingly detached from my body. My grip on the jug eased and my eyes fell shut with fatigue.

I was tired and heavy. It was time for me to let go.

Suddenly, the crushing pain in my chest ramped up, jolting me from my trance. It felt like someone had shoveled hot coal into my chest cavity, cracking each rib along the way to my heart, and then started slamming the shovel against my heart over and over again. My breaths became heavy rasps.

"Eight, please—no! EIGHT!"

It was as if a bolt of liquid fire ignited every nerve in my body. I seized up in a painful contracture, my muscles going rigid. My grip on the rock intensified uncontrollably as the ripple of electricity singed me to the bone. *I've felt this before.*

"Don't you dare give up."

As the spasm passed, my mind snapped back into sharpened awareness. I sparked with newfound energy and managed to lift one of my knees up against the rock and pull with my arms.

Grunting like an animal from the force of my effort, I pulled harder, lifting my body high enough that one leg was freed from the water. I found another hold behind the jug and used it, groaning and tugging with all the strength left in me to release my other leg.

Once they were both free I hauled myself up to flop onto the rocky surface and frantically cough water out of my mouth and lungs. As I lay there, trying to calm my ragged breathing, I noticed the water was no longer rising, as if satiated by the sacrifice Don had made.

My knees knocked against each other as I came to a stand on the first ledge and let myself look up at B and Rain.

B leaned over the rock as far as he could without falling and reached for me. The contours of his face were sharpened by fear. He looked completely unhinged by what had just happened.

Rain's face was still streaked with dark rainwater but I could clearly see his eyes were swollen from crying and his mouth was frozen open in a silent scream.

I gave the deadly river below me one last glance, looking over its downstream expanse. I felt myself crying and realized with some surprise that my tears weren't for me but for Don, wherever he was now.

I reached up with both hands to B. He didn't hesitate as they made contact and hoisted me up next to him.

The rain had stopped abruptly, almost as quickly and as strangely as it had begun, and the riverwater began a slow retreat from the surrounding rock we rested on. I shivered at the uncanniness of this place and from the cold.

The cold never seemed to leave me.

I let B move me into a sitting position and let him slip my pack off my back. He unzipped his jacket and then pulled me into him, wrapping his jacket around me while I clung onto him for warmth. Our jackets, all of our clothes actually, seemed to be drying somewhat quickly.

A gift from the After, I registered dully.

In the calm of the moment, and B's gentle embrace, I let myself break. The tears I had been shedding ever since Don slipped under the water became shattering sobs that coursed through me. The image of Don's face disappearing below the surface and the one of the tree trunk breaking the rope between Lily and Harley ran through my head on unrelenting replay.

B's arms never let go but held me tightly the entire time. After a while I became aware that Rain had unzipped his jacket also and was pressed against my back to mimic B. Cocooned between the two of them, I gave way to my grief with my hands scrunched into B's shirt, and moisture running from my nose and eyes to soak B's shirt anew.

B lifted a hand from my back and brought it down on the crown of my head then slowly caressed to the nape of my neck. He continued to stroke me as he said, "it's okay to cry for him, Eight. Keep crying. Keep feeling. Keep fighting. Keep *raging*. That's the only way we know this will be worth it in the end. If we fight against this with everything we have, even if it brings us to our last breath. It will be worth it. *You* are worth it." He leaned his head down as he spoke and his lips brushed my ear.

"I almost gave up," I admitted shamefully in a whisper.

"I know," he said and his voice caught.

I heard Rain say something behind me, but I didn't quite catch it. "What, Rain?" My eyes were so heavy from the force of my tears. It felt like I had expelled every bit of water my eyes were able to produce.

"Until the end," he said and hugged me tighter.

"Until the end," I whimpered.

Eventually, the three of us came apart and stood to take stock of our situation. My limbs felt like they were made of glass. Just removing them from around B's body made me feel like I was going to shatter into a million pieces.

B gently helped me out of the rope that I had forgotten was still around my waist. He untangled the knot that had attached my and Don's ropes together. I watched stoically as he wound up the coarse length of it, then started on Don's.

I looked away, unable to stand seeing the sheared-off end where Don had cut himself free. Instead I gazed down the river. I was about to look away in fear of coming upon Don's corpse when I saw two people downstream, waving manically at me. I squinted my eyes and realized that Lily and

Harley had found safety similar to us on top of a rock. A bit of relief shifted through me. *I didn't have to grieve for anyone else.*

I waved back, not able to muster as much enthusiasm as Lily and Harley were putting into their waving. Rain followed my gaze and began to bounce up and down with excitement, matching their energy more easily than I was able.

B handed my rope back to me and offered me Don's as well. I took both numbly and laid them in my bag, which had also dried quickly. I accepted them both because, who knew, maybe the ropes could be useful again. B pretty much carried Rain's permanently now. It was only fair if I took the remainder of Don's.

While placing them in my bag, I hesitated when I saw the light chocolate. I knew I should probably eat a bite after the amount of energy I had burned, but I couldn't bring myself to. I told myself it was because there was likely a layer of grimy water coating the bar, but I knew it was actually from oily guilt in my stomach.

I shivered thinking about Don.

"Do you want to put my jacket on over yours?" B offered.

"I'm okay," I said, but I wasn't. I felt like I would never be warm again, as if ice penetrated deep into my soul.

"Are you sure?"

"Let's just get this over with so we can make a fire somewhere," I said, my voice a monotone of misery.

We climbed down from the rock to discover the water had receded so that just an inch covered the riverbed.

Lily and Harley cut a diagonal line towards us as we trudged towards the forest on the other side of the river. Our pace was slow, but I hardly considered the time it took, consumed by my jumbled emotions. B had picked up Rain to help him get across the riverbed and I vaguely registered his heavy breathing.

Eventually Harley and Lily made their way to our side, huffing from the effort as well.

Lily eyed us up and down and then cast her gaze outward. "What happened to Don?"

Harley frowned knowingly, shaking his head and looking down.

"Where's—"

"Gone," I said bluntly.

"Eight, what if he isn't though? Lily and Harley are okay. What if he is too?" Rain asked, turning his hopeful doe eyes to me.

"He's not." I didn't bother softening my words for Rain's benefit. This was something we all had to get used to, the finality of death.

"But—"

"No, Rain. He's not coming back. Let it go," I said, a bit too harshly.

"Eight—" B started.

"Let's *go*." I shoved past the group, not stopping to observe the looks they were likely giving each other at my heartlessness.

It took us a while to make it to the other side, all of us continuing to need the support of rocks to make it through the sticky riverbed.

Finally, the trees came into better focus. I could see cracks ravaging their colossal trunks. The leaves were various shades of brown, offering a slight changeup to the grey landscape we had just spent days in. Dry muted yellow grass and dirt made up the forest floor.

Sintra's white marble form was visible in the treeline. They watched us intently, and I knew they had waited for us mortals patiently throughout the entirety of our struggle.

Once we were within hearing distance, Sintra began speaking. Their marbleized lips moved with words that I barely processed through the anger that began burning in me at this being. This *suffering* they were subjecting us to.

"Welcome to the other side of the river, mortals. You all did well. We mourn the final moments of Don, but know I am currently ushering him into the warmth of his eternal resting place. He will know no more pain, no more strife. He will find peace," they beamed proudly, as if Don joining the After was some grand accomplishment that he had achieved. Sintra didn't even acknowledge this was the second horrific death Don had experienced.

I saw Rain's face fall as he apparently had not lost hope that Don had magically survived after being sucked under the current, but my gaze was focused on a gleaming gold key in Sintra's right hand, reflecting brightly on the marble of their skin.

As we got closer Sintra leaned down to make eye contact with Rain. "Do not fret, child. The After is a joyous place, he will be looked after, cared for, just like—"

I strode up to Sintra with fury radiating off of me despite my pain and exhaustion, grabbed the key out of their hand, and spit at their feet.

"Eight," I heard B warn from somewhere behind me.

I looked over my shoulder at him. I took in his expression of worry and fear for me before I turned my gaze back to Sintra.

"I hope you learn suffering, Sintra. I hope you know what it's like to wish for someone to survive and then watch them die in front of you. I hope it haunts every waking moment of your life. I hope you always usher mortals to peace, but never actually find any yourself," I seethed.

"You know nothing of me," Sintra said with a sneer carved on their face.

"And I hope to never know anything more about you."

I walked away, shoving the golden key in my pack unceremoniously.

I heard grass and crunching leaves behind me as the others followed me. I had no idea where we were meant to go, but I didn't care. I didn't really think it even mattered. The suffering was lurking for us in the rivers, trees, grass, and very air itself. If we didn't find the tribulations, they would find us.

After a few minutes, I felt a small body at my side. Then I felt a dirt-caked hand grab onto mine. I looked down and saw Rain smile at me sadly, his hair stuck together in clumped locks. We kept walking, and the silence stretched endlessly between all of us.

Considering what we all had been through, we didn't walk for as long as we had on previous days, although we made sure to put a healthy distance between us and where we had last seen Sintra.

Once we found a grassy clearing, we decided to call it camp for the night. B and Harley set to making a fire for the group silently, their interactions still strained. The fire they built was better than the other nights' fires as they had large fallen branches to work with and ample dead grass as a starter. They made a shallow pit in the ground to keep the flame from spreading to any nearby grass.

I placed my sleeping bag in front of the fire's warmth and sat down to take off my shoes and socks. I sat them next to me and then laid down and curled up on my side to watch the orange flames dance and listen to the occasional pops and crackles the fire made. The group ate their light chocolate together, made small conversation, and occasionally glanced at me while I remained motionless.

Once the fire died down I slipped into my thankfully dry sleeping bag and laid awake as Don's last moments on the rock played over in my mind. Eventually I heard Lily say she would be on watch, then I heard the others get ready for sleep, then the gentle sounds of their slumber soon after. A distant part of my brain said I should be sleeping as well but I couldn't and just stared into the darkness for hours.

The next morning I was bone weary and even though I had passed on dinner the night before, I couldn't bring myself to eat breakfast.

B and Rain asked me about it, but I shrugged them off and pretended I had eaten before either of them woke up. I know I didn't sell this lie to B, but I didn't have the energy to be more convincing.

My body felt like one enormous bruise. I was surprised nothing was broken from the slamming river. I vaguely remembered feeling like my ribs had cracked open while trying to get to the top of the rock B and Rain had reached. Though they were sore, they didn't feel as painful as I imagined broken ribs would be, so I let the thought go.

I stumbled a lot as we walked, my feet finding everything possible to catch on—a tree root stabbing up through the ground, a rock, a small crater in the dirt. Once it was even an imaginary hill I thought I needed to step up onto that sent me sprawling to the ground. I could feel my eyes growing cross once or twice from lack of sleep.

After I had fallen for what felt like the thirtieth time, B placed his hand under my elbow, helped me to stand, and then stated firmly, "we are done for the day." We had walked for just two hours, but everyone knew I needed to rest. I was too proud to admit it, but I knew I was responsible for slowing everyone down and that the rest would do me good.

As we made camp, we noticed a small pond a little ways from where we set up. I think all of us were hesitant to be near water again, but further investigation proved we had nothing to worry about. The pond was about five feet deep in the center and it was fed continuously by a brook that passed through it. The water wasn't murky like the river but was instead so crystal clear we could see all the way to the dirt-covered bottom. Harley put his hand in and reported the water was cool but not freezing and suggested we were being presented with an unexpected opportunity to wash ourselves and our clothing. I wondered if the pond was an apology from the After for our first tribulation.

If only.

B and Harley made a fire again—their tension seeming more smoothed over—and then Harley, Lily, and Rain took turns washing themselves in the pond. Lily gently helped Rain cleanse himself, shooing him away once it was her turn. After he had bathed, Harley ate his chocolate, tucked himself in his sleeping bag a few paces away and was instantly sound asleep. Rain came over to where I sat and got down on all fours to kiss me lightly on my forehead.

"Goodnight, Eight. Feel better," he said.

I had been staring into the fire but I glanced up at him briefly. "Night."

With a small pout, he stood and walked over to where B sat across the fire from me. He hugged B hard and in return B gave him a long hug. Letting go he leaned back and looked into Rain's face.

"Goodnight, Rain. Wake me up if you need anything?"

"Okay," Rain said, smiling at B before he walked over to his sleeping bag by Lily's side.

The fire started to go out, having not been fed since Harley put on the last branch before going to sleep.

"Better go wash if you want to dry off before this fire...dies," I said, hesitating on the last word.

"Not until you eat and wash yourself," B challenged.

I was too tired to fight. "B—"

"No, don't. You haven't eaten in, I don't know, a full day maybe? You've barely moved besides whatever that stumble through the forest was earlier and you look like you haven't slept in months."

I closed my eyes. "But—"

"No, I don't want an excuse. Get up, please, Eight. I will throw you in the water myself if you don't do something, *anything,* to take care of yourself."

I shot daggers at him with my eyes. "You wouldn't dare."

"You want to bet on that?"

I groaned as I made myself sit up and prickly stiffness traveled through my body with the movement.

B handed me my light chocolate, as if he'd been waiting for this moment all night. I managed a bite and was instantly relieved of the hunger I'd been ignoring.

I looked into his eyes, emotion washing across my features. "I know I'm not okay, B, and I'm sorry. I just...I don't know how to help myself right now."

He traced my jaw lightly with his hand, his blue eyes steady on me, centering me with their strength. His thumb brushed my cheek. "Will you let me help you?"

I searched his expression, my eyebrows pinched together as a tear slipped from my eye. He wiped it away before it slid past my cheek.

I leaned my face into the warmth of his hand and took a deep breath, closing my eyes.

"Yes."

Chapter Ten

B kept his arm around me while we walked over to the pond, offering me unspoken support. When we reached its edge, I stared down into the water—and jolted back with a sharp inhalation as an image of Don's gasping face seemed to lurch toward me through its surface.

"It's okay. I'm right here with you, you aren't alone," B said gently.

I shook the image from my mind, knowing my sleep-deprived brain was playing cruel tricks on me.

I stepped out of the safe embrace of B's arms and looked up at him.

"Do you want me to turn around?" he asked.

"Sure," I said, clearing my throat awkwardly. I looked over to make sure no one in their sleeping bags would be able to see me strip down to my underwear. Luckily, they were far enough away with plenty of trees blocking the view of the pond. I also knew how hard this group slept and they would be out until the early hours of the morning. Maybe even longer, given how much we had exerted ourselves in the last couple of days.

B turned away and lifted his grey shirt over his head, flopping it into the pond once it was off of him. I was momentarily dazed, lost in thoughts about the river while I watched his shirt sink.

"Eight?"

I blinked, my concentration broken. When I turned to him to respond I sucked in a surprised breath instead and B quickly spun to face me. "What? What's the matter?" he asked. Though the sight of his trim chest and immaculately cut abs that disappeared into the waistband of his pants was breathtaking in itself, what had startled me was the two-inch wide band of bruising I'd seen on his low back, and which I now saw wrapped around his waist too. Angry and red at its center, it spread out in a tie dye of blue and purples. It must have been caused when the tree trunk impacted the rope that had connected him to Lily and Harley.

"B..." Without stopping to think, I lightly traced my finger over a part of it near his hip.

He shuddered.

"You have to be in so much pain," I whispered, my brows furrowed with worry.

He smiled reassuringly. "Looks worse than it is."

I glared up at him. "God forbid you admit you're in pain."

With a little sigh, he put a finger in the air and twirled it in a circle, gesturing for me to turn back around.

I huffed, but obeyed. I heard the sound of more fabric shuffling and a soft plop as it hit the water. I noticed one sock floating on top of the pond.

Plop. Another sock.

Splish. His pants.

I moved to take off my shirt and groaned. My arms felt like boulders from how tired and sore they were and I could barely raise them. I gave up on my shirt momentarily and lowered my pants down and off my body instead. I stood in my underwear, legs exposed to the cool air. It was cold on this side of the river, but not nearly as icy as the air had been on the other side. I heaved my pants into the water and then tossed in my socks. I made an attempt at my shirt again and grunted in irritation when I couldn't lift the hem more than two inches.

"Everything okay?" B asked.

"Yes... just...uhm..." A moan of pain slid past my lips as I struggled.

"Remember when you said I could help you?" His voice was tentative and soft.

"I do."

"Can I help you now?"

I paused as a mix of hesitancy and anticipation swelled in my chest. "Okay."

We turned slowly to face each other, and I noticed how his eyes shone in the dim glow of the sky.

He reached out and his fingers brushed the skin above my hip so gently, like I was made of porcelain. He gripped the bottom edge of my shirt and then slowly worked the material up my torso, his knuckles brushing my skin along the way.

I started to lift my arms above my head, but sharp pain punched down into my shoulders in response.

"Breathe," B whispered tenderly.

I took deep breaths in through my nose and pushed them slowly out through my mouth. I kept raising my arms higher while I breathed. Higher, higher, until they were extended in front of my face.

He worked with it, fingers drawing lines up my back as he lifted the shirt up to the neck hole and then over my head. He freed me by pulling my shirt down my arms, leaving me facing him in my bra.

"There," he said. *Plop.*

Suddenly bashful, I looked up at him and then away quickly. "Thanks," I mumbled.

He held a hand to me in invitation. "Shall we?"

My stomach coursed with tiny currents of electricity when I took his hand, and then we walked into the pond together.

He let me take my time getting used to the water, and let me lead the way as we stepped deeper into the pond. He didn't question when my eyes widened with fear at the feeling of the liquid around me, just held my hand and let me work through my turbulent feelings in silence. My grip tightened when the water passed my waist, then squeezed his hand painfully, I was sure, when it reached just below my breasts.

"Let's stop here," he offered.

I nodded as I looked at him, then let out a breath I hadn't realized I had been holding.

The bottom half of my hair soaked into the water, releasing the greasy black film the rain had left on it.

B let go of my hand and plunged himself fully under the chilly water. He quickly resurfaced, then stood and snapped his head back. He wiped his face with both hands and pushed back his hair, squeezing some of the water out. When he glanced at me, he frowned at my expression. "What?"

I shook my head and said, "I won't be getting that clean tonight, that's all."

"Come here."

I didn't know what he wanted, but butterflies suddenly raced around inside me at his direction. I cut through the water towards him.

When I stood in front of him, my head inches from touching his chest, he cupped a bit of water in his hands in front of me.

"May I?"

I nodded slowly.

He let the water gently trickle over my right shoulder. When I didn't flinch, he repeated his actions, pouring water over the filth coating my body. He slid his hands down my arms and across my shoulders, worked handfuls of clean water into my hair and scrubbed away at the dirt gently.

I let myself be brave and shifted my legs to lower myself in the water until it covered my shoulders. I tipped my head back to let my hair fan out behind me while he tangled his fingers in the strands and massaged my scalp soothingly.

For the first time in over twenty-four hours, I relaxed. I listened to B's breathing as his fingers removed more and more dirt from my body. I let myself soak up being cared for. I didn't know if anyone had ever done anything like this for me in the Before, but at this moment, it was novel.

Tears welled in my eyes. I didn't deserve this, not after yesterday. I was here with B when I should've met my final death. Instead, I was being *pampered*.

B gave my hair one last run through and nudged me back into a standing position. Tears fell from my eyes as he took more clean water in his hands and smudged dirt away from my face, cleaning my tears in the process.

My tears kept falling in a silent, woeful, release.

B looked at me and tipped his head to the side. "Talk to me, please."

I looked away as I tried to piece together the words for my feelings. "It's just...hard to process it all. I don't...*didn't* even like Don. I know that sounds bad, maybe it is bad but, I..."

B patiently waited for me to continue.

"I thought he was going to be the reason for my final death. When I saw him freeze up in the river, I knew he was lost. I thought it was like how he'd tried to hide behind me when we came across that blood-sucking creature. But this time, I knew he was going to get us both killed because it was too much like his last moment in the Before...I slapped him, B. I've never slapped anyone like that before. Well, I actually don't know if I've slapped anyone like that before, but I don't think so because my knuckles fucking hurt afterwards and I think I'd have better form if I backhanded people regularly like that..." I trailed off.

"I thought he'd at least try to come to me. I thought in his panic he'd still have the desire to live, but no, he just cut the damn rope and sacrificed himself...for *me*. I never thought he would be capable of something so...*brave*...or selfless. I wasn't even nice to him. He still let me go and I don't understand it. I don't understand it for one second."

Tightness coiled in my chest at the memory of watching Don die. I wanted to convince myself there was nothing I could've done to make sure we both survived, but "what ifs" dashed around my brain. What if I had pulled on the rope with one hand to help him get to me while holding onto the rock with the other? What if I had screamed harder at him, and was more encouraging, would he have braved swimming to me and made it without dragging me underwater? What if we both had just held on longer, would the rain have stopped and we both could've made it?

I told myself I had been fighting for my life, trying to hold onto that rock while his weight pulled me down. That there was nothing I could've done differently. But I doubted my recollection, thought perhaps I was making my memory of the situation more futile than it actually had been and I really just didn't try hard enough to help him. I didn't care enough that he was traumatized by water. I just willingly let him give up and die so that I could live.

I thought back to how Don said he knew he'd end up pulling us both down. I thought he knew he would kill me if he tried to get to me and that was why he cut himself free instead. This should have brought me a tiny measure of peace but it didn't—because I didn't know what I would've done if the situation had been reversed. My selfish will to live might have resulted in the both of us arriving in the After together.

"I don't know what I was like in the Before," I said to B. "But here and now, I don't know that I would've made the same choice that he did. That *kills* me. The feeling is eating me alive." Silent sobs rocked me.

B put his hands on either side of my face, stroking away my tears.

"Why, B? Why me? I'm horrible....just...*why*?"

He leaned back and searched my eyes, still lightly holding my face. "You're strong, Eight. You're so strong and you don't even give yourself any credit for it."

I scoffed. "I'm *strong*?"

"Yes and don't laugh when I'm complimenting you because I'm right. You are the only person who isn't afraid of Sintra. The first person to watch out for Rain. The one whose quick wit sparked life into me when I felt alone, confused, and like the world was ending." He was quiet for a moment as he appeared to wrestle with what he was about to say next. "I almost asked Sintra to take me to the After that first day."

"B..." I couldn't bear the thought of him not being with me through this journey.

He twisted his lips to the side as he looked away from me. "I'm not proud of it," he said and then brought his gaze back to me. "But it's true. Then I heard you say you wanted to fight and I realized I was being weak, about to give up without even trying." He shook his head at himself.

"You aren't weak."

"And you aren't horrible."

One last tear slid down my cheek and slipped into the water.

B took my hand in one of his and—his eyes never leaving mine—placed a chaste kiss to the inside of my wrist.

I melted as his soft lips brushed the sensitive skin. I couldn't look away from him. I was bewitched.

"You're the bravest person I know, B. And that says a lot because Harley's pretty damn tough."

He lowered my wrist, a deep chuckle escaping him. The sound brought a little laugh to my lips as well.

"Harley, huh? I think Lily is also made of steel. I'm actually in last place for bravery when it comes to this group."

"You can just take the compliment."

He moved closer to me and wrapped both his arms around my waist while he looked down at me.

"I couldn't possibly," he said, "because usually when you don't take the compliment you end up getting more. And I really want to hear you say more nice things about me."

I splashed his face with water and laughed again. "You're such a pain."

"A pain because I'm painfully handsome?"

I pretended to consider that for a second. "Or irritating, but I guess both can be true," I decreed.

He continued to hold me with one arm as he pushed back a strand of hair that had fallen into my face, and tucked it lightly behind my ear. His gaze was reverent when he looked at me.

"As long as you think so."

We stood there together for a little while before breaking apart to finish cleaning up. Occasionally a splash of water in the other's direction led to a playful debate as to whether or not it had been intentional. We laughed and splashed each other quietly so as not to wake the others.

We gave our bodies and clothing a final rinse in the brook that fed the pond, then gathered our stuff and made our way back to the hot coals that were all that remained of the fire. Our clothes were made of quick-drying material, but we draped them over some nearby branches and B added some wood to the embers, coaxing flames to return to help them dry even faster. Not sure how close to sit after what we had shared in the pond I plopped myself down near the fire but a couple feet from B. But that felt too far away so, unsure, I inched closer and was rewarded with him casually putting an arm around my shoulder. I rested my head against him and allowed myself to relax again. He hummed a light tune while we stared into the flames, melodic and soothing, a balm to my nerves.

My eyes grew heavy, my blinks growing longer each time. A tranquil warmth settled into my limbs.

I hadn't realized I had fallen asleep until I woke up to him shifting me under the covers of my sleeping bag. "Goodnight, Eight," his breath whispered over me, his hand caressing wisps of hair away from my face. I smiled sleepily in response.

That night, my sleep was restful and dreamless.

Chapter Eleven

I awoke facing the blackened wood of the fire that had long since been extinguished but with a warmth inside me that was difficult to explain.

Not ready to face the day, I turned over in my sleeping bag. My eyes landed on a wide-awake and grinning B, still in his own sleeping bag and facing me.

"Well, good morning to you too," I grumbled. I checked my watch and blushed slightly when I saw it was 22:00. I wondered idly if he had been counting the time it took for me to wake up while he finished his turn on watch.

"About time you woke up," he teased.

I laughed. "What happened to making sure I was well rested and all that? Now we're impatient, are we?"

"How do you feel?" he asked, his smile growing a little more serious.

"Still tired, sore, a bit like someone rolled one of these tree trunks over me while I slept. Besides that, I'll live, I think." I saw the hint of bags under his eyes. "How about you? How's your...bruise?"

"I'll be okay, Eight. It's not like you don't have your fair share of bruises on your arms and legs."

I resisted the urge to lift up the top of my sleeping bag to verify that statement. Last night, I had been so focused on the emotional damage the river crossing had caused I hadn't worried about physical damage. B obviously had taken care to look me over at some point. A little frisson ran through me at that thought but I couldn't tell if it was mortification or something else.

Just then Harley called out in a knowing tone, "you two decent over there?" I sat up to tear into him for being rude and apparently insinuating something, but then my sleeping bag slipped down my torso to reveal my bra. I quickly pulled it back up while my mouth gaped open and shut on my aborted comeback, no doubt convincing Harley that something more had happened between me and B the night before.

"I... we..." I started.

"Uh, huh," Harley said, smirking as he nodded.

"No! Not *uh huh*, we did not!" I said defensively.

"Whatever you say, Eight," he teased again, taking a bite of his light chocolate, still wearing his sly smile.

"How dare you—" I tried again, throwing in a pompous tone for effect.

"Do you need help reaching your pants?" Harley offered, tilting his head to the side where B and I had hung our clothes.

I groaned and threw myself back into a lying position. Whatever Harley had been thinking, I definitely had just made it worse. Knowing that made my face burn with embarrassment.

I stared straight up at the trees, refusing to turn over to look at B even though I could feel his gaze on the side of my face, his mouth pressed together to hide a laugh.

"I think you handled that rather well."

"Shut up."

I grabbed my clothes and managed to put them on while still within my sleeping bag. B wasn't nearly as bashful as I was and got up to put on his clothing without hurry. I wanted to hide my red-stained face as I watched him but I couldn't look away, regardless of my embarrassment.

My eyes latched onto his bruise and I tried to determine whether or not it had gotten bigger overnight. My torso hurt just looking at it circling his core. I looked away when my view was broken by him pulling his shirt over his head.

After I had eaten my light chocolate and put my stuff away, I found Lily. She was leaning against a tree next to the pond, watching the brook burble softly. Rain sat about ten feet away with his back to us playing with something that looked like a tiny doll.

Lily turned when she heard me approaching and noticed my confusion as I looked at Rain.

"It's a toy I made for him," she explained.

"That's really kind of you, Lily. What is it exactly?"

She shook her head and turned back to watch the brook.

"Well, it's supposed to be a person. I made it from the easiest to work with grass I could find for him. I'm not sure exactly what it is or why I know how to make it, but it seemed like something a child would want in this place," she said and looked at Rain again as a smile lit up her face.

Rain traced the figure along a root, making whooshing noises as he set it flying through the air. He was so invested in his own little game that he paid no mind to us.

"Rain?"

He twisted his head around and looked at me with a smile. Then his smile fell and he looked concerned when he realized it was me calling him and not Lily.

"Eight?"

"Hi Rain," I waved awkwardly. "I think I'm a little better now," I said softly.

He ran to me and hugged me around my waist, burying his face in my stomach. I leaned down and wrapped my arms around him, giving him a big hug even if my sore arms made it an effort.

"Good, B and I were scared for you," he said.

My chest tightened painfully with emotions. "You don't need to be scared for me, Rain. I'm a grown up, it's my job to look out for you. I'm sorry that I didn't. I got lost there for a moment, but I'm back now," I told him while I rubbed the back of his head, his brown curls soft now that mud no longer covered them.

"I can help you too sometimes," he whispered.

I hugged him tighter, smiling. "I know and you do, trust me." I released him before I started to tear up again. "Now, go hang out with B. He needs another big strong man to help him put away his sleeping bag."

Rain rolled his eyes. "Harley's over there."

I leaned in conspiratorially so only he could hear me. "Harley looks big, but I think you're stronger. I don't even think he can lift that branch in front of him and throw it to us if we asked him."

"Really?" Rain asked, his eyes widening.

"Yeah, watch." I turned my attention to Harley and yelled to him through the trees. "Hey, Harley! Can you throw me that branch in front of you?"

He looked at me in confusion, then narrowed his eyes in suspicion. "Why?"

"Because I want it."

He continued to look suspicious of me, like I was going to do something criminal with the branch. "Come get it yourself."

I looked back at Rain and shrugged. His mouth hung wide with disbelief. "Told you," I said.

"Okay, I'll go help B."

He ran off to where B was eating his light chocolate against a tree and I saw their faces brighten at being together.

"That kid is completely obsessed with you and B," Lily said without turning towards me.

I watched her profile, her face breathtaking from every angle. "He's a good kid," I said.

She nodded distantly.

We shared a moment of quiet. The silence didn't feel awkward or uncomfortable between any of us anymore.

"Do you still want to see what you look like?" she asked after a couple of minutes.

"What? How could I?" I asked her, confused.

She lifted her chin towards the pond. "It's not very bright around here but for some reason I can see the trees reflected in it. I think we could probably see our faces in there if we wanted to."

"But—"

"I saw you peering at your canteen."

"Oh," I said, remembering when B had helped me piece my appearance together. I paused for a moment and let myself think about her question before giving her an answer. *Did I?*

I had been desperate to see myself at first. I wanted to see if my face would jog any memory in my mind of myself, of my life before. I felt certain that it wouldn't work that way, but still I couldn't help but try. Every time my mind tried to reach for that blank space where I felt my memories once existed, I was thrown back out, my mind shutting the door on itself. Maybe looking into the pond would at least set that door a little bit ajar.

At the same time, I was afraid to look at my face now. It was easier to lose myself in the people around me and forget that I had an identity, a look, that everyone with me was used to seeing. The thought made me feel panicked.

I was also afraid that I wouldn't like what I saw. I realized the way B studied my face intently, the way he looked at me, made me feel beautiful. What if I looked at my reflection and didn't like my appearance, if I thought B had just been being kind?

"Did...you look?" I asked her.

Still not looking at me, she shook her head. "I waited. I...didn't want to do it alone."

Maybe she felt the same apprehension I did.

I leaned down and took one of her hands in mine, thinking to comfort her. She pulled her hand back sharply, thoroughly startled.

"I'm sorry!" I apologized, holding my hands in the air in front of me. "I didn't mean to scare you, I just...was trying to be comforting." Her eyes were wide and she was suddenly breathing hard.

"I should've asked first," I said and shook my head, annoyed at myself for thinking that people found comfort in touch like I did.

Lily closed her eyes and took a deep breath. After letting it out, she swallowed hard and said, "it's okay, I'm sorry. I didn't mean to seem afraid, I just wasn't expecting that. I know you didn't mean to...hurt me, I—" she cut herself off, swallowing again.

I offered a small smile in the awkward moment.

"Here," she said, turning to me, and held out her left hand.

"Are you sure? You don't have to do that for my sake," I replied.

"No, I want to. I was just lost in thought for a moment. It's fine, I'm fine. Please, take my hand, Eight." She waved her hand again pointedly.

I tentatively took her soft, dainty hand in mine and we took a deep breath together.

"Do you feel ready?" she asked.

"Honestly, no, but I'm glad we have each other."

She shook her head and a slight tremor passed through her as she looked back towards the pond.

I swallowed, then laughed nervously. "I'm afraid of seeing someone I don't know. Like the picture I've created of myself in my head won't add up to what I actually look like. Do you know what I mean?"

She didn't look at me. "I'm more afraid of seeing someone familiar."

Before I could ask what she meant by that, she tugged my hand and started moving toward the pond. We stepped towards the clear water, watching in silence. It was difficult to see anything at first, but as we got near our faces waved into view. We knelt by the side of the water to get a closer look, remaining a few inches away so as to not get ourselves wet.

And we both stared, transfixed by our reflections.

I scrunched up my face and shock coursed through me when I watched the face in the water do the same. I knew it was me making the face, but without memories from the Before, I was a stranger to myself. I did look how B had described me, which I appreciated, but the longer I stared the more I realized I didn't care whether or not I was beautiful. It honestly didn't matter even a little to me as I took in that I was starting to get to know myself completely outside of my physical appearance. I got to set vanity aside while I confronted the ugly, selfish parts of me, but also the parts of me that yearned for peace, for friendship, for love. The parts of me that fought, that endured pain and *survived*. Nothing about that version of me could be shown by this simple glimpse of myself in the water.

Seconds before I had been worried about whether or not I was just *beautiful*. As if beauty even really mattered in a place like this. The river wouldn't have let me live only because I'd had a pretty face. The Before didn't swerve the car away from me for that singular *accomplishment*. The world kept going whether someone who was simply beautiful in appearance lived or died. Why would being beautiful even matter? Yes, B had told me I was beautiful, but he also told me that I was witty, that I was strong, that I was *worthy*. How could being beautiful ever measure up to any of those other words? How ridiculous that I had been afraid of not liking what I looked like. How absolutely *absurd*.

I laughed, and watched the eyes of the face in the water crinkle at the corners. I started laughing harder and harder, to the point I couldn't stop myself.

Lily squeezed my hand encouragingly, as if giving me permission to enjoy myself, while a small tear coasted down her cheek and into the pond, slightly distorting her image through the ripple.

We continued to hold hands while we stared at our reflection, two women whose faces were unfamiliar but whose minds were sharp as whips. Two women who had the deck stacked against them, but who would persevere.

Chapter Twelve

A gain without a specific destination, we entered the gnarled forest the next day. I had asked Lily to check on the progress of B's bruises. Luckily they were starting to take on greenish hues, the edges becoming a sallow color that faded into his skin. Lily was certain, based on the fact that he was still standing and hadn't keeled over dead yet, that there was no internal bleeding present from his ropelash.

"Thanks doctor," B told Lily when she asked him to pull up his shirt during a rest break on our aimless walk.

"I'm not a doctor!" Her words came out in forceful annoyance.

"You're really selling that, Lil," Harley said pointedly as he looked at her holding up B's shirt with one hand while she observed his bruise, the pointer finger and thumb of her other hand framing her chin in a check-mark.

She sighed and rolled B's shirt back down stiffly. "You'll live. I don't think I need to keep looking at it."

"Got it doc—"

"Don't call me doctor again!"

B snapped his mouth shut. I could tell from his awkward expression he hadn't realized he'd pushed her that hard, that he'd only been trying to joke with her. She had been exceptionally snappish since we left the pond, even more so towards B.

"Everything okay, Lil?" Harley asked her, training his face into a placating expression.

"Yes," she grumbled, "I'm just going to walk alone for a little bit."

She plowed ahead without another word, her elegant legs finding a quicker pace.

"Can we play a game?" I looked back to see Rain tugging on B's shirt, pleading mercilessly with his doe eyes, an expression I knew B wouldn't be able to turn down.

B's face quickly changed from confusion to amused delight. "Why don't we make a story together? I'll start with one detail, then you have to pick the next, then I'll go…" I tuned out their conversation as B continued explaining the rules to Rain while they walked after Lily, even though I was impressed by their boundless imagination.

Then it was just Harley and me.

At first silence stretched between us, but it was comfortable. We had grown from the first days of dislike towards each other and built a foundation of friendship. I recognized Harley was centering to our group. He was firm and decisive. No matter how much I teased him, there was strength in his presence and I was grateful for it.

"Don't want to play their game?" Harley asked, his scar visible as he turned his head towards me.

"I'm not really sure I'm suited for stories that children like," I replied dryly.

He chuckled, tipping his head towards me in agreement. "Yeah, you're probably right, I doubt you are too."

I laughed. "Glad we agree."

He winked at me, bringing my attention back to his face.

"Did you know you have a scar?" I blurted before considering whether or not my question would be appreciated.

Harley's expression deadpanned. "I lost my memories in the Between, not the sense of sensation in my hands, Eight. I can definitely feel the scar on my face."

I grunted out a laugh, feeling like an idiot for not considering that. "Yeah, you're right. That was stupid of me."

As we walked, I could see him in my peripheral vision, studying me with a grin on his lips. After a beat he said, "there once was a man named Harley with a scar on his face..."

I looked at him with a surprised smile as I asked, "what, are we playing Rain and B's game without them now?"

"We sure are, I'm interested in your not-suitable-for-children story-telling skills."

"Well, I never said I had skills, so don't be too disappointed."

He nodded and said, "still interested to see what you got, Eight."

After a few moments to think I said, "there once was a man named Harley with a scar on his face. He road motorcycles to feel like he was a big, tough man, but it was all just compensation for his negligible—"

"Alright, I take it back. We're done with this game," Harley cut in with a scowl.

I pretended to look disappointed. "Damn, I was just about to get into your *riding skills*."

"I think I get the point."

We smirked at each other before we looked to the forest ahead, while B and Rain's voices carried on excitedly. Lily had put a good distance between the rest of us, but she still remained in view.

"How are you feeling, Eight?" Harley asked quietly, hiking his backpack further up his shoulders. "I mean, more...emotionally, how are you doing? After Don?"

I furrowed my brows and glanced at him questioningly. The two of us hadn't had a serious conversation since arriving in the Between. It felt...uncharted.

"I'm...okay. Sometimes I feel like everything is going to be fine and that I'll move past his last moment and then others it's all I can think about." I trailed off, peering at his face and then looking away, unable to meet his gaze. Though his expression appeared free of judgment, filled with only concern, I still felt the weight of guilt pinning my eyes to the yellowed grass along the forest floor.

Harley nudged me with his shoulder, breaking my gaze from the ground. "I know I didn't see what happened, Eight. I don't know exactly what you are struggling with and you don't have to talk about it with me if you don't want to, but you can't fault yourself for whatever you did for your own survival. You're human and there's nothing wrong with wanting to make it out of here alive."

I swallowed, struggling internally to accept what he was saying. I didn't know if I truly believed that I wasn't at fault for doing whatever I could to live. It felt too convenient for my guilt to vanish that easily, for my sins to be washed away in the name of survival, but I appreciated Harley for trying to help me anyway.

I pursed my lips before murmuring, "Harley, he sacrificed himself so I could make it to B and Rain."

I saw the split second of confusion cross across his face, as if for a moment it was as difficult for him to believe as it had been for me this whole time. He recovered quickly, assuming a neutral mask within a blink. It was too late though, I had seen the look before he could cover it up.

"Surprised?" I asked, unable to help my curiosity.

"I just...I figured that he drowned because he was too afraid of the water to fight for his life again."

I moved my head side-to-side as if debating whether to let my thoughts out, but I didn't really feel like I had to worry about being judged by Harley. He already knew that I was an asshole, so I had no reason to sugarcoat my thoughts for his palatability. "I wouldn't say that wasn't a part of it, honestly. He choked up and almost got me killed first. I can't help but feel surprised that he decided to do it, that he willingly let himself drown for me."

Harley's dark skin glowed in the purplish light of the sky, and his deep brown eyes shone with resolve. "At the end of the day, don't blame yourself for protecting you. We come into this world alone and leave it that way, so you did what you had to do, Eight."

"Jesus, Harley. You make it sound like I murdered the man."

A smile cracked through his solemn expression. "I knew you were ruthless from the beginning, but not like that. You may act like you have a tough shell, but deep down we both know that you give a shit about the rest of us."

I smiled sweetly. "I don't know, maybe you should watch your back. I could just be a really good liar and actually be a sociopath."

"Nah, I watched you pretend to be nice to Don. You're not a good enough actor to pull that one off. You couldn't even kill that fucked-up looking coyote." He smirked at me, his eyes twinkling now.

I pretended to be offended. "What? I have no idea what you're talking about..."

"Just like that, you're not selling it to me."

I rolled my eyes. "Fine, I do give a shit."

He placed an arm lightly around my shoulders and gave me a few comforting tugs towards him before he dropped his arm. "I know you do," he said, "and we give a shit about you too. So don't disappear on us again."

We looked at each other and smiled, and a deep feeling of appreciation towards Harley passed through me. I was so thankful for these people around me, for their willingness to patch me back together after Don's death, each of them breathing a wisp of acceptance of myself into me.

For B for allowing me the space to process my feelings and assuring me I wasn't horrible, for Harley encouraging me to embrace the parts of me I felt ashamed of, for Lily holding my hand through the panic and fear of myself, and for Rain's relentless embrace of me that knocked down all my walls. Each and every one of them took their turn gluing me back together.

"You got it, Harley."

We walked through the forest for many days and didn't encounter any tribulations. Each night we built a fire and huddled around it, making conversation, joking with each other, or sitting in companionable silence. We got along surprisingly well despite constant hours of forced proximity. Rain and B continued their nightly games, B and I stole moments away from the others a few times, Harley and I ribbed each other at every opportunity, and Lily no longer sought solitude with just her own thoughts for company.

However, as the days wore on, nagging anxiety grew within me like a stubborn weed. I was on edge, constantly expecting Sintra and their saccharine smile to step out from behind the next tree to yank us into another awful experience.

I mentioned my unease to Harley while we were walking one day. I thought he might offer some comforting words but instead he asked, "Do you think Sintra's head would crack or break apart if you hit it with a hammer?"

"What? Harley, were you even listening?..." I trailed off and found myself pondering his question. "Unfortunately, no. Or I would find a way to make a hammer from a stone and a branch. I don't think I built anything in the Before, but I'd be willing to get creative for Sintra's death."

"You really got an issue with her, huh?" Harley replied.

"First of all, yes, I have an issue with anything that decides I have to earn my ability to return to living; second of all...you think Sintra's a *she*?"

Harley reared back. "Well, yeah, I mean—what, you think she's a guy?"

I was certain Sintra would have found the need to assign them a gender amusing. All the things we didn't know about them—how did they live? were they born or simply just *were*? what were they actually made of?—and this is what we wanted to discuss. *Or how bashable their head was.*

I shook my head. "I don't think beings in this place consider gender in the same binary standards a lot of mortals do. I think they're all encompassing," I decided.

Harley mulled this over, flexing his jaw in contemplation. He struggled to respond.

"What is Sintra anyways?" Rain asked from a few steps ahead of us. I paused, wondering if he hadn't just heard what Harley and I had said.

"Like, is Sintra an angel?" Rain tried again.

"I hope that's not what an angel is," I muttered bitterly.

"Maybe Sintra is an immortal of some sort. Could be more neutral than an angel. I'm not exactly sure what *the After* is either, if we're being honest," Harley said, more to the group than to Rain.

"Maybe Sintra's a demon," I offered.

Harley rolled his eyes. "Maybe Sintra is your personal demon and we're all being punished on your behalf."

I snorted with derision.

The topic of *what* Sintra was had crossed my mind before. I wasn't sure what I had believed prior to arriving in the Between, but the construct of the After left me confused. Was it related to a religion or was it its own entity? Was it heaven, hell, or something no mortal had ever thought to build a faith on?

"Sintra gives me the creeps," Rain said.

He had taken to holding my hand more throughout our walks. When he wasn't holding mine, he was with B either taking rides on his back to prevent fatigue or holding his hand while using his other to point at various scattered leaves or branches. B was exceptionally good at distracting Rain with games, I'd give him that.

I could completely understand Rain's feeling, as I felt it too when I thought of Sintra, but couldn't help asking while the time was ripe. "Why is that?"

"I just feel funny when they're around," he said. "Sintra always looks at me. I don't know...what they want?" he questioned, scrunching his face up in confusion.

Harley's voice interrupted before I could ask more about Rain's thoughts on Sintra.

"Are y'all seeing that?" He squinted his eyes towards the distance, his scar flexing with the movement.

I looked ahead to see what he was concerned about. Something massive was up ahead in the far distance, but the trees and the dim sky made it difficult to determine what it could be. It looked like a small hill...or a dark wall of some kind. I craned my neck but couldn't see around it to the right or to the left.

"Is that a mountain?" Rain asked.

"I don't think so," Lily said. "It might be a hill, but it doesn't rise above the trees so I don't think we can consider it a mountain."

"That's a technicality, Lil," Harley muttered.

She cut her eyes to the side to look at him in annoyance.

"We need to go to it," B said in resignation.

We all stopped and looked at him, hoping he wasn't implying what we thought he was implying.

"He's right," Harley said after a few beats.

I inhaled sharply and almost choked on my own saliva. "You both feel it?"

Harley looked at me with a pained and almost regretful expression. "I understand now what you meant by the river. We have—"

"—to go," I finished for him, nodding in a way I hoped was validating.

B shook his head. "It really does feel like death is beckoning."

We walked toward the thing with apprehension. After a while we got close enough to see it was a wall made of downed trees, grass, and mud mashed together that stretched endlessly to the left and right.

"Are we supposed to climb it?" I asked as we came to its base, all of our necks craning upwards to look at it. I shivered, imagining scaling that high off the ground. If any of us fell, there's no way that wouldn't spell death.

"Or do we go around it?" Lily asked.

"God, we'd probably be walking for days even if we *could* get around it that way," I said.

"Fucking stone prick didn't even give us a goddamn axe," Harley snapped as he kicked the base of the wall, a hollow echo sounding when his foot made impact.

Then the wall started to groan.

"What did you do?" B exclaimed, turning on Harley quickly in accusation.

"Something, man! What were you going to do, stand there and hope it parted like the damn Red Sea for you?" Harley stepped to B in challenge and pushed him in the chest.

I heard Lily cry out and watched her grab Rain and back away a fair distance. Turning back to Harley and B, I yelled, "what the hell has gotten into both of you?" and jumped between them. "Feeling like shit because of the tribulation is not an excuse to get in each other's faces!"

"No!" Lily squealed.

I thought she was agreeing with me but when I glanced at her in thanks I saw she'd raised her hand and I turned to see what she was pointing at. Then I grabbed the two stubborn men by their shirts and hauled them backwards with me as clumps of mud began to fall from the wall.

"What in the—"

The ground shook as the muddy wall screeched apart, thousands of branches snapping in a loud crescendo. When it finished moving, we could see the entrance to a passage between high walls of more mud and trees. Even open to the sky above, it looked darker than the forest around us but not so dark it would be impossible to walk through.

The real problem was how narrow the passage was. At best, two of us could walk side-by-side through it, but we wouldn't be able to make it through as a group. My heart beat with growing panic and my palms grew clammy. How did we know the passage's walls wouldn't close up while we were in there and crush us to death?

I shook my head. "N-no...maybe we should look for a way to go around."

"We can't," B said with bitter factualness.

I started to tremble and must have made a sound of distress because Rain rushed to my side and looked up at me. "I can protect you, Eight," he said as he grabbed my sweaty hand in his.

I tried to quell my alarm. "Thanks, you're helping me a lot," I said, albeit in a somewhat shaky voice.

B looked at me. "Are you going to be okay?"

What did it matter? Even if I wasn't fine everyone was going to have to go through that passage. But I nodded anyway. "Yeah, I'll be...alright.

Echoing my thoughts, Harley said, "let's go two at a time. Lily, you and I can—"

"No."

With the way Harley and B had been acting a moment ago, I didn't blame her for not wanting to be around either of them. I told myself that if we made it through this tribulation we'd all have to talk about ways to better handle it when we felt annoyed with each other.

"Oh, uh...okay."

"I'd like to walk alone, that's all," Lily said quietly with her eyes cast on the ground.

"Well, Rain is my protector and Lily wants to walk alone. Can you two be trusted not to kill each other right now?" I asked B and Harley flatly.

B gave Harley a once over, which was quickly reciprocated by Harley.

"We'll be just fine, won't we B?" Harley asked a little mockingly.

"Perfectly," B replied sarcastically.

"For fucks sake, you two," I muttered and hugged Rain a little closer to me.

We entered the passage with Harley and B in the lead, Rain and I following them, and Lily behind us. I wasn't sure exactly what had set her off, but she had grown withdrawn again. I thought about trying to engage her in conversation but I knew she wanted space. And besides, my ability to stay mentally composed was hanging by a thread as we walked through the tight space.

I tried to soothe my anxiety by looking up and reminding myself I could still see the hazy sky above us. Each time I did, Rain squeezed my hand and when I met his gaze he'd offer me his most reassuring smile.

"Eight?"

"Yes?"

"Thank you, fear."

I let out a breath. "Yes...thank you, fear."

"For protecting me."

"Actually, Rain, thank *you* for protecting me," I said and tousled his hair. He beamed back at me, pride filling his face.

In front of us, Harley had drawn his lantern out of his bag and switched it on. *Smart,* I had forgotten about those but was thankful for the light making the passage seem a little less narrow. As we walked I peered into the overlaid trunks and branches now visible in the walls, wondering how the wall had been created. I startled when I felt something drop on my backpack and looked up, wondering if it was about to rain again. I distantly registered whatever had landed on me felt much weightier than a rain drop though. I turned my head to look at my backpack and let out a wail.

A scorpion-like thing about the size of a softball perched at the top, inches from my face. It stood on four legs and dark spikes covered its body, except for the tip of its curved tail curled up over its back. Spikes were concentrated around its neck, like a sharp lion's mane. Horns on its head curved down and along its jaw, which opened to reveal fangs. Six golden eyes stared at me with malice, the thing ready to strike.

I yanked my hand out of Rain's so the thing couldn't scuttle down my arm and onto him and was about to scream when something flashed in my vision and the creature went sailing to hit the wall on our left.

My heart was thundering as I looked at Lily, who had her backpack half pulled in front of her, the tail of her rope in her hand. She had used it to whip the scorpion off of me.

"Lil—" I started, but she wasn't looking at me, she was looking up and in horror. I followed her gaze, and almost lost the contents of my stomach.

Hundreds of the creatures were descending towards us on the wall on the right, weaving in and out of the branches, crawling over each other to get to us.

"Shut the lights off!" Lily shouted at Harley, who was gaping dumbfounded at where Lily had thrown the first scorpion.

He followed Lily's gaze and suddenly the light was gone.

"Get the fuck out of here! NOW!" I yelled, grabbing Rain's hand again and shoving B and Harley forward, wanting to be done with this tribulation immediately.

I could hear Rain breathing heavily in fear, but no one lingered, we all started running further down the path. I was itchy all over and on the verge of hyperventilating.

Manticore.

The word popped into my head. *Was that what those things were?* I didn't know why, but the name didn't feel exactly right, like the things we'd just seen were too small to be manticores. Really? *This* is the information from the Before that managed to pierce the veil that blocked my memories? That's all? Wait, no, there was one more piece of information that floated into my awareness—manticores fed on flesh. I wanted to cry as I heard the creatures skittering along the walls.

The walls suddenly widened out dramatically and we found ourselves in a room, although one without a ceiling. We huddled with our backs to each other as we caught our breath and looked around us. We saw a tall stone table but that was it; no doorway led out of the space. We were trapped.

We weren't alone, though. Manticore-scorpions—manticorpions—coated the walls about fifty feet up, crawling around actively but not descending upon us like they had when Harley's lantern was lit. It occurred to me they were staying near the top of the walls because it was brighter there. The sky above was purple but still lighter than where we were standing.

"There's no way out," Harley said, his voice uncharacteristically shaky.

"Did you all see this, though?" Lily said quietly, while she looked at the stone table.

Fourteen items were scattered across the top, all roughly the same size but different, irregular shapes. All had straight edges and were off-white and smooth, but some also had a spongy-looking texture on part of them.

The table was just a bit shorter than Rain so he stretched as he went to pick one up, but I grabbed his hand midair, not wanting him to be the first to touch the shapes. "Don't, we don't know what those are."

"They're made from bones," Lily whispered.

A chill ran through me.

"Human bones?" B asked.

Lily shook her head, looking at the items. "I have no clue."

I looked up to verify the manticorpions were still uninterested in us. "So now what?"

"I'm assuming we're going to have to do something with these things to get out of here," Harley grunted.

No one moved so I picked up the item closest to me hesitantly and studied it. After a few seconds of nothing catastrophic happening, I passed it to B and grabbed another one. Harley, Rain, and Lily each picked up an item then and examined it before trading it out for a different one.

"Are they meant to be weapons of some type?" Harley asked, touching the sharp end of one of the triangular pieces.

"I find it hard to believe we're meant to fight hundreds of insects with a couple sharpened triangles," I mumbled.

"Maybe there's a place in the wall we're supposed to put them in, like a key that would open up a way out?" B offered.

"Or it's a puzzle," Rain said, more focused on the stone table than the bone pieces.

"Rain..." I said, "that's genius!"

He looked at me, thoroughly pleased with himself and smiled hopefully. "Really?"

"Yes, you gifted child! It's Archimedes's Stomachion!" I said excitedly as my brain wrapped around the task at hand.

"A—whose—what?" Harley asked.

I pulled Rain to me and gave him an enormous hug. "It's an ancient Greek game and, exactly as he said, a puzzle."

Chapter Thirteen

"And how do we solve this puzzle?" Harley asked skeptically.

"You have to arrange the shapes into a square," I said, studying them. They were familiar and so was the puzzle, but no knowledge about how to solve it came to me.

"That doesn't seem too bad," B said, turning over a shape in his hand.

"I don't think it's particularly hard, but...I'm not sure what the catch is." I looked up to make sure we were still being left alone.

Rain grabbed a couple of the pieces and turned them over in his hands. "B, it's kind of like our dirt game where you have to make sure the shape to the side of the other shape will match in size on one side or you don't get points."

"It looks like you'll be taking the lead on this one then," Harley said, grabbing his canteen from his pack and taking a swig while looking up the wall. He capped his canteen and shifted his focus back to Rain. "Don't disappoint us."

B slowly raised his eyes from the bone in his hand to look at Harley. "What the *fuck* did you just say?"

Harley looked at B in confusion and then at the rest of us. "...what?"

"Why would you *ever* think it's okay to make a child feel like they could disappoint you?" B barked at him.

I stared at B, surprised by the anger in his voice.

"I didn't...I don't actually think that, man. I was just saying—"

"Well, *don't*," B snapped, stepping in front of Harley.

Lily backed away, putting distance between her and the two men. Rain had laid some shapes on the floor and was focused on them, unaware of what was transpiring.

"I didn't mean it like that! You need to relax!" Harley said defensively as he crossed his arms over his chest.

"I don't care what you meant," B said in a threat-carrying whisper. "Don't you ever, *ever*, make Rain feel like a disappointment again or I will—"

"What are you going to do, huh? What are *you* going to do?" Harley said, uncrossing his arms and puffing his chest out.

Before I knew what was happening, B had shoved Harley backward and Harley reciprocated by shoving B so hard he stumbled back into the stone table.

"Stop! Harley! B! You still have bruises, stop hurting each other!"

They ignored me as B righted himself only to push Harley even harder so that he stumbled into the wall behind him.

And Harley screamed.

The impact had caused a few hissing manticorpions to fall from the wall and land on him. He furiously tried to brush the things off even as they stung him repeatedly.

"Shit!" B yelled. Swiftly he grabbed two of the bone shapes from the table and rushed to brush manticorpions off of Harley, while Rain jumped to his feet and moved around to the far side of the table. I grabbed a sharp-edged shape and stabbed at them as they flew off and landed on the ground, managing to sink the bone right through a gold eye of one and the back of another.

Another one scrambled into a small opening under a tree trunk in the wall and disappeared before I could kill it. I looked back to see Harley still slapping at himself and breathing hard while B stomped the last manticorpion under his boot.

"Harley!" I ran to his side but Lily was already there, looking him over.

"It burns!" He clutched at his shirt, vigorously trying to rub at whatever marks they'd left. A red welt was forming on his neck, discoloring the dark skin.

"Let me see!" Lily lifted the edge of his shirt to reveal more welts all over his abdomen.

Just then Harley turned to the side and vomited. When he finished, his breathing was rapid and shallow. Lily held her index and middle fingers to his neck to check his pulse. "We have to get him out of here, his heart's racing and I think it's from the venom in the stings," she said, looking at me.

I glanced at B who stood stricken, his face pale at what had happened. "Harley, I'm sorry...I..." he said, his hand reaching out to Harley, who swayed on his feet. B jumped to grab his arm to steady him.

Rain had resumed his spot on the floor now that the manticorpions were gone and I could see him arranging and rearranging the pieces, working the puzzle as quickly as he could. "Rain, you heard Lily, right? We have to get out of here quickly. How can I help you with this?"

"Can you bring me the rest of the shapes?" he asked.

I wiped some blood off of the piece I still held and handed it to him, then reached over and grabbed the two B had dropped to the floor in order to hold Harley up by both hands. Harley's eyes were spasming and drool ran out of the corners of his mouth.

I handed the two pieces to Rain and pulled some more from the table. I handed them down to Rain on the floor and saw he had nine shapes fit together already. *He was so smart.* I kept handing him pieces and he rotated and shifted them with the others, working furiously. After a moment he had eleven pieces fit together. I was about to tell him he was doing a great job when I heard Harley vomit again, followed by his gasping for breath.

"His lips are turning blue. Hold him more upright, don't let him slouch," I heard Lily urging B. "It's harder for him to pull in air if he's slouched."

A few seconds after I handed the last two pieces to Rain he shouted, "that's it!" and lined up the fourteenth shape with the others to form a complete square.

"Rain, you did it! You saved us," I yelled and waited for a door or opening to appear in one of the walls around us.

Nothing happened.

"I don't understand, we solved the puzzle, shouldn't something happen now?" I wondered aloud. A moment or two ticked by and then Rain looked up at the table and then down at the square he had formed on the floor and then back at the table again. "These pieces were on the table when we got here, maybe they need to go back there?" he asked.

I looked at Lily and B on either side of Harley for their input but they just stared back at me. "Let's give it a shot," I said. I picked up a corner piece of the square and set it on the table. Before I could reach for the next piece, the first one lit up with a soft green light.

And the manticorpions above us stirred in response.

Fuck.

I whipped the piece off the table and they stopped moving. *Great*. I was going to have to get all of the pieces on the table as quickly as possible and hope that it would be fast enough for something positive to happen before we were overrun and stung to death.

"Everyone get ready to move quickly. Those little shits are going to get active again as I put the pieces together on the table," I warned. Not waiting for a response, I held my hand out to Rain and he put the second shape in it. I quickly set it and the first one down on the table and they started to glow and fused together. The manticorpions stirred again, making little scuttling sounds over our heads. Working quickly, Rain handed me a piece at a time and I set it in its place. When I moved the tenth shape into its place, it glowed red instead of green.

"What—Rain, help!" I cried.

I heard a couple manticorpions hit the ground, then Lily springing into action, stomping on them.

Rain's head popped up and he analyzed the puzzle.

"Wrong spot! Up at the top not down at the bottom."

I moved the tenth piece to where Rain had instructed and it glowed green and fused with the one next to it. Relieved, I held out my hand and Rain handed me more shapes and soon enough I held the last one.

Before I could set it in place, a manticorpion dropped onto the stone table, right where the last piece needed to go.

"Oh, fuck *you*," I spat at it, and slammed the last bone shape into place, smashing the creature between it and the table.

A green light illuminated the space.

Then the table cracked in half and the room, with its thick walls made of trees, mud, and grass disappeared from around us and we were back in the forest.

A shimmer caught my eye and I saw a glorious, golden key lodged in the crack in the table, along with a small vial. I grabbed the key and pondered what could be in the vial.

"Lily, look," I said, pointing to it, figuring if anyone had a clue of what could be in there it would be her. "Any thoughts on what that could be?"

Her brows furrowed and she pulled at the strands of her hair, tension bracketing her features. "I'm not sure..."

I cut a quick look to Harley, seeing the shallow rise and fall of his chest.

"...but if it's here, it might be related to those crawling things. Maybe it's poison to kill them?" She pondered for a moment. "Or maybe it has to do with the poison Harley got from being stung? Like an antidote?" She frowned. "It seems pretty likely that if we don't do something, Harley will die, so maybe we should give him what's in the vial," she whispered so only I could hear her conclusion.

"But what if—" I started.

"Now is not the time for what-ifs, Eight. It's next to the key and the key is overall a good thing. So let's just hope this is too."

My mouth went dry, but I nodded, taking in Lily's resolute expression. I didn't want Harley to die, but I also didn't want to increase his suffering. I trusted Lil, though, and couldn't refute her logic.

"Such a predicament you find yourselves in."

I looked up to see Sintra, arms crossed, leaning back against a tree behind where B was now kneeling while holding an unconscious Harley.

I growled, but followed Lily as she grabbed the vial and pulled its stopper as she ran to Harley. With B holding him, she forced his mouth open and poured the vial's golden liquid in, then shut it quickly so he couldn't spit it out if he regained consciousness.

Harley's body grew taut suddenly, his back arching, startling B enough that he accidentally let him go. I sucked in a breath and held it. *Did he just...?*

After a few seconds, Harley's muscles relaxed and he gasped, taking in deep, wheezing breaths as his eyes flew open.

Lily and I both exhaled simultaneously.

"Harley...I..." B started.

Harley held up a hand and closed his eyes while he took in air, shaking his head in B's direction.

"It is fortunate only one of you had gotten stung," Sintra spoke, uncrossing their arms and standing upright, golden eyes glinting with curiosity. "I would have been interested to see who would have gotten the vial if more of you had been."

I looked at Sintra, shocked horror filling my expression.

"Congratulations," Sintra said, arranging their indigo robes so they didn't catch on the grass as they walked towards Harley, who was still laying on the ground gasping while B hovered over him. "Feeling better?"

Harley just stared with wide eyes at Sintra, unable to speak through his wheezing.

"You will."

They smiled insincerely and then they were gone.

After Harley said he felt good enough to do so, we walked for a few hours and then made camp for the night. Harley insisted on taking watch; he said he felt like the manticorpions were still crawling all over him and he wouldn't be able to sleep anyway. Other than that, he had completely recovered physically, not even scars from the stings marred his skin.

The next morning we decided to stick around for a few days so that we could all catch a break mentally and physically. Harley gave B the cold shoulder, rebuffing B's attempts to discuss what had happened and hash things out. B gave Harley the time and space to come to him for a conversation, but I could see the remorse he carried grow each day.

Rain had some newfound confidence after the last tribulation and insisted B play their dirt game with him each night. B tried to get out of it at first, but after Rain argued that playing a similar game had saved their lives he couldn't refuse.

Lily and I were watching Harley try to get the fire started one night while B and Rain played their game.

"You're going to need something flat to fan it," Lily laughed, watching Harley's face turn red as he blew on the initial flames to get them to grow.

"Well aren't you just an expert in all things, Lil?" Harley said, obviously agitated at looking foolish.

"I wish I could help the knowledge that comes to me without my permission, *Hal*, but that's not within my control," she grinned back at him.

"We can't all be thinkers, *Hal*," I added.

Harley stood up, flustered and annoyed at having to interact with us. He looked over to B and Rain playing their game and sighed.

I pretend to pout. "Aww, c'mon Harley, just sit back down with us." I patted the spot next to me for emphasis.

He made a noise that sounded like "ick" and walked away, aggravated by everyone's presence.

"No, that's not fair, B! You can't do that!" An unexpectedly grumpy shout from Rain rang out.

"Hey, we made the rules together, Rain. It's only fair we *both* play by them, not just me," B told the little tyrant diplomatically.

"Yeah, but you keep winning. I haven't won once tonight!" Rain's arms crossed his small chest in defiance.

"Rain, you just saved us the other night, we're just playing for fun. It's not life or death," B tried to reason with him.

"You might as well quit while you're ahead, B. I think you're going to lose either way if you keep playing with him in this...mood."

"Shut up, Eight!" Rain yelled at me.

We all stopped and looked at him in bewilderment. He was not one to snap, but his face was contorted with rage. He looked so angry, too much so for the nature of their game tonight.

"Rain, I think maybe it's time we take a breather from playing," B offered, rubbing a hand gently on Rain's shoulder.

"I'm not a baby!" Rain screamed into B's face, and shoved at his shoulder.

A look of stunned hurt crossed B's face before he calmly said, "I...didn't say you were."

"I'm tired, I'm going to bed." Rain stomped off to his sleeping bag, away from the fire.

I started to get up, thinking I'd go after him to see if I could figure out what was bothering him.

"Don't, he might need space. I'll go keep an eye on him though and make sure he stays close," Lily said to me and B as she got to her feet.

I nodded, trusting her completely to take care of Rain in whatever way she saw fit.

"Don't wait up, I'm going to go to sleep after I check on him," she said, turning to make eye contact with me momentarily with a sly grin on her face before walking away.

I hadn't spoken to Lily about my attraction to B but it seemed she could sense how I felt, which, frankly, I struggled to put a finger on. I definitely found him extremely handsome and I admired the way he looked out for Rain. I liked being near him and felt safer at his side than I did anywhere else in the Between. But what did any of that mean?

As I watched Lily walk away, I saw B look at me with a soft smile. "What do you think about going for a walk, Eight?"

Chapter Fourteen

W e strolled together in silence through the forest, in the opposite direction of where Harley had wandered off in a huff. After a while, though, I asked, "so...would you like to talk about it?"

B sighed and looked away. "I...don't feel good about what I did," he admitted.

I took his hand in mine. "Hey, I think we all have things we regret here, you're not the only one." I pulled on his arm and stepped in front of him when he stopped. I waited until he turned back to meet my eyes before I said, "you're not alone."

He shook his head, his face solemn, "I know...I just I don't know why I snapped."

I nodded, understanding the sentiment completely. "I don't think we'll ever fully understand some of our actions here while we're missing some parts of ourselves." I thought about Don momentarily, how something about his personality had been exceptionally grating to me and how I knew I'd still regret how I treated him until I met whatever end in the Between.

We continued walking together and I didn't let go of his hand.

"Do you think you're going to talk to Harley?" I asked.

B let out a heavy breath, "I am and I'm going to apologize. I shouldn't have escalated that."

I squeezed his hand. "Would you do it differently if you could?"

He looked at me, his blue eyes shining in earnest. "Yes, a hundred times yes."

I nodded. "Then can you stop beating yourself up and just tell him that instead?"

He smiled wryly. "What a simple solution you have for me, it seems."

"Well, just try not to push him when you apologize and I think you should be alright. Can you manage that?"

He threw his head back and laughed and I joined him, happy he was feeling better.

"I was thinking about something after this last tribulation," he said, once his laughter died down.

"Oh?"

"You seemed to recognize that game from somewhere. Maybe you were a historian in the Before?"

I smiled, thinking about that. Maybe I wasn't a lawyer after all. I guessed arguing over historical relics and their purpose could fit my personality.

"Or maybe I just really like games?" I said lightly, knowing that wasn't completely true, considering Rain had solved the puzzle, not me. A shiver coursing through me and my teeth chattered as I spoke.

He let go of my one hand and brought both of his to either side of my arms, working their way up. "You can tell me if you're cold and we can go back to the fire. Or if you want my jacket?"

"I'm fine," I said, rolling my eyes and grinning at him playfully in return.

"You always are, aren't you?" he mused, and then he bent and wrapped his arms around my upper thighs, lifting me off the ground.

"B!" I screamed, a hysterical, choked laugh leaving me. I was completely unprepared to be airborne. I grabbed onto his shoulders with both hands.

He turned in a few small circles while wild noises escaped me in momentary joy.

"Put me down!" I tried to order him through cackles. He grinned broadly at my helplessness. "Seriously, you're going to make yourself tired! Let me go!"

"Never."

I tried to squirm out of his grasp, afraid he was going to exert himself too much while holding my weight. He relaxed his hold just enough for me to slide down his body. He allowed me to drop until I had to wrap my arms around his shoulders and my legs around his torso to keep from hitting the ground.

His smile turned into a mild grimace.

"I'm sorry!" I attempted to untangle myself. "I forgot about your bruises, I know they haven't healed fully yet."

Ignoring me, he pulled my legs tighter around him and walked until my back was up against a tree.

"I...don't want to hurt you..." I said as tingles ran up my spine. I shifted my arms so I could put my hands on each side of his neck. For a second I worried they might be clammy but if they were he didn't seem to notice or care.

"Do you think you could? Hurt me, that is?"

I tightened my grip around his neck. "I'm something of a masochist, actually, so I think I could be very capable, yes," I said with a wink.

His face inched closer to mine and I felt his whisper dance across my lips. "Well, do your worst then, Eight."

Our gazes met, questioning, probing, waiting to see something in the other's expression.

Then his nose touched mine gently. His blue eyes bore into mine and he let go of one of my legs. I tightened my thighs to hold on. As he nuzzled my nose with his, he pulled one of my hands away from his neck and tipped his head to gently kiss my wrist.

My head fell back against the tree, my eyes half opened, as I relished the moment.

"What do you want, Eight?"

"You, of course." It briefly crossed my mind that I almost said it was him that I *always* wanted, but the gravity of that statement felt too defining, too certain given where we were. If only I had always to promise him. I *wished* I could bind him to me like that indefinitely, instead of feeling like we were living on borrowed time.

B let go of my hand and his mouth met mine with a desperation I felt deep in my bones. I shoved both of my hands into his hair and his warm, soft lips moved against mine. He tasted sweet, like a dessert of some sort. I couldn't help my tongue reaching out to experience the taste more fully. His gentleness turned fervent as his tongue met mine.

Something snapped in him. I tried to turn my head for a quick gasp of air but he grabbed the back of my neck, holding me in place as he licked my lip. "Don't stop, please."

I pulled my head back and gasped, "insatiable, you are completely insatiable."

His nose traced my cheekbone and I could feel his smile ghosting my jaw while he melded my body to his. "You have no idea how impossibly I want you, Eight," he groaned.

Abruptly, I felt coldness, like ice, trickling down my spine. I froze and looked at B, my eyes searching his face for any sign he felt the same thing. Trepidation galloped through me at a steadily increasing beat.

Our eyes locked and I could see he was equally as panicked as I was. I wasn't alone in the looming feeling that had taken root deep within me.

"Do you feel that?" he whispered, as his hold on my body turned stiff with worry.

"I...do..." We stared at each other, not wanting to be right about our intuition, wanting to stay in the joyful moment we had found, wanting to forget where we were and any reason for being there besides each other. It hadn't been that long since the last tribulation and it had happened in this forest. *Surely we couldn't be facing another one already.*

"Hello, mortals."

I ground my teeth together as tears sprung to my eyes at the loss of the moment. I didn't know what was coming, just that it would surely be ruinous.

I slid down B's body, letting my feet return to the dirt. I put my hand in his, not wanting to sever contact.

"Sintra," B said, breathing in ragged pants as he moved to stand in front of me.

Sintra tilted their head to the side studying us slowly.

"It's unwise to form attachments such as you appear to be doing," they said finally, a chilling smile chiseled to their face.

"Can't stand to see anyone enjoying moments between their little sufferings, Sintra? I don't think I got enough of a break since seeing you last," I bit out.

"I cannot control how you mortals decide to feel for each other, but I also cannot stop your tribulations either. You have to meet the challenges you willingly committed to regardless of how closely in time they occur, and even if you form an ill-advised connection to one another."

Bile rose up my throat and I desperately wanted to vomit on their flawless skin.

"Welcome to your third tribulation."

They snapped their fingers once. Twice.

And the ground around them burst into flame.

Chapter Fifteen

I couldn't stop staring at Sintra, even as the dry grass around them burned with an intensity that foreshadowed an inferno. Amid the growing heat, my rage was singularly focused on them. All I wanted was to be back in the moment with B, to hold onto the joy I had been feeling. If I could have, I would have erupted with enough frustration to set off a Sintra-ending explosion. *We weren't ready for another one.*

"Better run, little mortal," Sintra snickered.

I snarled at them and bared my teeth. I was ready to lunge for them, risking the flames for the sake of spite alone.

"Eight, we have to go! We need to get to the others!" B grabbed my hand and tried to tug me away from my stare down with Sintra as smoke stung my nostrils in warning. I wished I could watch the Sintra's marble skin melt, watch their luster drip into the dirt where it rightfully belonged. But even if I had known a way to kill them, they were protected now by a wall of flames—and those flames were spreading, eating up the grass between us.

With a parting glare at them, I let B pull me away. We broke into a run back to the camp, trying to reach our friends ahead of the fire.

"Hey! HEY!" I screamed as we tore through the trees, my progress slowed by the roots I tripped over. Other than our racing footfalls and the sound of the fire crackling and snapping behind us, the forest was eerily silent. B's long legs had eaten up the ground quicker than mine and he reached the others ahead of me. I heard him shout at them to wake up, that we had to go quickly.

I arrived at our campsite to see B run straight to Rain and yank him out of his sleeping bag without second thought. Lily bolted upright at B's sudden appearance and scrambled backwards.

"W-what's happening?" she cried, eyeing B in fear, as if he were about to pounce on her.

B yelled a quick explanation and I ran over to where Harley was slumbering in his sleeping bag. Incredulity flared through me—it was just utter horse shit that he could sleep soundly even while death came for him.

"Hal!" I shook him as hard as I could. "Wake up, please! HAL! We have to go, right now!"

He tried to shove me away in his sleep.

Given the circumstances, I didn't feel the need to be gentle about getting him awake as quickly as possible so I shoved a fistful of dirt in his face.

Harley shot up, spluttering and rubbing at his eyes. He looked at me fiercely and bellowed, "the hell you think you're doing, Eight?!"

"You wanna die? Because I don't think so and I'm trying to prevent that!"

He looked behind me and took in the forest fire coming toward us.

Harley's jaw set. "We just barely finished the last tribulation. That sonofabitch really does want us to die," he growled.

"Exactly—but I'm not ready to let Sintra get what they want and I doubt you are either, so get the hell up and let's go!" I could feel the air warming around us and the sound of crackling and hissing flames growing louder.

Harley grabbed his bag and shoved his sleeping bag in it without care. I ran to my own bag and as I packed my things quickly, I squinted, straining for a glimpse of Sintra through the haze and flames. I didn't see them, though; they must have already released themself into a glittering breeze, off to wait for us at whatever finish line we reached.

Rain, Lily and Harley were up, their stuff collected in their packs. We were ready to make our escape.

I ran to them, past our campfire that was still calmly flickering in the night, unaware of its ugly twin about to absorb it in a fiery embrace.

"It's gaining traction, let's go!" I cried.

I grabbed Rain's hand and B grabbed my other. The five of us took off with B leading the way. Our shorter heights meant Rain and I were pressed to keep up but we ran as hard as we could. Still, it wasn't long before we felt the heat of the fire at our backs and the way before us was blanketed in smoke.

I let go of B's hand to cover my mouth and nose, hoping I wouldn't breathe in too much smoke. I felt Rain's small hand in mine tighten, then the weight of him pulling on me, then my hand was empty.

"RAIN!" He was sprawled face-down, barely moving. I reached for him frantically, more terrified in that moment than I had been in the river.

No, no, no.

I crouched at his side and turned him over, screaming at him to get up but he didn't respond. I didn't have time to figure out what was wrong with him as the fire danced closer to us so, coughing and choking on the smoke, I stood and put my hands under his arms and dragged him backwards in escape. Flames raced forward toward his feet and he let out a small scream as they made contact, making my heart seize. I stumbled as I tried to run backward with him and could feel wisps of hair around my face start to singe.

Harley and B suddenly appeared next to me and Harley pulled Rain's limp body from my hands. He threw Rain over his shoulder and started running again. B grabbed my upper arms as I was about to sink to my knees, wheezing and my throat raw from the smoke.

"Don't you dare give up on me again, Eight! If you die, I will follow you. Don't for a second think I'm willing to face any of this without you!" he yelled.

My lungs felt like they were going to give out, but I let him force me back into a run to catch up with Lily and Harley and Rain.

We managed to make it to a clearing made up of dirt, no dry grass to fuel the approaching flames. Harley laid Rain on the ground before leaning over with his hands on his knees as he panted furiously. We all huffed to catch our breath, and I wondered where we were supposed to go. Would this be what the next few days looked like? No sleep, just running away from the ravenous flames?

I grabbed my canteen from my pack and took desperate gulps, hoping to cool my burning throat. Lily and Harley followed suit, chugging from their canteens. When B didn't, I looked to find him staring at me with a horrified expression and my stomach bottomed out.

"I didn't grab my pack."

I gasped, "B...is it back—"

"It's gone, everything, back at the campsite. All my supplies are gone." His hands scraped down his face. "I ran for Rain and I forgot it was across the fire from you. I'm a goddamn *idiot*!" he shouted in fury and frustration.

I grabbed hold of his arm and shoved my canteen into his chest. "It'll be okay though, we'll figure it out. Here, drink!" As he drank, my gaze darted around and I realized we were about to be trapped—the flames had made it three-quarters of the way around the edge of the clearing, except for a ninety-degree gap.

I pointed with a shaking hand. "We have to go!"

Harley picked up Rain and threw him over his shoulder again, and then we were all running through the gap with Lily leading the way.

We made it out of the clearing with only moments to spare before the fire closed it off.

We kept running and after a while I felt my legs start to weaken, each step getting harder and harder, and I knew I couldn't keep up the pace much longer. I was so hot and it felt like my lungs were going to explode. It was so tempting to stop and rest, just for a moment.

But no—I couldn't start to give up this time. I wouldn't let myself give into my head telling me to slow down and accept my death. If I allowed myself to succumb, B wouldn't hesitate to stop with me and we'd both end up in the After. I couldn't let that happen to him.

I pushed myself harder, sweat running down my face and into my eyes.

The number eight flashed before me.

A car hit me.

My foot burned as it was run over.

I screamed, raged, demanded to be heard.

I was spiraling, falling, a curb greeting me with open arms.

"STAND. UP. NOW!" Harley's deep voice boomed down to me from above, leaving no room for debate.

I was on the ground and not sure what had happened until I looked around and saw that I must have tripped over another goddamned tree root.

"Rain?" I panted.

"B got 'im." Harley sounded equally as winded.

"Hal—"

"UP!" He shoved his hands under my arms, pinching tender skin in the process, and yanked me into a standing position.

"I—"

"Move!" he yelled and shoved me forward. I coughed and sputtered and my eyes watered as I thanked whoever would listen that Harley had come back for me.

We ran side-by-side, not letting one take the lead over the other. The fire had gained momentum and raced into a hollowed-out tree to our left. The fire hit the empty space within the trunk, causing it to explode and wood projectiles to shoot towards us. I screamed and ducked my head but we kept running. Ahead of us I could see the forest beginning to thin out, the trees getting fewer and farther between.

I felt Harley slowing down next to me. *Unacceptable.* I looped my left arm around his right and forced him along, pulling more of his body weight than I was expecting.

"Hurry, you ass!" I cried at him.

A grunt. "I'm...trying."

I was sure that if we could get out of the trees we'd be safe but Harley's gait had turned into a stumble and we were slowing down even more. I held on to him with all I had left in me, knowing I wouldn't let him go down, I wouldn't allow this to be his final moment because he chose to come back for me. I would find a way to drag him out of this forest if necessary.

"So close, Hal...we're almost there," I whispered hoarsely and then we tumbled out of the trees, out of the forest and away from the flames that couldn't follow us. Harley and I let our packs slide off our backs and then we fell to the ground and sucked in lungfuls of blissfully clear air.

I turned my head toward where B stood holding Rain, Lily next to him. "Please tell me someone got that damn key already," I rasped.

"Got it," Lily said in a panting breath and flashed its glowing light to me before quickly tucking it away in her jacket pocket.

I turned back to Harley, about to make a quip about his slow pace toward the end. I wanted him to know how thankful I was that he had saved me, but jesting was our love language.

But before I could say anything my eyes fell on a huge, jagged piece of wood sticking through Harley's left side.

Chapter Sixteen

"Harley!" I scrambled to my hands and knees and crawled over to him, and the others joined me by his side. I stared in horror at the mangled branch that jutted out of skin.

Breathing shallowly, Harley tried to sit up but pain or maybe just the branch's weight had him flopping onto his back instead.

"How bad is it?" he asked, his scratchy voice barely audible. He looked up at the sky, his eyes resolutely avoiding his injury.

"It's..." I trailed off. The branch was sticking out from his side, one end embedded in his oblique muscle. I had no idea how to figure out whether the damage was fatal or if he could recover from this.

"Bad," Lily finished, kneeling by him. She assessed his predicament clinically.

Sweat continued to bead on Harely's face. His normally rich brown skin began to turn sickly. His lips were dried and looked as if they'd crack open and bleed with each intake of breath.

Harley scowled. "C'mon, a final...death by... tree? That's pathetic..." he panted before his eyes fluttered shut.

Suddenly, his body went rigid and Lily and I jumped back in shock. He let out a rippling scream, and then his back arched off the ground and blood gushed from his wound. The veins on his face looked like they were about to burst open from the strain. His fingers dug into the ground, knuckles turning white. It reminded me of the way his body had contorted after he drank from the vial after the last tribulation.

"I won't! I won't give up!" he screamed to seemingly no one when his body finally relaxed.

Still panting in the aftermath of his fit, Harley inched his fingers down his abdomen until they grazed the branch. Blood pooled on the ground underneath him, thickening in a scarlet puddle. I was so worried about Harley, I didn't even notice when the blood reached where I knelt and coated my knees in a sticky layer.

"Don't you *dare* rip out the branch yet," Lily growled at Harley, pushing his hands away.

"What, am I supposed to live with this thing in me Doc?" Harley seethed through clenched teeth.

"No, *idiot*, I'll take it out of you. You aren't even looking at it while you're thinking of yanking it out. You might do more damage to yourself in the process," she said. Though her words were harsh, she gently laid his hand on the ground next to him.

"I need someone to grab me one of the medkits, *now*," Lily said calmly. She was so together, so collected, even while she balanced Harley's life in her knowledgeable hands.

B gently set a crying Rain on the ground before grabbing the kit from Harley's bag and handing it to Lily.

She searched through it expertly before grabbing a pair of those weirdly-angled scissors and cutting through Harley's shirt around the branch.

"Lil, I only have one of these shirts," Harley grunted to her.

"You also only have one life, but would you rather me save your shirt instead?"

He promptly shut his mouth.

Once his shirt was completely open, the damage the branch had created was on full display.

I turned away from Harley as I gagged and my stomach clenched in dry heaves.

"Your reassurance is…helpful, Eight," Harley deadpanned.

Lily glared up at me. "Seriously, leave if you can't handle this."

I took deep, steadying breaths. "I'm fine," I croaked unconvincingly.

Lily didn't acknowledge my response, just focused on what she was doing for Harley.

"B, I'm going to need you to take that piece of shirt I just cut off and be ready. Fold it tightly into a pad. Once I pull this branch out, you're going to apply steady, firm pressure to his wound with it. It will bleed more than it is currently, but we can't let him lose too much more blood. I'm going to get a needle and thread ready for stitches. Hand me that water canteen," she directed him, waving her hand to the water at B's side. "Eight, when I tell you to, I need you to light a match for me."

I stared at her in confusion.

"I need to sterilize the needle! Don't give me that look, just do what I tell you!" she snapped. She pulled a bottle of brown liquid, a needle, and some thread from the medkit and laid it all out neatly on top of the kit.

I scrambled for my pack and grabbed out the matches.

Once more, Lily assessed the branch's point of entry in Harley's side. Then she made eye contact with B and then me. "Are you all ready?"

We nodded quickly.

Lily gently placed a hand on Harley's chest, and met his eyes with hers. Tears streaked down his face while Lily remained calm.

"Are you ready?"

"I trust you, Lil," he stated, trying to put on a brave expression. "Just do it."

She gave him a small, reassuring smile.

And then yanked the branch from his side, giving him no warning whatsoever.

The sound that escaped Harley was one I knew I would not soon forget. His strangled scream was so feral it made my stomach churn.

"Now, B! Apply pressure!"

Without hesitation, B shoved the shirt pad onto the open wound, eyes wide and arms shaking with the pressure he applied against Harley's side.

"Light the match, Eight."

I struck the match on the ignition pad and held it out to Lily, who dipped the end of the needle in the flame. I shuddered, thinking of the reason we were here with Harley fighting for his life. This flame danced around so innocently. How could something so small and tiny brew into such tremendous destruction?

"Okay, keep the pressure going B, just a little longer."

As Lily worked to thread the needle, I watched Harley's face, contorted in pain.

"Harley, do you want my hand?" I made sure to ask for permission before touching people now, not wanting to cause him any more stress than he was already going through.

"Dear god, she's being nice to me. This has to be bad," Harley said, his breath heaving.

I narrowed my eyes on him. "Oh sorry, do you want me to tell you that you look like absolute shit right now?"

He tried to smile, but it was more of a grimace through the pain.

"Yes, please, Eight," he agreed and turned his wide, frightened gaze to me, nudging my knee with his fingertip.

Tears began to well in my eyes as I scooped up his blood-slicked hand. "You're going to be okay, Hal," I said, not really sure if that was true.

He squeezed my hand. "Trust me, I'm too stubborn to die like this."

I laughed as a tear made it down my face. "I'm counting on that."

Lily was oblivious to the moment, lost in her task of staving off death. When she was ready, she turned to B and said, "okay, when I say three, remove the pressure, B."

He nodded his head in confirmation, sweat trickling down his face.

"One...two... three!" Lily said. B leaned back and out of the way quickly, pulling the pad off Harley's skin. Lily poured water from the canteen onto the wound, clearing away any blood that had begun to slide out of the opening.

I think the pressure from Harley's hand on mine could have broken all my knuckles. I tensed in on myself, leaning towards Harley, and bit my tongue hard to keep from screaming. I watched as Lily made precise stitches, sewing Harley's skin together. His grip on my hand slowly started to lessen.

"Harley?" I choked out, concerned he was slipping from us.

"Keep him awake, Eight! He's lost a lot of blood," Lily said, focused on her handiwork.

Harley's eyes were half open and unfocused. "You hear that? You're not allowed to sleep on me! Especially because you're *such* a pain in the ass to wake up, Hal," I said, lightly slapping his face.

"I am fighting, trust me," he said in a soft whisper.

My eyebrows pinched together, bewildered. That didn't make sense—I hadn't asked him to fight, I told him not to fall asleep. I looked at Lily.

"He might be hallucinating from shock. It's normal," Lily said confidently. This brought me a measure of comfort, but I still needed him to stay awake.

"Tell me something, please, Hal. Tell me anything," I said, rubbing his cheek until his distant eyes found my face.

He seemed lost in a sleepy thought, and his eyes flickered shut before opening to latch onto me again. "I thought you were...an asshole...at first."

I laughed, the first smile on my face since we made it out of that horrible forest. "You know, I recall you actually telling me that too."

I could see the effort it took for the small ghost of a smile to make it to his lips. "I don't mince words."

"Which is why you and I get along so famously," I said as I rubbed his cheek again and tried not to notice his hold on my hand was weakening once more.

He closed his eyes.

"Okay, the stitches are done. Harley, this next part is going to hurt. Keep a hold of Eight," Lily instructed.

I braced myself for another hand crushing, but Harley didn't appear to have heard her.

She poured the brownish liquid from the medkit on his wound.

Harley screamed and let loose a steady stream of expletives as his grip did, indeed, become crushing again. Lily placed her hands on Harley's shoulders to keep him from thrashing against the pain while I tried not to pass out from the bones in my hand grinding against each other.

"You better not rip my stitches, Harley, or we're both going to be pissed at each other," Lily said, face red with the effort of restraining him. After a few moments, Harley stopped shifting around so Lily grabbed gauze from the medkit and placed it over the two and half inches of stitches she had just threaded into his side. Next she pulled out something that looked like a piece of transparent skin and placed it over the stitches, sealing them and the wound shut.

Now that her work was done, she sat back on her heels and wiped away sweat from her brow with the back of her shaking hand. She, B and I were all covered in varying amounts of Harley's blood, but she most of all.

"I need you to eat something and drink some water before you fall asleep, Harley," Lily told him as she got up on wobbly legs. "I'm going to go check on Rain."

B and I set to work, forcing Harley to follow Lily's orders. B knelt and gently raised Harley's head and shoulders enough that I could hold a canteen to his lips. After a few sips, he nibbled a little of his light chocolate.

Behind us, Lily removed Rain's boots, which had melted around his foot. Luckily it seemed the outside of the thick material had taken most of the damage, but there were a few parts where it had melted into his skin. Lily was gentle as she applied some ointment to each burn but Rain still cried out in pain.

I tuned out his whimpers as best I could. I'd had enough of watching my friends suffer for the day. Later, once I had a moment to myself, I could be there for Rain. Right now, Lily was there for him and that's all I could ask for.

B and I laid out Harley's sleeping bag and got him settled on top of it and he dropped into slumber. The fire continued raging in the forest behind us, ash drifting down onto us like a morbid snow, but we were far enough into the safety of this new, barren terrain that the flames couldn't reach us. Besides, we couldn't move an injured Harley and Rain with our own tired legs so B, Lily, and I decided to set up camp for the night.

A while later, Harley was sleeping even more deeply than he usually did and Rain's little feet were bandaged. His boots were absolutely ruined, but that was a future problem since he needed to be carried for a while anyways. Until his burns made noticeable progress scabbing over, according to Lily.

Lily, B, Rain, and I sat quietly and chewed our dinner. With his pack gone, B was sharing my supplies.

"Huh," he said after taking a bite of my light chocolate.

"What?" I looked at him, shaken from my own thoughts.

"Yours is sweet," he said, chewing thoughtfully.

I looked at him as if he had grown a second head. "What, yours wasn't sweet?"

He shook his head side-to-side. "Nope, mine was savory. Almost like a meat of some type...I'm not sure. It was tasty though. Yours is sweet, like a dessert. It definitely tastes different from mine."

Lily had been watching our exchange as she swallowed her small bite of dinner. "Mine tastes like a berry, I think."

We all looked to Rain who, once his cries of pain had subsided, had been extremely quiet. We all knew why and didn't push him to participate in the conversation if he didn't want to.

"Cheesy," was all he said.

"So they're all different then." I looked at my light chocolate, perplexed. "I wonder why?"

"I wonder what Harley's tastes like," Lily said.

"Yeah, and Don's." It was out of my mouth before I could stop it.

We fell silent then, no one wanting to continue talking about our fallen and injured friends further.

We stayed in our camping spot for the next two days. A fine layer of ash coated everything around us, making our throats dry and causing occasional coughs and wheezes. Regardless, no one was in any particular hurry, or physical or emotional shape, to face a long walk. Lily checked Harley's wound every so often, seeming to mentally track any changes it made. I didn't feel brave enough to look at it myself, so I asked her how he was doing. She seemed to avoid my questions, never meeting my eyes and only giving me vague shrugs in response.

While Harley was sleeping that day, I used some water from my canteen and tried my best to wash the blood out of the scrap of his shirt B had used as a pad. Lily had removed the rest of Harley's after our first night in camp, saying it would make it easier to tend to him. I took care to wash the rest of his shirt as well.

After the shirt had dried by our camp fire, I grabbed it and pulled a thread and needle from my medkit. B sat down next to me.

"What are you doing?" he asked, gesturing his chin towards the shirt in my hand. He watched as I started stabbing the needle through the fabric.

"I'm stitching Harley's shirt back together. He seemed pretty attached to it. Might make him feel a little better when he wakes up again," I said. I was not exceptionally talented at sewing, it turned out. I tried to mimic the movements I had seen Lily make when she stitched together Harley's skin, but I wasn't nearly as adept. My stitches were uneven and left gaps in the shirt material. I wanted to ask Lily for help, but she seemed worn out between caring for Harley and Rain so I just jabbed along as best I could. It was the thought that counted, even if it looked like shit.

"That's nice of you, Eight. I'm sure he's going to like that."

"I guess we'll see. Have you talked to him yet?" I asked.

"No, but I will. I just needed the time to find the right words, but you've inspired me. Once he's up and better, I'll do it. I think now he just needs some rest. I don't want to stress him out by bringing it up now," B said, sweeping a stray hair that had fallen in my face back and tucking it behind my ear.

I smiled at the gesture.

His face was next to mine suddenly, and he kissed me lightly on the cheek. I breathed in sharply.

"Ouch!" I waved my finger, bringing the tiny injury I'd just acquired to my mouth.

"Sorry, didn't mean to distract you," B whispered into my ear, his hot breath causing little shivers to race down my neck.

I glared up at him. "Liar."

His nose grazed mine. "You're right, I am a liar."

We sat like that for a moment, our foreheads resting against each other. His hand reached out and stroked my cheek softly.

"You scared me, Eight. I couldn't see you through the smoke, didn't know where you were. I was so panicked looking for you and then Harley ran to me and shoved Rain in my arms. He was back there by your side before I could stop him. I...I had to get Rain out of there," he said in a strained voice. "I thought I was going to lose you. I don't think I would have survived that."

Tears welled in his eyes.

"You would survive though, B. If something happens to me, I want you to. For Rain. Survive for him, please." I looked into his eyes, the blue shimmering with the unshed tears. When they finally spilled over I kissed them away.

"Please don't ask that of me, Eight," he choked out.

"Would you not ask the same of me?"

He shook his head, then grabbed the shirt, needle, and thread from my hands and set it on the ground next to me. He lifted my right hand, turned it over and kissed my wrist, a butterfly wing's brush that sent shudders through me.

He held my wrist lovingly to his cheek. "Okay, Eight. Then let's promise each other, if something happens to one of us, the other has to continue on. No matter how much it hurts, no matter how much we want to search for the other in the After, we survive. We do it for Rain."

A tear slipped down my face as my heart contracted. He brushed it away.

I gazed at him solemnly for a moment. "I promise."

He nodded and cupped my face in his hands, and we sealed our bargain with a soft kiss.

Chapter Seventeen

Harley's death was not a quick one.

It was not the quick intake of water and drowning that had snuffed out Don's life. It wasn't a few moments to contemplate the After before disappearing into a warm golden glow. It wasn't a quick rupture of an artery or break of a vertebrae and subsequent loss of consciousness.

No, for better or for worse, Harley was a fighter.

When Lily insisted on the second day being another down day, Harley started to fuss, saying he was ready to get up and start walking again. He even stupidly offered to carry Rain on his back, because that's the kind of person he was. One who was willing to help those he cared for, even if he ripped his stitches open painfully in the process.

"If you lift anything, even your backpack, I will kill you," Lily had said sternly when she overheard him talking to Rain. "We're resting again today."

Harley held up his hands in defeat and I pretended not to notice them quake.

Later, Lily did her routine check of both Harley's and Rain's bandages. She knelt where Harley had stayed stretched out on his sleeping bag and lifted up his mended shirt. Her face fell as she looked over to me with grim resignation.

"What is it, Lil?" I asked. Harley's breathing had seemed more labored today, but he'd still been present, still mentally sharp. He was just healing and tired. That's what I had been telling myself at least.

Tears brimmed in her eyes, and Lily slowly shook her head. I went and stood next to her, taking a deep breath to prepare myself for whatever I was about to look at.

I glanced at Harley's uncovered wound and inhaled sharply.

The skin around the injury site was puckered up, swollen with rage, like it wanted to consume all the stitches in its path. Under the skin, red streaks branched away from the wound, the poison of infection on its way to lay claim to the rest of his body.

Lily stared at Harley's body helplessly. "I...there aren't any antibiotics in the medkits," she choked out.

"Can't you just clean it again?" I asked desperately, pleadingly. Harley lay peacefully and he barely opened his eyes to join the conversation. "That brown stuff, it's to help clean it, right? Put more of that on it, Lil!"

She shook her head, freeing tears from her eyes to run down her cheeks. "Iodine won't help now, it's too late. It's in his bloodstream. He needs antibiotics that we don't have."

I shook my head. "No, there's something, look through the kit again. There has to be something in there, Lil. Just look one more time!"

"There's nothing, Eight!" she yelled. B looked over when he heard her shout and I gestured for him to stay where he was sitting with Rain. "It's been getting redder and I've been hoping it would get better on its own somehow because I can't do anything! I've *never* been able to stop this, so don't ask me to perform a miracle...please!"

I reeled back at the vehemence in her words, then reached a hand towards her tentatively. "Lil..."

She nodded, granting silent permission. I placed my hand on her back and rubbed soothingly while tears slowly crawled down my face. To my surprise, she turned and wrapped me in a hard hug, letting out a wail. She held me tightly, her body shaking.

"I tried, Eight. I tried, I don't know..." she sobbed. "I want to save him, I want him to be okay. I did everything I could...I..."

I buried my face in her hair, knowing nothing I could say would take away the pain she was feeling. There was nothing that could heal this type of heartbreak. This was all I could do, cry with her for our friend neither of us were ready to let go of.

I got on my knees next to Lily at Harley's side but I could tell he didn't see us, couldn't focus on our faces. He knew we were there, though, when I picked up his left hand with mine.

"It's okay...I'm going to be okay," he rasped, the faintest smile touching his lips, attempting to reassure us as he gazed towards the sky beyond.

I reached out to gently stroke his face. I could feel the fever burning hot and bright, almost as hot as the fire the other night. This time, the inferno raged within him.

I cried harder.

B carried Rain over to us and set him on the ground next to me. He leaned over and rested his head against me, crying softly. Then B knelt on Harley's other side, grabbing his right hand while tears streaked down his face.

"Harley...I...*fuck*," B's voice cracked.

Harley's eyes momentarily focused on B, as if for a single second he was lucid again. "Don't live with regrets."

B cried harder, lifting Harley's hand to his forehead while he wept.

"You're going to be okay," I lied to Harley while I continued gently stroking his face.

His dry lips smiled slightly and his eyes fluttered shut. "I'm sorry," he said just before he breathed out a ratting sigh.

His eyes never opened again, the smile never left his face.

For several hours after, none of us could move. We sat huddled together, holding and crying into each other. None of us felt capable of moving Harley's body—and where would we have moved it to? We only knew we weren't ready to leave it.

I didn't even look up when Sintra appeared.

"He is well, mortals. Do not fret," they spoke softly.

I shook my head, painful sadness filling me. I'd been so used to wrapping myself in a blanket of rage in the Between to protect myself from feeling more vulnerable emotions like despair, hurt, or loneliness. But I couldn't find my familiar anger to protect myself, couldn't feel anything but choking misery, could only let the tears flow down my face.

Sintra didn't offer us any more comfort. They, and Harley's body, just diffused away on a breeze. A glittering of gold flecks on the ground mixing with ashes from the fire was the only thing left to remember him by.

We didn't move from the spot we had lost Harley at for several days. We grieved and rested, trying to pull ourselves back together as best as we could before having to walk towards another tribulation.

Rain had scooped up a little bit of gold-flecked, ashy dirt and put it in his bag, saying it made him feel like Harley was still with him. He cried off and on over the days we rested, and I hugged him when he did. At night I let B take my sleeping bag and I shared one with Rain, stroking his hair gently, until his tears subsided and he fell into a restless sleep. B always stayed within arms reach, while Lily slept away from us. B took the longest watch most nights, keeping an eye on our little group vigilantly. He hadn't fully patched things up with Harley before he died and that would be a wound he couldn't heal. I think it comforted him to at least make sure Sintra didn't creep up on us while we slept and send us on to our next hellish experience.

The night before we broke camp, I couldn't sleep and looked at my watch to see it was 04:00. Sighing, I turned my head to where B sat staring into the distance. He must have heard me shift because he looked down at me with a small smile that didn't quite reach his eyes. "Hey."

"Hey," I replied. After a few moments of silence I asked him, "what do you think it's like in the After?" I took care to keep my voice low, so as to not wake Rain. He stirred restlessly, but snored lightly, telling me he was asleep.

B stared up at the purple sky. "I hope it's pain-free."

I wished the same, for both Harley's and Don's sake. "Why do we keep doing this? Why do we keep going just to lose more of us to these tribulations? It feels like the odds of any of us surviving to the end are definitely against us. If the After is peaceful, what's the point of all this suffering? Just to get back to a world we don't know if we'll even be happy in? What if this is all pointless and the better option is to just let go? To just skip this part and move on to the After?" I was so tired and sad.

B spun his head to me, a shocked expression on his face. "Let me ask you this, do you feel peace right now, Eight?"

I didn't have to think about my answer. "Absolutely not."

"I don't either. I don't know what's waiting for you in the Before, I don't know what's waiting for me, or Rain or Lily either. I do know one thing though. If it wasn't worth it to return, we would feel peace. Do you think about who might be missing you in the Before, waiting for you to wake up? I do. I wonder if I have friends or family who are heartbroken, waiting to see if I wake up or not. I think that's what makes it worth it; if we don't give up, if we *fight*, we get to stop their heartbreak."

I sighed again, knowing he was right. Everyone in our group had asked for a chance to return to the Before and we got one. We had to continue, to fight to go back to a real life, to loved ones who might be waiting for us.

"B...do you think we'll remember each other when we get back?" My voice cracked a little at the thought of not seeing B's kind, caring, handsome face ever again. My chest tightened, even though I had cried all my tears away over the past few days.

"I don't know, Eight. But I hope so. I hope we know each other somehow, in some way, even if it isn't the same way we know each other here." He reached out to caress my face.

I pressed my face in his hand, hoping that was true. "I don't think I could forget you even if I tried."

His thumb brushed across my lips and his eyes locked onto mine. "We'll find a way to make it back to each other, I know it."

I nodded, holding onto this moment of hope. I wished to whoever was listening in the universe, whatever benevolent being was out there, that we would have that small request granted to us after we survived the tribulations.

Chapter Eighteen

Before we broke camp the next morning, we gathered around the spot where Harley had died to honor whatever life he lived in the Before and the brief one we all knew together. The life that was ripped away before any of us were ready.

We stood, holding hands, and looked down at the golden flecks left from Harley's departure twinkle against the ash and bland, brown dust. Silently, we all said goodbye to our friend.

After a little while, we drifted to where our things were and started gathering our stuff. I knew B didn't want to, but he kept Harley's pack seeing as his had been destroyed by the fire. He dusted the dirt off Harley's old sleeping bag, trying his hardest not to cry for our sake before he shoved it into the depths of his new pack.

I held his hand and looked up to his face. "I'm here, you aren't alone. It's okay to be sad, to be afraid."

He looked down at me and squeezed my hand. "Thank you, fear."

I nodded. "Thank you, fear."

We walked, the days quieter, Harley's absence stretching between us. This wasn't like how it felt after Don's death. I knew the big difference was that I hadn't really liked Don while Harley and I had grown close. I couldn't say for certain how B, Rain, or Lily felt at Don's passing, but there was no doubt that Harley had been more personable, that he had helped hold the group together with his grounding energy. When I tried to set my bias aside, I realized none of us really got to know Don in the short time he was a part of our group. He had been shy, not often participating in conversation. Though I wished neither death had happened and sharp guilt had been wrapped up in Don's, Harley's had a much greater effect on me.

This time, I had lost a friend, and the experience was novel. Without any knowledge of my life in the Before, this was, for all intents and purposes, the first time I'd ever experienced the loss of a loved one. I had loved Harley as a friend, and I desperately wished our ending could've been us hugging goodbye as we parted ways happily to return to the Before.

B and I held hands while we walked, whether he was carrying Rain or not. I felt we were cut from the same cloth, whatever that was, and found comfort in each other's touch. Even so, my neck often prickled with the feeling of being watched, and I occasionally heard that voice in my head again, pleading with me. And I know B was still struggling. When we made camp each night and gathered for dinner, I knew it was hard for him to eat the light chocolate that once belonged to Harley, that it weighed on him to drink from Harley's canteen. B had what he needed to continue trying to make it through the tribulations but only because Harley was gone.

Lily was also having a hard time. She had taken personal responsibility for Harley's recovery only to doubt her abilities when she couldn't save him. She was still breathtakingly beautiful, but her face had lost its glow and looked drawn. She still evaluated Rain's healing burns on a daily basis, but grew quieter, more aloof, and continued to sleep away from us. I gave her space because I knew what it was to feel smothered by another's death.

If Harley had never come back for me in the fire, I would've been the one the group mourned. However, the one thing I knew from processing Don's passing was that no matter how much I wished to, I couldn't take away another person's choice to save me. I couldn't force them to not cut a rope, to not run back through a fire. I missed and mourned Harley, of course, but I knew that I couldn't go through the same guilt I had felt at Don's passing. I could no longer let that feeling eat me alive, couldn't let myself give up, couldn't leave B with the burden of surviving without me.

One night I was able to convince B to get some sleep while I kept watch, and as I sat up while the others slept, I mulled over the conversation B and I had had about returning to the people we loved in the Before. In theory, I cared about the people that were waiting for me, if they really were. In reality though, I only cared about not leaving B, Rain, or Lily alone here. I didn't want to be the cause of the same heartbreak that I'd experienced and witnessed at Harley's death. I didn't want anyone to feel responsible for tending to my survival. I needed to do that on my own.

And I had to help Lily move through the guilt she felt, like B had helped me that night at the pond after Don died.

The next time we made camp, Lily sat on top of her sleeping bag away from the rest of us. Instead of laying out my sleeping bag next to B and Rain, I set up next to Lily, knowing that she wouldn't mind my presence. She never cared when it was me or Rain.

She didn't acknowledge me, just stared at the horizon and picked at the material of her sleeping bag. For a while, I just sat with her and offered her the comfort of my presence. I breathed in and squashed the desire to start a conversation.

We might have sat there for an hour, staring at nothing before she said, "I wasn't honest when I said that I didn't remember what happened in my final moment before."

I don't know what I had been expecting Lily to want to talk about—probably something about Harley—but it hadn't been her last earthly moment.

I turned my head to her, waiting for her to continue, the way the B had for me. When she began speaking, she sounded distant, as if she had detached herself from the moment.

"I'm not sure why I didn't feel safe to talk about it. Everyone here feels like friends...a weird little family of sorts, kind of, but I didn't know how to, didn't know what to say. I didn't really want anyone to offer me any consolation or comments," she said, still looking to the horizon. I knew Lily would stop speaking if I kept looking at her, so I turned my head to match her far away gaze.

"I'm here," I said, "whatever you need, Lil. Whatever I can offer you, I'm here and I want you to know that."

She placed her hand on top of mine in an unexpected gesture but didn't look at me.

"I did see lilies when I died the first time. I'm not sure where I was, but I think it was a kitchen. I think it might have belonged to me, the me in the Before. I was in there with a little boy." I could hear a slight tremor in her voice now. "He looked like me in my reflection," she said, "the one that we saw together in the pond. I don't know who he was, but I think he was a part of me in some way. He smiled with so much...love...in his face..." She shuddered then, and seemed like she was struggling to hold herself together.

"Then someone came into the kitchen, a man. His face was so angry and all I can remember is feeling confused and afraid."

My heart skipped a beat. I slowly turned my hand so I could take hers gently into mine and rubbed soothing circles in her soft skin.

"That little boy's face fell when he saw the man come at me, pointing his finger at me aggressively. His face looked so scared, so tiny, he looked not much older than Rain does now." Lily's voice shook as she continued, "he screamed so loud when the man twisted my hair around his fist. He begged and pleaded for me when this man punched my face and I heard my nose crack.

"The little boy grabbed the man and tried to hit him, *yelled* at him to stop. I knew my heart was never going to be the same again when I saw the man shove the boy away from him hard then saw him curled up on the floor. He was still breathing, but I was terrified."

Lily was crying now as she glanced down at where I held her hand and my chest squeezed painfully from the look of shame on her face.

"I said something to the man, something I can't remember, no matter how much I try to pull the thoughts from my brain. I want to answer this question that's been...haunting me...what *did* I say? How did I bring on so much rage towards me?" she gasped out between sobs.

"What kind of person was I that I would let someone like that near a child? Why didn't I *protect* him?" she wailed painfully.

Unable to keep myself from looking at her tear-stained face, I turned and ducked my head to catch Lily's eyes. "You are *not* the reason why that little boy was hurt. *Nothing* you could've done ever justified being treated like that. Do you hear me, Lily?" I shook her hand, wanting to get that through to her.

She looked at me with bloodshot eyes. "I should've done more, I could've done more and I didn't."

I shook my head emphatically. "No. You had to have loved that little boy. You probably loved that man too, Lil. Sometimes we love people that we shouldn't. Sometimes we love people that are toxic to our souls, but we still can't let them go, even if we know we should."

Tears were still running down her face. "I will regret loving that man for what he did to that boy as long as I live if I make it back to the Before," she said in a voice full of anguish.

We sat quietly for a few minutes, the only sound the juddering breaths Lily took to calm her tears. I kept holding her hand.

"After he twisted my hair into his fist, I screamed and cried. I shouted things at him I'll probably never remember. I couldn't stop looking at that perfect little boy's crumpled body, terrified that I couldn't reach him. He snapped my head so painfully, I can still feel the spot he grabbed me when I think about it. He smashed my head into the tiled countertop. The tiles had lilies on them. That was the last thing I saw until I woke up here."

Slowly, hesitantly, I brought my other hand up to her face. She watched me the whole time, unflinching. I tucked a strand of hair that was hanging in front of her eyes behind her ear. Her lips twitched as more tears fell.

"I couldn't save the little boy and I couldn't save Harley. I'm broken...I'm...I...can't help anyone." Her body began to shake again.

"You gave everything you had to Harley, Lil. He was sick, you didn't have what you needed to heal him. If you did, you would have saved him. If you weren't being held by that man, you would have helped that child too. Listen to me—*you did nothing wrong*."

Lily stared at me for a second and then slowly she leaned toward me and rested her face on my shoulder. This time the sobs wracked her body and it seemed her heart must have shattered. She looked so fragile, so breakable. I wished there was something as easy as a bandage to fix this type of injury. This was a wound to the soul, though.

I put my arm around her, trying to offer as much comfort as possible. She had been bottling up so much pain for as long as we knew her, pain from her time in the Before.

"That man is going to get what he deserves," I whispered fiercely against the top of her head. "I don't know anything about what happens in the After, but I don't think people like that get a second chance. I don't think they get to know peace."

After a long while, her sobs eased enough for her to wipe her tears on my shoulder and say, "I hope that's true, Eight. I really fucking hope you're right about that."

"You are a goddamn blessing to this group, Lil. It's not fair, it's not *right*, that anyone has ever laid their hands on you without your permission, but I feel damned lucky that I get to walk through this shitty fucking realm by your side. I'm so lucky to have ever known you, whatever the future holds for us. And Harley was lucky to have you until the end."

She nodded a little bit but I don't think she believed it yet.

I would keep reminding her. Keep helping her see her worth, do what I could to help patch herself back together. I would not give up on her beautiful soul.

"God, life sucks," I said, shaking my head.

A tiny laugh escaped her, one that quickly turned into another sob.

I held Lily until she eventually pulled away and laid down to rest, thoroughly exhausted. I lay by her for the rest of the night. I didn't sleep but watched our surroundings, angrily daring anything to cross me at that moment. I was willing to fight to the death.

While Lily slept, I kept her as safe as was humanly possible.

Chapter Nineteen

I was on watch the next night and scanned the horizon methodically while I sat on my sleeping bag, even as my thoughts wandered from Harley to Lily's abuser. It was so unfair Lily was suffering in the Between while, presumably, her abuser was walking free in the mortal world, coming nowhere near the pain that Lily was going through. *It's such a load of shit that this place prides itself on being fair to all.*

"Mortal."

I leapt up and whirled around to see Sintra standing behind me, their indigo robes billowing around them even though the air was still as usual. I opened my mouth to shout for the others but they raised a hand to stop me. "No need for that, this is a...personal visit. Not a tribulation."

I narrowed my eyes in distrust. "Personal, huh?" What could Sintra possibly have to say to me *personally?*

"Yes. Walk with me for a bit," they said, nodding their head in a direction behind them.

I looked at my sleeping friends then back to Sintra's marble face. "I'm kind of busy making sure they wake up alive, if you can't tell."

"You have my word no harm will come to them," Sintra offered stiffly. "Please, this will not take long." I didn't trust Sintra for one second but there was something oddly entreating on their part. I knew there was every chance I would regret it but I didn't feel like I could refuse their request.

"Alright then," I said as I stepped over a sleeping Lily, "but no springing anything life-threatening on me."

Sintra smiled tightly. "Well, all of life is threatening in one way or another but, again, you have my word."

We strolled without speaking across the empty landscape until Sintra stopped suddenly. "You cared about Harley very much, but you did not care about Don. Why?"

I inhaled sharply at this unexpected jab to my mental wounds. "I...I didn't know Don, not like I did Harley. Harley was...not afraid. He was solid, like a rock. I don't know, but he and Don were different."

I squinted at the ground, feeling so confused at what the purpose of this interrogation was.

"You thought Don was weak."

I snapped my face to see Sintra studying me closely, like a scientist watching a mouse in an experiment. I opened my mouth to defend myself but found I couldn't. I *had* thought he was weak. I'd be lying to myself if I denied it.

I looked away, resolutely setting my gaze ahead of us while I started walking again. After a pause, Sintra joined me.

"Curious, mortal. You surprise me."

"How so?"

They tilted their head to the side for a second, weighing their words before speaking. "You dislike weakness and yet you rely on those you deem as strong as a crutch. You allow others to die in your stead. Your survival seems to have no bounds."

Sharp anger rose in me. "What do you *want*, Sintra? Just to piss me off even more?" I asked defiantly.

They sighed, a bit dramatically I thought. "No, I do not." They turned to face me and we stopped walking again. They looked me over slowly, assessingly.

"You are a survivor, mortal. Others flock to you for it."

"...thanks?"

"That is not a compliment. Others also die for it."

Don and Harley's faces flashed in my mind and I looked away.

"This is for the boy," they said and held out a pair of kid-sized boots in their hand. "For when his feet are healed and he is able to walk again."

Taken aback by this unexpected generosity, this kindness, I looked at Sintra as I slowly accepted the boots. For a moment I thought I saw their expression soften a little bit.

"I...that's...thank you."

They nodded, and I knew I wasn't imagining it, they were looking at the boots almost wistfully.

"Take care that he wears them."

"No shit," I said, but there was no heat to my words. It felt like a truce had been drawn and I didn't want to ruin it but I still had to ask.

"Sintra, what...why...for Rain? I don't understand." It was great they were replacing the boots that had been melted in the fire, but it was like offering someone a stick to paddle a rowboat with. It wasn't like they were offering to remove Rain from tribulations much more dangerous than being shoeless, after all.

Sintra stared remotely at where I held the boots by my side, their expression blank now. "Mortals come and go through this place more than you can imagine. Many are forgettable, uninteresting, turn to dust before my eyes. Plenty of them deserve it, some do not, but I do not trouble myself with weighing the goodness of a mortal, it is pointless. You are all capable of kindness, but also have the propensity to commit such atrocities in the short breath of your life. There are few that find themselves here that are misplaced."

Their golden eyes flicked to my face and captured my stare like a predator trapping its prey in its claws. "I trust you will not allow him to perish for your survival?"

I set my jaw. "Never."

"I hope you mean that, mortal," they said in a low voice just before they disappeared.

I quickly paced back to camp to find everyone still asleep. I sat on my sleeping bag, my mind whirling, as I tried to shake off the weird interlude with Sintra. I tried not to think that my will to survive meant that others died, but they knew exactly which of my nerves to pluck, how to *hurt* me. But even as they were hurting me, Sintra seemed to care enough about Rain's wellbeing to give him a new pair of boots—which he'd be wearing as he fought for his life through Sintra's tribulations. Their kind gesture was also so cruel.

When the rest of the group woke up later, I presented Rain with his boots.

"Where did those come from?" B asked, his eyes glinting with curiosity.

"Um...Sintra."

He froze. "Sintra was *here*? When?"

I shook my head reassuringly. "It was a personal visit, they said. They tried to ruffle my feathers a little and then gave me these for Rain."

He looked at the boots like they were another puzzle tribulation, like our lives depended on figuring out what it meant.

"Odd," was all he said.

And I didn't speak of it further. I wasn't going to think of Sintra as anything other than the villain just because of one small act of charity.

In the days that followed, I wouldn't have said Lily returned to how she had been before Hal's death, but she tried. I could see that Rain was the main reason she started coming back to herself again. She had deemed his feet healed enough that he could walk for short periods of time and when he wasn't being carried on B's back she was at Rain's side, holding his small hand. At night, she set up her sleeping bag near him whenever I slept between him and B.

Maybe she allowed herself to feel close to Rain because of the little boy she felt she hadn't been able to protect in the Before, even though the blame for what happened to him was never hers. As if protecting Rain so that he could return to the Before, was an atonement of sorts. I understood; B and I had promised each other to do all that we could to make sure Rain returned to the Before, to people we assumed missed him terribly, whose hearts were breaking as he hovered on the edge of life and death. The violence and grief we all experienced would be worth it if Rain survived.

After interminable days of walking, we noticed the air became warmer and the ground became a dull orange color, like the rusted bits of a nail. One day, we came upon a small body of steaming water surrounded by low trees that had many twisted and naked branches. We had ditched our jackets and put them in our packs when it became so warm that sweat dripped down our backs and salt crystals began forming on our shirts. We had all been washing ourselves as best we could with the water from our ever-replenishing canteens, but it had been many days since the pond and we all relished the idea of a good soak. I crossed my fingers the water wouldn't be too hot to prevent us from getting in.

B bent over and stuck a finger in the water and quickly removed it with a little cry, as if he had been scalded. A blistered fingertip wouldn't be nearly as traumatic as burnt feet, but we didn't want to use up supplies in the medical kits if we didn't have to.

"It's pretty damn hot..." B said finally, staring at the water, then at his finger as if waiting for it to whisper some answer to him.

"Like too hot for us to use, to get clean and relax a little?" I asked disappointedly.

He contemplated his finger for another second. "I'm not sure. It felt pretty hot to me, but not in a way that would cause burns. It startled me, is all—I thought it would be cool like the pond was. I think it's safe for you to test it out yourselves at least."

Lily and I approached the oasis's edge, discarding our boots and socks to the ground. We both stuck our big toes in the water then pulled them back out. After a second I stuck my whole foot in and let out a moan of pleasure. Lily soon followed, letting out a pleased sound as well.

"B, you're insane, this water is *perfect*," I said. My sore feet instantly felt more relaxed than they had this entire journey.

He scrunched his face up in confusion then removed his boots and socks as well. He dipped a toe into the water, clearly wondering what he'd missed with his first test. He pulled back his foot so quickly it was like he thought the water was about to bite it off.

"That's hot! Are you both serious?!" He looked between us like we were about to dive into a lava pit.

"B, are you afraid of a little hot water?" I teased him.

He shook his head, clearly finding us delusional. Lily and I laughed and I realized with a pang that it had been many days since I'd done so.

After an agreement to have the boys set up camp facing away from the oasis, Lily and I stripped down to our bras and underwear, tossed our discarded clothes into the water to rinse out, and stepped in up to our shoulders. The water smelled slightly sulfuric, which made me want to gag, but I shoved the feeling away quickly. Nothing was going to stop me from enjoying the way the water was getting my aching muscles to release their tension.

We floated there for a while, then rinsed out our hair and helped each other find parts of our bodies we missed in our attempts to scrub away dirt. We probably spent an hour or more in the water, luxuriating in the heat before we gathered our wet clothes onto the edge of the oasis and climbed out so B and Rain could have a turn.

With our backs to the boys we hung our wet things on some of the trees' low branches to help them dry even more quickly and then set out our sleeping bags and crawled in. I laid mine so that Rain would be between me and B. I didn't say anything when Lily laid hers out on the other side of mine. Deep down, I hoped her willingness to sleep closer to the rest of us was because she felt safer around B despite what she experienced in her final moments before arriving in the Between. I hoped she recognized he wasn't like the disturbed soul who had abused her in the Before.

I could hear B gasping and panting as he slowly eased himself deeper in the water. I tried to stifle a giggle at his struggle.

"I can hear you laughing, Eight," he said. It sounded like he was talking to me through gritted teeth.

I grinned at Lily who was doing a much better job at hiding her chuckles.

"B, stop being such a wimp, that water is a perfectly reasonable temperature," she said.

"Where's cold pond water when you need it," he said under his breath.

"So dramatic, B." I rolled my eyes, the grin still plastered to my face.

Despite his complaints, B fell quiet after a few minutes.

"Everything okay back there?" I called, trying to quell my anxiety at the sudden silence.

"He's okay, Eight," Rain yelled.

"You just got awfully quiet there for a second," I said. "Are you, perhaps, enjoying yourself now?"

"If you don't move around too much, I guess the water isn't so bad," B called back. Lily and I giggled again and then I heard B explaining to Rain to take off everything but his underwear, like he had, and throw it all in the water to rinse out. Then he told him he'd hold him in the water so that his feet didn't get wet. Rain was developing calluses in the place of the burns but Lily had said the hot water might aggravate them. After they had finished soaking and hung their wet clothes to dry, they got into their sleeping bags as well and we all nibbled on our light chocolate and chatted.

Later, it was my turn to keep watch again so I sat up, my arms around my raised knees, occasionally scanning the empty space that stretched around us or staring at the mauve sky. After a while I heard stirring next to me, and looked over to see B sit up and follow my gaze to the sky.

"Not able to sleep?" I asked him.

"Don't really sleep well these days," he explained in a whisper.

I nodded. "Me either. In the time we've been here I think I've only had one night of real sleep that I actually woke up feeling refreshed from."

He raised his eyebrows at me. "Yeah? Which night was that?"

I took in his handsome profile briefly before he turned his gaze to meet mine. "The night by the pond."

He smiled innocently. "Did you know that you snore?"

I gaped at him. "I do not!"

"It's really quite cute actually. Your face kind of...leans back with it. It almost sounds like a little mewling kitten. I like it." He imitated my alleged snoring, throwing his shoulders into it for dramatic effect.

I shoved him playfully. "You're just messing with me."

He grinned wickedly in return. "Am I?"

"I don't know how you do it," I said with a smile.

"Do what?"

"I hate this place, hate that I'm here, but I don't hate being with you. I just feel...normal, almost, when we're talking. Like I could be anywhere and this wouldn't be some life or death moment for any of us," I admitted.

B leaned over at that, cupped my face in his hands and kissed me.

My insides brimmed with tingling sensations. I kissed him back, caught up in the feeling of normalcy and passion. Stopping for a moment I stood up, stepped over to him, and then lowered myself onto his lap, resuming the kiss.

He smiled and admonished me softly. "Now, now, Eight. Don't forget we aren't alone."

I let out a small laugh and glanced at Lily and Rain in their sleeping bags. "I know we aren't, but they're asleep. We don't have to go any further...I mean, we can't...I know that, but let's just have this moment and not think too much about anything else."

He brushed his nose against mine and wrapped his arms around my waist, pulling me closer to him. We were both in our underwear and the places where our bare skin met were electric.

One of his hands drifted up between my shoulder blades as he pulled me into another deep kiss. I lightly grazed my teeth against his lower lip, he threaded his hand into my hair, gently tugging my head closer. I was breathless, my whole body swept up in the gentle warmth of desire.

I wound my arms around his shoulders, and somehow he managed to pull my body even closer to his, as if we were joined as one in this moment.

His tongue pressed against my lips, asking for permission, permission that I instantly granted. Our mouths moved against each other, our tongues danced, and we let ourselves go while Lily's and Rain's breaths were heavy with sleep.

After a while, we pulled apart, drugged by desire. He spread his legs and shifted me so that I sat between them, his arousal present, with my back to his chest. Heat flushed my face at the sensation, but neither of us mentioned it and instead we stared blearily at the horizon, content.

"I should probably get up, it's my watch," I whispered.

He stroked a hand up and down my arm soothingly. "Let me take the watch for the rest of the night."

"It's my turn though."

He kissed my temple. "Get as much sleep as you can, Eight. I'm fine, I'll take the watch."

"Well, you're making it really hard for me to sleep when you're being so nice to me," I whispered as I tipped my face up to him.

He looked down at me with a smile that turned suggestive. "Need help sleeping, Eight?"

My breath left my body. I wasn't sure what he was going to say next, but I deeply wanted to know where this was going.

"Yes, I think I do," I murmured.

He looked over at my sleeping bag. "Go lay down."

I opened my mouth, liquid heat pooling in my core. I slowly removed myself from between his legs and did exactly as he said. Once I was stretched out on my bag, B got up and knelt at my feet.

"B, maybe we shouldn't..." I said quietly.

"Shhhh," he returned.

My insides quivered as I waited for his touch on my skin. I was completely at his mercy, but I wasn't afraid. I only felt trust, excitement, and devotion toward him. I knew without hesitation that I would give him anything he wanted.

Slowly, his eyes locked on mine, he reached out and took my right foot in his hands and began making firm but soothing strokes along the arch with his thumb.

My eyes drifted shut and I pressed a hand against my mouth to silence the moan of pleasure that wanted to escape.

B's thumbs dug expertly into my heel next, rubbing gently, before they moved to the pads of my feet. The massage was the final straw—I began to drift into sleep and it was just moments before I was snoring gently with a smile on my face.

That was the second night in the Between that I slept deeply, not waking up once.

Chapter Twenty

Time stretched on in the desolate orange landscape we now inhabited. We walked, day after day, but unlike the previous times between tribulations, it didn't seem like we felt on edge or anxious about what was coming.

Rain and B had taken up their dirt game again whenever we stopped to rest or camp for the night. Lily and I would watch them sometimes, or pass our time in conversation, or other times just sit in companionable silence.

One day we noticed what looked like a crack in the ground in the distance, running parallel to the horizon. Over the hours we walked toward it, the crack appeared to widen. I tried to ignore the worry that began building as we got closer.

"Is it another river?" Rain asked, his eyes fixed ahead of him.

"Only time will tell, little one," Lily replied patiently to Rain's apparent dissatisfaction.

"Is it warm enough here that it could be a mirage? Maybe our minds are playing tricks on us," I said to no one in particular.

By day's end, we had reached the fissure and discovered it was the edge of a vast canyon.

I didn't need the incoming-doom feeling to spread across my body to know that this cliff signaled something unpleasant was in store for us.

"I...feel..." Lily started.

"Bad, horrible, like your insides are trying to twist in on themselves until you vomit, that death is beckoning and we have to go toward it?" I asked as I searched the canyon for some way to get across it.

Lily snapped her head toward me, a look of dread on her face. "Yes."

I let out a heavy sigh.

We decided to make camp for the night, thinking it would be best to get some rest before we faced whatever was down in the canyon. I slept poorly, tossing and thrashing. I even woke myself up whimpering a couple of times and knew it was the proximity to the next tribulation that made me extra restless. I don't think the others slept well either; everyone was groggy, touchy, and anxious when we decided to get started the next day.

The canyon was relatively deep and B and I spent some time arguing about how to get down into its depths.

"What about the rope?" B asked.

I looked up at him with horror. "You really want to try the rope thing again after what happened the last time we tied ourselves to someone?"

He shrugged. "I don't know, maybe we could lower ourselves in there somehow."

"You better just call Sintra for me now if you're going to try to lower me in there with our ropes. They aren't long enough, they could maybe make it a quarter of the way down that ridge at best," I muttered.

B rubbed his hand across his face, scrubbed at his eyes and then scratched the stubble along his jaw.

"Let's keep walking, we don't have to rush down there. I'd rather have a solid plan than get ourselves killed because we were impulsive," Lil said with her predictable rationality.

We continued to move along the cliff edge until we reached the beginning of a steep path carved into the canyon wall. It was only about four feet wide and as we peered down its length we could see it zigzagged in a series of switchbacks. Here and there boulders—some taller than others—seemed to block the path. Were we going to be able to squeeze between them and the canyon wall to get past? If not, what were we going to do, climb over them? My stomach lurched at the thought. This was going to be harrowing.

"Maybe the test will just be getting down into the canyon?" I suggested halfheartedly.

No one responded, probably afraid if they did it would jinx the opportunity for this to be over with quickly. I knew that wouldn't be the full tribulation anyway—Sintra wouldn't let it be that simple.

With no other options, we started down the path; B led the way, followed by Rain, then me, then Lily. B made Rain walk the whole way, afraid that if he carried him on his shoulders and took one wrong step, one slip, they'd both meet their final death in a plummet to the canyon bottom.

"Pick your feet up Rain," I said, watching him sulk down the switchbacks.

"I am!" he said with a huff, clearly annoyed at my prodding.

"I can literally see you dragging your feet in front of me. I'm not too keen on watching you tumble over the side, so please, Rain. Pick up your feet with a little more oomph."

He grumbled something at me I didn't bother trying to decipher. His footsteps became more pronounced and that's all I really cared about, not whether he liked it or not. I think he was making them dramatically large to spite me, but it brought me comfort, so I didn't critique his form. His listening was enough.

We discovered the boulders we had seen didn't block the path completely. Most of them left about a foot of room for us to squeeze around, although a few were a little bigger and the squeeze was tighter. I was just thankful we didn't have to climb over any and risk falling off to our deaths.

It got noticeably cooler the lower we got into the canyon. Somewhere in my head I thought that most lower parts of canyons were supposed to be warmer than the upper parts, something to do with the canyon walls trapping heat but everything we'd encountered in the Between had been weird so why not this. Calling a halt to our trek, I shrugged it off as I carefully pulled my jacket out of my pack and put it on. The others did the same.

When we reached the canyon bottom, I checked my watch and saw it was 11:30. The bottom was almost as empty as the top surface had been. There were loose stones here and there but also a number of cairns.

I wondered if the stones had been stacked and left behind by mortals who had walked this terrain before us. Perhaps they had left them to help direct us where we were supposed to go. I hoped they survived, had beat the odds of this place.

We sat down around one of the cairns to grab a quick drink from our canteens. We refueled with our light chocolate, unsure when we would get another opportunity to eat again.

Rain played with his grass doll that Lil had made for him and I realized he had become expert at finding ways to distract himself from fear. It twisted my gut that he was getting used to death, to his life being at risk in this cruel place. It took effort to keep my light chocolate down at the thought.

After a while we stood and started getting ready to walk some more. Rain put his doll back in his pack as he stared at a cairn. "What are these rocks doing?"

B, Lily, and I looked around and shrugged, not entirely sure ourselves.

"Maybe other people left them here to help us? To try to point us in the direction to go next. I think that's a thing that happens with hiking..." I trailed off, not entirely sure. There was a vague idea about that in my head, but like I said, I really didn't think Before me was a hiker.

Rain picked a stone off the ground and lifted it up to one of the cairns and dropped it on top, as if to help guide the next mortals who crossed this way.

An eery, oppressive feeling suddenly descended on the four of us.

A vibration shook the ground, slowly at first, but then more vigorously. We looked at each other in apprehension, not completely sure what to make of it. Then the loose rocks started moving, slowly sliding across the ground to collect at the bottom of the path down into the canyon.

At first we sidestepped the rocks easily, moving out of their way and watching them scrape past us. But then they started moving quicker and the next thing we knew they were airborne and zooming past us like they had been shot from a cannon. For a brief moment we stood frozen, not sure what to do but then I saw a large stone hurtling towards B.

"Watch out!" I shouted and shoved him hard to the side, knocking him over and landing on top of him.

"Rain!" Lily screamed. I turned my head to see Lily using her body as a shield to prevent him from getting stoned to final death by flying rocks.

"We have to move!" B shouted and I rolled off him ready to get up and run. Before I could, a few rocks whizzed past my head and I ducked. I looked up and before I could warn her, I saw a rock smack Lily in the back, sending her sprawling awkwardly to the ground.

I crawled towards her, ducking and dodging although small rocks pelted my arms and legs in the process.

"Lil, please tell me you're okay," I gasped when I finally made it next to her. I knelt up in front of Rain, trying to block rocks from hitting him as best I could. I threw my hands quickly over my head as I dodged a particularly close call.

Through gritted teeth she said, "my shoulder, I think it's dislocated."

B crawled over and we saw her shoulder sagging oddly, the socket sticking out in an unnatural way. I swallowed hard. "What do you do with that?"

"I need you to shove it back in."

"You need me to do *what*?!"

"SHOVE IT IN, NOW!" Lily screamed, her face turning red with pain.

"I don't know what I'm doing, Lil! I don't want to make it worse!"

She shouted at me frantically. "If you don't push it back into the socket, I'm as good as dead, Eight! Just *do* it!" The calmness she showed when she was healing others disappeared when it was her.

"Goddammit, okay...okay, fine...Do I count to three?" I squeaked.

Before I could do anything, Lily let out a frustrated noise then gripped her arm and shoved it back towards her shoulder where it made a dull popping sound. Her scream of pain carried over the sound of the rocks cracking into each other as they reached their pile.

My jaw went slack at what she'd just done to herself. *How?*

I searched her face. "Are you okay?"

"I'm going to be fine," she said, still gritting her teeth and now guarding her shoulder.

I looked at B then and grabbed both sides of his face when I saw his nose was bleeding.

"B, what happened? Did you get hit anywhere else?"

"We have bigger concerns right now than my nose, Eight," he said as he glanced pointedly over my shoulder.

I realized the rocks had stopped flying past us and knew who I'd see even before I turned to look behind me.

"Greetings, mortals. The After and I are excited to announce your fourth tribulation is about to commence."

I groaned. Of course the tribulation hadn't been as easy as dodging flying rocks. That had just been the warm up.

"After you complete the tribulation, you will find the golden key over there," Sintra said, pointing to the newly-created pile at the foot of the path.

"What, under that pile of rocks?" B asked, confused.

"Yes, under that pile of rocks." Sintra's face shone with a smug, self-satisfaction.

The four of us looked at each other in confusion then stared at the rock pile. Was our fourth tribulation going to be just digging through it to find the golden key? So maybe the rocks careening at us had been the deadly part of this challenge after all. I was about to let myself relax when, with a rising sense of horror, I noticed the rock pile was moving—no, it was *breathing*—as it rearranged itself into a body, four legs, one tail, and four heads with razor sharp rocks for teeth on long necks.

"What the fu—" I began.

The newly-formed beast released a vicious, grating growl. All four necks lowered so the heads could assess us more closely with burning, golden eyes.

I also noticed something shiny wedged under its belly. *The key.*

Nausea slammed into my stomach.

Chapter Twenty-One

"**I**s that a hydra...made of stone?" Lily asked, her voice cracking with terror.

Rain ran behind the three of us, looking absolutely terrified.

I understood the sentiment completely; the hydra was horrific. The rocks had gathered in a way that created long lines of spikes running from its necks to converge into a single ridge down its back and tail. The tail had arranged itself from small rocks near the body, to large ones at its end, giving it an almost clublike appearance. Luckily the underside of the beast, including its tail, was layered in smooth rocks. Hopefully that would make it less dangerous when it was time to recover the key.

The hydra stood, its four heads swaying, as it waited for the go-ahead to charge its next meal.

"What a horrible makeover you've given yourself, Sintra," I spat at them.

"I thought perhaps you would enjoy meeting more inhabitants of the Between," they smirked at me. "It has been awhile since your last encounter."

"Charmed," I growled.

All at once, the four heads let out roars that sounded like a rock slide tumbling down down the canyon wall. The four of us flinched and covered our ears immediately.

"Simply retrieve the key, mortals, and your fourth tribulation will be over," Sintra said, serene and unbothered by the monster's noises.

They acted as if doing so would be *easy*, as if approaching the colossal beast was similar to catching a stray cat. The hydra was likely thirty feet tall and perhaps forty five feet long. It could easily split one of us in half with a crunch of one of its four jaws, spear us to death with its tail, or even just step on us and we'd be dead.

"Do we get any special weapons to battle this?" B asked, his eyes narrowing in determination as he stared at the hydra.

"No."

I could feel panic wanting to well up in me but I couldn't let Rain see that. I gave myself a mental shake and took some deep breaths, fighting for calm.

I looked at Lily, who was still holding her aching shoulder, her eyes wide with terror.

"We can figure this out, between the four of us. We won't lose another person, not to this monster," B said, making eye contact with each of us in turn. I couldn't tell if he really believed that or if this was his way of trying to rally us together, hoping to give us more confidence before going into battle.

"Though you will not find any weapons, you may find items throughout the canyon to be of service to you. I hope you can find a way to use them to your advantage. Best of luck," Sintra said before evaporating on their signature golden breeze to watch us from a different vantage point, I was sure.

As soon as they were gone the hydra began stepping towards us, jaws snapping, its necks weaving back and forth like snakes and grinding against each other in a chilling sound when they met. We tensed, realizing we had a minute at most to think. I was completely lost at what to do, how to strategize against something like this, and I could feel myself wanting to just slip away from the challenge it posed.

"We have to see what's placed around here, find the items Sintra mentioned, find something that could be useful to us," Lily said. "B, give me Hal's old jacket."

B handed it to her without question and watched her wrap her arm and shoulder in it as a makeshift sling.

"I'll take Rain and go left. Lily, Eight, you go right. One of you try to get behind it and see if there's anything against the far canyon wall. The other one of you look against the rightmost wall. Keep yourselves spread out, that'll make it more difficult for that thing to target us," B instructed.

"It has four heads, I don't know that it matters how far apart we spread," I muttered.

"Eight, look at me," B said sharply, his voice commanding. I pulled myself together and looked at him.

"Don't give up before this has started." He searched my eyes. "I will not let anything happen to you"—he looked around—"to any of you. Be smart, be fast, and *survive*."

I swallowed and forced myself to inhale a deep breath through my nose. I let the breath exhale out of my mouth. *I will survive this. For B, for Lily, for Rain.*

For me.

"I go back, you go right," Lily said to me.

"Got it." I glanced back at the hydra and a second later all four of us took off. B had Rain do a long, wide arc to the left and then run up against the canyon wall we had come down so that he was protected from the hydra while B ran a more direct line toward the beast, adding in some zigzags as a diversion. Lily and I picked up on the strategy, and she mimicked B's back and forth movements, holding her arm while she ran to keep it from bouncing around painfully. I ran a wide arc to the right to see if I could find anything useful against the canyon wall.

The one thing about a hydra made from rock was that its heads had a lot less mobility to twist around than a flesh and blood beast would've had. It lacked the flexibility of ligaments, like in a snake's neck, which meant a head could track just one of us at a time. The heads would need to coordinate their attack.

Which they didn't do well, I noted as they snapped at each other, apparently disagreeing about who to go after first.

The hydra's indecision gave us all a moment's advantage to run as fast and as far as we could before it apparently reached consensus and swung all four heads toward Lily.

"Lily!" I yelled as one of the heads reared back to lunge down and snap at her.

She looked up and with lightning quick reflexes born of terror rolled forward with a muffled scream, barely avoiding the hydra's jaws by inches. She was up and running again in seconds, more agile than I had expected her to be, despite holding her injured shoulder with her left hand. The head that had almost had her howled in frustration while the other three made attempts of their own to snatch Lily. But she was quick as she ran towards the back of the canyon, managing to stay ahead of the hydra as it turned to follow her.

Lily had to be in pain with her shoulder slowing her down more than she'd like.

I looked around for anything that would provide a distraction for her. I had reached my part of the canyon wall and found a pile of rocks that hadn't been incorporated into the hydra. I grabbed three of the largest I could find, wrapping them in my arms while I ran towards the beast.

"HEY!" I screamed and lobbed a rock towards it that bounced off the side of its dragon-like body. The beast slowed down momentarily and the head closest to me turned to the side, amber eyes blazing with anger as it let out a rocky hiss.

"That's right, you ugly little shit, look my way," I whispered under my breath. If a few spare piles of rock was Sintra's idea of help, they could go to hell.

I threw another as hard as I could but this one missed entirely and sailed between two heads. The head that had looked in my direction turned back towards Lily who, fortunately, had gained ground and nearly reached the back canyon wall.

I hefted my last rock with a quick request to the universe that I made contact with the hydra on my next throw.

I ran towards it once more and threw the rock with all my strength.

It struck one of the heads, dead center, on the back, before falling to the ground. I had an insane urge to giggle.

The beast turned its whole body toward me quickly, all four heads now howling in rage. I covered my ears and then quickly turned on my heels and dashed for the side wall.

I could hear four jaws crashing together as the hydra picked up speed. *Shit.*

The ground shook, rocks bouncing up from the force of the monster's body crashing towards me. I eyed the length of the wall while I ran towards it, hoping to find some type of salvation. My heart raced but I pushed myself, *faster*. My lungs were on fire, my mind buzzed with adrenaline, my vision blurred from the effort.

I felt the ground lurch and made the mistake of looking back only to see one of the hydra's heads smashing into the ground as it tried to throw me off balance with the impact's resulting vibrations.

I screamed, high-pitched with fear, as my body swayed and I fought to keep my balance. I faked as if I was running to the left and when I felt confident the hydra had turned its body to follow me, I pivoted and ran to the right. The monster screamed in frustration, unable to change directions as quickly as I had. I heard the grinding of rocks and assumed its heads must have crashed into each other again as the hydra attempted to course correct. It struck me then that its inability to move more fluidly was possibly our only chance at beating this thing.

I reached the wall and scanned up its length and was surprised to discover a U-shaped hook embedded at about hip height. Shouting in frustration at how useless that was, I turned and ran several steps before my legs suddenly cramped painfully. My focus interrupted, I tripped on a rock and fell, a cloud of dust pluming up around me as I landed in a breath-stealing flop.

It felt like an eternity before I could breathe again and try to stand. The ground was shuddering again, though, and I could only get on my hands and knees to steady myself. I could feel the hydra getting closer so I turned over and started scooting backwards like a crab, using my hands and feet, to get away from it.

As four snarling heads loomed toward me I realized I was practically up against the canyon wall. I stared into the hydra's eyes and saw it savoring the moment. It relished having trapped its prey and was about to enjoy its kill. Fear consumed me as the heads lowered but I didn't look away—if this was the moment I died, I would face it straight on.

"EIGHT!" B screamed.

One of the hydra's heads turned to look curiously behind it to see what was making a commotion. I flicked my eyes toward the sound of B's voice and saw him lift a large boulder over his head and bring it down to shatter a section of the hydra's tail.

All four heads reared up and back as the hydra screeched, apparently in pain.

I didn't hesitate. I shot to my feet and ran toward B as he shouted, "Eight! There's a wheel anchored in the wall on the other side where Rain is, with a rope attached to it! Get to it while I lure the hydra away! There has to be something on the other side of the canyon to connect it to!"

Just as I reached him he sprinted off and I knew the hydra had managed to turn to face him. "I got it!" I screamed and kept running, my chest heaving with effort. I spotted Rain waving wildly and raced to where he stood, a large coil of rope on the ground beneath a wheel in the canyon wall, just as B had described. When I reached him, gasping to catch my breath, I turned to see how B was fairing. He had reached the canyon wall and was running flush alongside it. The hydra's heads snapped at him but were too large to get close enough to the wall to pick him off.

I grabbed Rain's shoulders. "Where is Lily?!" I shouted.

I looked in the direction he pointed and saw Lily had made it about forty feet up the path we had followed down into the canyon. She was wedged between a large boulder we had passed on our way down, with her back against it and her feet braced against the canyon wall.

I knew what she was planning and another idea bloomed in my mind.

"LILY!" I shouted and she turned her head to look at me over her shoulder.

"Wait for me to yell your name! When B draws the hydra close to you, have the boulder ready!"

"Okay!" she yelled back to me, voice strained with effort.

"Rain, stay here and don't move, I'll be right back, I promise."

I grabbed the rope next to Rain and with its heavy length uncoiling behind me I ran back to the U-bolt on the opposite canyon wall. I hated leaving Rain behind but I had to get the rope secured to the bolt as quickly as possible. B was doing a good job of outpacing the hydra, but I didn't know how long he could last.

I was running hard and was three-quarters of the way to the bolt when the rope snapped back, pulling me to the ground with it in shock. *Fuck, the rope wasn't long enough!*

Sintra was probably having a good, maniacal laugh over this one. *Asshole.*

I whipped my pack off my back and frantically dug around in it until I found the rope that had once tied Don and me together. I grabbed the severed end where he'd cut himself free and did two quick overhand knots to connect it to the rope I had been pulling. My knots weren't nearly as elegant as Don's had been but I had no time to work out another way to tie the ropes together. I should've watched him while I had the chance.

I got up and sprinted for the bolt. When I reached it, I quickly tied the now-long-enough rope to it and then turned around to head back for Rain.

While I was running, I looked across the canyon to Lily, seeing her in place at the boulder, ready for my signal.

Then I glanced at B, who was tracing the back end of the canyon now, starting to turn, making a run towards the switchbacks hoping he could reach a height that provided some protection from the hydra. When he made it to the second switchback, the hydra appeared to lose interest in him and turned its heads toward Rain. Its eyes seeming to blaze with delight, it shifted to lumber in his direction.

No.

I ran faster towards Rain, my strides eating up the ground furiously. It couldn't have Rain, nothing could. Not Sintra, not this hydra. *Nothing.* He would get back to his family. I would not let him die here.

When I was close enough, I screamed at the hydra. I put all the anger, the frustration, the injustice of the tribulations into it. The hydra swung its heads to me and for a moment we roared at each other in a bizarre, primal standoff. I held my ground, letting all the rage flow out of me, unrestrained. "GO! DIE!"

The hydra heaved its body around to me. I waited until it was right where I wanted it, right below where Lily was positioned on the path up and out of the canyon, then took a deep breath and screamed one more time.

"NOW, LIL!"

Lily hollered painfully from the effort, flexed her legs, and pushed her back against the boulder until it rolled off the edge of the path onto the base of one of the hydra's necks and crushed it. The other three heads wailed, their necks thrashing around angrily and uncoordinated.

Trying to recover, the hydra stepped sideways, then forward, and then backwards. It lurched forward again but made it just two steps before its front legs stumbled against the rope I had secured. The rope strained against the monster's jerky movements but held. The hydra lost its balance and, after teetering for a moment, fell heavily on its side.

It was *over*.

I could see the golden key in its underside, just a twenty-foot run away.

"No, Eight! Stop!"

It was too late, I was dead set on retrieving it, knowing the end of this terrifying challenge was within reach. Lily was up on the path and B had run down and over to Rain to protect him. No one else could do it. I ran to where the monster lay, its legs flailing as it tried to figure out how to right itself again.

Perfect.

Ducking so I wouldn't get crushed, I ran between the legs and snatched the key, the tingly rush of victory sparking through me. I had made it through this tribulation unscathed and it was over now that I had the smooth, golden key in my hand.

I was smiling as I noted something flying toward me at the edge of my peripheral vision. I had a split second of recognition that I wasn't going to be able to move in time before the hydra's tail struck me in the stomach and threw me ten feet up and back, towards a screaming Rain and a terrified B.

I hit the ground on my side with a thud.

My stomach twisted violently and I vomited.

I saw the key still in my hand.

And then all was blackness.

Chapter Twenty-Two

I could feel my body shaking violently but I couldn't see anything. Had the hydra gotten up and was charging me, making the ground quake? If so I had to get up, and quickly. But I was so tired and felt like I was drifting away, slowly. I thought I heard someone shouting.

"Stay with me."

It was that voice again, the one I'd heard before that caused chills down my spine. It seemed like it was coming from far away but reverberating around in my head at the same time. My body felt like it was being zapped by bolts of lightning, every part of it being singed.

"Wake up!"

I groaned.

"Wake up, please."

I wasn't ready.

"EIGHT! WAKE UP!"

My eyes abruptly shot open and I saw B's face hovering over mine, desperate concern lining every feature. I tried to breathe in but broke off with a cry of agony when it felt like a thousand knives stabbed me inside my stomach.

Unable to speak, I focused on B's beautiful face, his blue eyes, strong jaw, the mole under his right eye centering me.

"Eight, please, are you okay?" he cried.

I realized I was on my back so I rolled my eyes to the side to look for Lily and Rain. They were kneeling next to me and worry lined their expressions too.

I lifted my shoulders to sit up but searing, sharp pain stopped me. B put a gentle hand on my shoulder, keeping me still.

I glanced down and saw my shirt had been lifted up to underneath my breasts. B moved his hands to the sides of my face drawing my gaze back up to him. "Don't look, Eight. Okay? Keep your eyes on me."

I felt both too hot and too cold suddenly and when I tried to ask what was going on I started coughing and choking on my own saliva. B moved quickly and turned me on my side so I could spit. I forgot the violent pain in my stomach for a moment as I stared at the ground, unable to look away.

Everything I had just spit out was blood.

"What...?" I trailed off. I rolled to my back again, cold sweat trickling down my face. I started shaking and balled my fists against another wave of searing stomach pain. Dimly, I became aware of feeling something digging into my right hand. I looked down in confusion and slowly opened my fist to see a golden key pressed against my skin.

I turned my head to where the hydra had struggled to stand and remembered the excruciating blow of its tail. Instead of the hideous beast that hunted us relentlessly, the hydra had returned to a still pile of rocks. I wanted to be glad but the burning and twisting in my stomach made me scream in agony.

"B..." Lily said, her voice weak.

"No, don't you dare!" B's stern words were for Lily but his eyes never left mine. He looked so angry but at what I didn't understand.

"It's internal, I...I can't...she..." Lily tried again.

"NO!" B shouted, this time turning his head to snap at her so quickly he looked like a serpent about to strike. His rage was palpable and terrifying clarity suddenly rushed in. *I was dying.*

Lily jolted away from B in fear.

He turned back to face me, and I saw tears forming in his eyes.

"You're going to make it through this, Eight. I will not allow anything else. You're not allowed to leave me like this." His voice held so much command, as if he sat at the crossroads of life and death, determining who went in which direction.

"B, it hurts...so bad," I whispered, the tears in my eyes matching his.

He put his forehead to mine. "I know, Eight. I know it does, but it'll be okay. This will all be okay."

"I...don't...think you can...promise...that," I murmured.

He lifted his forehead from mine and stared into my eyes. "I can and I will. I promise this is not your end, Eight."

I opened my mouth to tell him I loved him before I had to go, and felt a glob of wetness slide out instead. At the same time, it felt like something inside me was slowly deflating and the pain was unbearable.

"SINTRAAAA!" B demanded at the top of his lungs and shot to his feet.

"GET DOWN HERE, SINTRA," he screamed again, the cords in his neck straining against his skin.

Suddenly, Sintra appeared to my right, smiling down on me with unrestrained malice.

"Looks like only three mortals will be making it this time," they said, crouching to kneel by my side.

No. I didn't want to go with them...I wasn't ready.

Icy panic began eating through me at the thought.

"Don't..." I started to say as Sintra's hand reached towards me.

"DON'T TOUCH HER!" B yelled and shoved himself in front of Sintra, blocking their way.

Sintra rose to their feet and stared B in the eye, a saccharine smile on their face. "It is her time, mortal. You cannot stop this," they explained and I could hear the hint of triumph in their voice at my impending demise.

Why Sintra would want to spend eternity with me was beyond me. It wasn't like we'd be braiding each other's hair like friends forever. Perhaps they wanted to usher me along out of spite; they knew I wanted nothing to do with them or the allegedly benevolent After.

Well, if that were the case then I would turn Sintra's time in the After into a living hell.

"Do you not follow your own rules?" B challenged Sintra forcefully.

Sintra turned an expression of utter boredom on him. "What meaning should I take from that, mortal?"

I saw the muscles in B's jaw twitch before he spoke. "When you explained the rules of this tribulation you said after the key was pulled from the hydra's body, once it was retrieved, this would be over. That we would win our fourth tribulation. She had the key in her hand when the hydra...attacked her."

My stomach lurched violently. I thought I could see where B was going with his argument, and wanted to hope, but I felt more blood flow upwards from my stomach and then out of my mouth. My eyes began getting heavy. *Please don't let this be it.*

Sintra's upper lip twitched.

B looked angry, yet smug. "Is the After not fair then?"

Sintra's eyes snapped to me. "The After is both fair and benevolent."

"When we first got here, you said you'd ensure the rules would be followed according to how you laid them out. Your rule was the tribulation was over once the key was retrieved. She should live," B said with blatant hostility.

Sintra and B stared at each other a moment longer, and I could see Sintra's eyes blazing. Suddenly they leaned down and brought their face within an inch of mine.

"Lucky you, little mortal, that you have someone watching out for you. A person who is finding loopholes to keep you alive. I will not make the same mistake next time," they hissed through clenched teeth.

With the little strength I still had, I spat a spray of blood onto their face. They leapt back in disgust and furiously tried to wipe it off with their indigo robes but only managed to smear it on their marble skin. Their face was contorted in fury and they raised their hand as if they were going to dissolve me into gold dust despite B's point but then something curious happened. I saw Sintra look away momentarily, as if gazing at someone next to them, and the briefest look of unease crossed their features. As quickly as it had come it was gone and their familiar blank look returned, even as their shoulders sagged seemingly in defeat.

Fear, that's what I'd seen. I was all too familiar with that feeling to have missed it even on carved marble.

What could Sintra possibly be afraid of?

Before I could wonder further, Sintra clapped their hands together and my vision exploded in white, my body raged with heat, and I arched my back in torment. It felt like all the cells in my body were fusing together, my abdomen churning and expanding. The pain was excruciating and I couldn't resist the pull of oblivion this time. As I began fading away I heard Sintra's voice distantly.

"Take care, mortals. The next tribulation will not treat you as kindly."

I woke up to a gentle, bouncing and swaying sensation. It was comforting and the desire to keep my eyes closed was strong. Regardless, I forced them open, remembering being near death not long ago.

The deep purple sky greeted me and I was thankful for the lack of sunlight because now I realized I had a raging headache to go with my fatigue.

I could see B's face above me, staring straight ahead. The bouncing made sense now—he was carrying me in his arms. My pack was in my lap, my hands resting on top of it. Lifting my arms up and around his shoulders, I locked my hands and shifted to pull myself up into a bit of a sitting position. My stomach was sore but I realized I wasn't in excruciating pain like I had been before I blacked out.

Feeling my movement, B looked down at me.

"You're awake." A statement not a question.

"I am...yes," I said.

He looked straight ahead again as he kept walking. "Good," he said, his voice flat and distant.

I thought he'd say more but silence stretched between us. Maybe carrying me was hard for him and he didn't have the energy to talk.

I looked around and realized we were still in the canyon, walking across to the other side from where we had come down into it.

"Are we stopping anytime soon?" I asked, looking up into B's face. I wanted him to look at me. I needed to see the intensity of his blue eyes and his soft smile reassuring me everything was okay.

"Yes," was all he said.

I decided to stop talking to him. Something wasn't okay.

Rain appeared at B's side. "You're awake, Eight! I was so scared and worried about you! Your tummy looked so scary, like it had been turned inside—"

"Enough, Rain!" B bit out, silencing him instantly.

I gave Rain a small smile. "I'm fine, Rain. Everything's okay now."

He nodded his little head and ran to catch up to Lily in front of us. "She's awake, Lil! She woke back up again!"

Lily stopped and looked back, smiling radiantly at me. "Glad to see you came back to us."

"Feels a hell of a lot better to be back this time than it did the last time I woke up." The small smile I offered her dimmed when I felt B's arms tense around me.

I caught the quick glance Lily threw B's way before she looked at me again. "I imagine," was all she said.

I slid my eyes up to study B. I did feel better than when I had come around after the hydra hit me, but I wasn't up for walking just yet. Was he mad he had to carry me? That seemed unfair. I mean, I'd practically died a little while ago and—oh. The realization struck me hard. I had almost died *again* and B had had to rescue me *again. I kept adding to the difficulties he faced in the tribulations, didn't I?* My stomach sank. I knew he cared about me but, still, he was mad because I wasn't pulling my weight. I had become a figurative and literal burden to him.

Before I could say anything, B stopped walking. "Let's call it a night." We were near the start of another zigzagging path up and out of the canyon. "We can get some rest before climbing up the switchbacks tomorrow. We all need it."

Lily nodded in agreement. I noticed then that she was still holding her right shoulder in the makeshift sling. I'm sure pushing that boulder off the canyon path had to have aggravated it and she'd be happy for the chance to rest.

B gently set me down and took my backpack. He pulled out my sleeping bag and laid it on the ground. Still exhausted, I crawled on top of it with relief.

"Hey, B," I said as he turned away to set up his sleeping bag next to mine.

He turned his head a fraction, barely looking at me over his shoulder. "Yes?"

"I just...wanted to say thank you. Thank you for everything." I tried to keep the quiver out of my voice. I was so tired, especially tired of crying so much in this desolate place.

He hesitated like he was on the verge of saying something, but looked away instead. After a beat he glanced over his shoulder at me again. "Sure, Eight. You're welcome."

I wanted to talk to him, to tell him I knew I needed to stop being a burden but Rain and Lily were setting up their sleeping bags on either side of us and I didn't want to talk in front of them.

"I'll take watch tonight," Lily offered.

"No," said B. "I'll be on watch."

We nibbled our light chocolate and drank some water in silence. My first sip tasted metallic and I remembered with a start the blood making its way up and out my mouth as I was dying. I chugged some water, swishing it around and running my tongue over my teeth, hoping to get off as much as possible.

Lily, Rain, and I laid down and B sat on his sleeping bag, his arms wrapped around his knees as he stared into the distance. I rolled toward him and lightly placed my hand on his upper thigh. He looked down at it, his expression shuttered. "B, I'm sorry, please, know that I am so damn sorry."

He kept staring at my hand, eventually laying his lightly on top of it. "Get some sleep, Eight, okay?"

He released my hand.

A tear slid down my face. "Are we not going to talk about it?"

He looked over at me and I could see pain, tiredness, concern, and terror all competing to overwhelm him.

"I just need...time, Eight. I need to process everything."

I nodded and swiped at my eyes. "Okay, I can do that. I can give you time." I meant what I said but I was impatient to set things right with him, with *us*.

I scooched down deeper in my sleeping bag, trying to ignore the concern I felt for B so that I could sleep. I needed to walk on my own tomorrow. I couldn't keep making him feel responsible for me. I could see it in his eyes, the toll it was taking on him to ensure our survival, to maintain the facade that everything was always going to be alright even as he mourned the friends we had lost.

I would give him the space he needed, but I wouldn't let this go. I needed to talk to him, to feel close to him again. I owed him my life.

Chapter Twenty-Three

We started up the switchbacks the next morning and I insisted on taking Lily's bag so she could let her shoulder rest. Lily and Rain led us off, holding hands and talking softly to each other. I followed them and saw her eyes light up every time she spoke to him and his answering smile beam back at her. B walked silently a ways behind me, which was just as well as I didn't feel like talking. I remembered Lily trying to tell B that the damage the hydra had caused, the injuries I had sustained, weren't survivable. I knew I was lucky I was experiencing only muscle soreness, like I had spent an entire day in a plank, and I was grateful but I kept hearing the torment in Lily's voice when she knew she couldn't help me. I hated to think how it would have affected Lily if I had died; she already felt awful about not having been able to save Harley...or the little boy from her Before.

The higher we climbed, the cooler the air got, which made no sense because it had been warm at the top before we descended. It crossed my mind that it would make sense if the next terrain turned out to be an arctic valley or a snowy mountaintop. I truly, *deeply* hoped that wouldn't be the case.

I strode a little closer and could hear Lily and Rain's conversation. "I bet my dad in the Before is something brave, like an astronaut or a firefighter. Or maybe my mom is one. I hope I have a sister or something when I get back, someone that I can show the dirt game to that B and I play together," Rain chatted at Lily while she nodded her head along, listening carefully.

"I'm sure they do something very cool and that you will have a lot of siblings you can show your game to," she agreed.

I wondered if that was true. Not so much about Rain's family as whether or not he'd be able to remember the dirt game. Would any of us remember our time in the Between, if we survived the tribulations and made it back to our real lives? B and I hadn't thought so when we talked that night after Harley's death, but maybe there was something we would be able to retain, some little glimpse of how hard we fought to make it back to our loved ones. Something that would let us know we had truly been brave in the face of death.

The idea of not knowing Lily, B or Rain made my heart heavy. I wanted to know these people for the rest of my life. We had been through something extraordinary together already, beating the odds of survival in four tribulations. I hoped we would somehow be tied to each other's lives when we returned to the Before.

"Who do you think is waiting for you, Lil?" Rain asked, not having any idea how the question would affect her.

I could see her body tense at the innocent question, knowing that it scraped painfully at her trauma.

"Hey, Rain, why don't you go back and walk with B for a little bit? He seems kind of bummed out and I think if anyone can cheer him up, it's probably you," I suggested.

Rain hesitated. "Are you sure...?" he asked, not looking excited at the prospect of spending time with him. He'd avoided B and his sour mood all day.

"Can you go try?" I asked, giving him a pouty face.

"Okay," he sulked, looking like I had just asked him to pluck each of his arm hairs out one by one.

I watched him stop and wait for B to catch up to him. B's eyes caught mine for the briefest moment before he glanced down to Rain who was asking him if he wanted to play their object color guessing game.

"Thanks," Lily said as I turned back around.

"Yeah, of course," I said a little distractedly, thinking about the awkwardness between me and B.

"He looks a bit like him," Lily said.

Brought back to the moment, I looked at her, feeling baffled. "Who? Rain and B?"

"No, not them," she shook her head. "I know B isn't him, but he has a similar muscular build and dark hair. Similar to the guy from my final moment in the Before."

I looked at her, my eyes widening. "Really?"

"Don't get me wrong, B is much more handsome than he is, but I found it confusing when I first got here. I didn't trust him, any of the men really. But the similarity is enough that I've felt afraid of B. It's been difficult to be around him," she said.

Stunned, I searched for something to say. "I'm sorry, Lil, I didn't realize," I offered.

"I know, and I'm not asking for your pity or apologies," she said, brushing her hand through her hair.

I didn't know what to say to that either, so I just closed my mouth and waited.

"I'm bringing this up for you, not for me. I know that B is not the same person as the man who tried to kill me. I know he would never do something like that to anyone. He has a big heart and protects his people fiercely."

I nodded. "He wouldn't hurt anyone, I've only ever seen him try to save us," I said, smiling gently at her.

She looked at me, staring deeply into my eyes, in a way she hadn't done before.

"Yes, I know he wants to help us all, but he also needs to be helped too. You were *dying* yesterday, Eight. I don't know what you recall, but he was beside himself. I don't think he would hurt any of us, but I didn't know if he was going to try his hand at hurting Sintra. He wasn't himself and he still isn't himself. He needs you right now," she said.

"Maybe you were actually a therapist, not a doctor," I commented as I looked away.

"Stop trying to avoid my point."

I rolled my eyes. "Look, I want to talk to him, but he doesn't want to talk to me. Last night he asked me for space to process, I can't force him to talk if he's not ready."

"Since when have you ever listened to anyone?" she asked, never breaking her stride.

I glared at her back. "People can change, okay?"

She kept walking but I heard her say, "some can...but not everyone."

Once we finally reached the top of the switchbacks, I glanced down into the pit of the canyon. I would be happy to never see a cairn again.

We rested briefly then kept walking, the environment changing slowly around us as the hours went by. The ground beneath our feet remained rusty-orange dirt but after a while a thick, off-white fog developed and curled ominously around our legs. We came to a halt, not sure we should keep walking when we couldn't see anything below our knees.

"I don't like the mist," Rain said worriedly.

I rubbed his curls lightly, trying to assuage my own anxiety. "Neither do I."

Suddenly he pulled away from under my hand. "Don't call me that," he snapped.

I looked at him in confusion. "Call you what?"

"Stop!" he said angrily and I saw his hands ball into fists at his sides.

I looked to see Lily and B watching us questioningly. I shrugged and mouthed, "I don't know," so Rain couldn't hear me.

I rested my hands lightly on Rain's shoulders and leaned down toward him. "Rain, what's wrong?"

"I'm not a baby!" he shouted at me.

I gaped, not sure what to say.

"No one called you that—" I tried again.

"NO! I'M NOT! STOP!" he screamed, his face turning red from the effort. He covered his ears with his hands and started rocking back and forth.

"Rain, please—" Lily said.

"Leave me alone! Stop talking to me!" He pulled away again and seemed like he was about to storm off, but before he could Lily wrapped her good arm around him. "Hey, shh, Rain, shhh. It's okay, you're okay," she murmured but Rain shoved her away and clapped his hands back over his ears. I was about to grab a handful of his shirt to keep him from running away when I saw B's hands settle over Rain's.

"Rain, please, look at me," he said gently.

Rain burst into tears, distraught by whatever he was experiencing. B pried his hands away from his ears and slowly pulled Rain into his arms. Rain fought him at first, but B held on and started humming like he had for me that night in the pond. He gently swayed side to side with Rain and the sound of his humming floated around us. Rain's tantrum seemed to wear itself out as he settled against B's chest. Still holding him, B looked over to me and began to sing.

A small part of my brain knew that he must be making up a song, that he couldn't be remembering a song from Before, but then I just let myself be awash in the sound of his voice. The rich timbre carried clearly into the empty space around us, filling me with an unexpected sense of peace. It reminded me of the radiant warmth of a wood fire on a cool day, the effortless glide of a shorebird above water, and longing built inside of me.

B kept his eyes on me while he sang and I couldn't look away, caught in the spell cast by his beautiful voice. I wanted to stay in this moment forever.

When his song came to an end he picked up a now-quiet Rain, cradled him in the shelter of his arms, and started walking. The fog had risen up around us while we had been transfixed by B's voice but I saw that it receded slightly as Lily and I followed him, drifting away just enough to provide about ten feet of visibility. Which was helpful because massive trees started to appear, looming up through the fog so high that the lowest branches were barely visible above our heads. The trees appeared to be covered in enormous, beige leaves and their trunks were so large I would barely be able to stretch my arms around a quarter of their circumference.

Large boulders were scattered around as well, some leaning up against trees, some toppled over on the ground. There was no grass, no brush in this eerie space. Just giant trees and boulders and endless silence. It seemed like a forest, but did it count as a forest seeing as there were just big trees and rocks? Was there a word for a rock forest? The trees were bigger so it seemed like they should get top billing...maybe a *forock*? Was that a word already? Had I just created a new word? I thought the chills dancing along my arms and back were from the thrill of inventing a new word but then I realized they were trying to tell me something—I was distracting myself from how I felt about our silent surroundings.

"I hate this place," I said, feeling smothered by the forock.

"Agreed," Lily said quickly. "This is giving me the creeps."

"Let's make it a short day then, get used to our surroundings, get some extra sleep," B said as he stopped. Rain had fallen asleep and his chest rose and fell in a steady rhythm when B knelt and eased him onto the ground. He pulled out Rain's sleeping bag and was getting it set up when Rain stirred awake and looked around sleepily. "Did we stop?"

"Yes," Lily said, as she sat down next to him and rubbed his forehead gently.

I smiled at him encouragingly. "Get some more sleep, Rain. We can never get too much of it in this place."

It was cold in this forest and I looked around, wondering if there might be some sticks we could use to start a small fire to warm us up a little. I was pretty sure I wouldn't find any but still wanted to check. I wanted to do something to take my mind off the creepy feeling of this place.

"I think I'm going to look around," I said. "I won't venture too far, I promise."

I started off through the fog when I felt a hand wrap around one of mine.

"Not alone. I'll go with you," B replied, tightening his grip as if I were a child about to take off in a defiant run from him.

"I want to go too!" Rain said, sitting up in his sleeping bag.

Lily pushed him back down. "No, Rain, they need some time. Stay here with me."

He pouted at that so I shook off B's hand and went over to place a kiss on Rain's forehead. "We'll be back soon, okay? Keep Lil company."

I turned to B who now had his arms folded across his chest and was looking warily at me. "Ready?"

I wasn't sure what he meant by that. If I was ready to talk? Ready to go on a silent walk with him? Ready to apologize again? I didn't know, but I nodded regardless.

"I am."

Chapter Twenty-Four

We walked through the mist-covered forest, not speaking. I was careful to remember landmarks that we passed, to make sure we could find our way back to Lily and Rain. Considering how quiet it was, though, I wasn't that worried. If they called for us, their voices would likely carry a fair distance through the stillness.

After about fifteen minutes, I stopped and ran my hand along the smooth trunk of a tree that had a boulder wedged up against it. Like the tree, the boulder was massive, and I stood under a chunk of it that stretched out almost like an awning.

B had stopped a short distance from me. The fog and mist moved around us, but the leaves on the trees didn't stir. Everything was quiet, especially B.

"I wonder if I've ever seen anything like this in the Before," I said, desperate to make conversation. I was so uncomfortable with his reticence all I wanted to do was reach out to him, grab his hand, wrap my arms around him. *Anything to get us back to where we had been.*

I looked over and saw his strong form standing tense while he stared at me intently.

"B..." I pleaded, turning to face him. I wasn't sure what I was pleading for exactly, but any type of response would be a good start. I stepped closer to him, and when he didn't move back in response I continued toward him, but carefully, like I'd approach an injured animal.

"I know you're upset with me and I want to give you the space you need, I really do...but I'm so anxious not knowing where we stand. I'm sorry you have to keep saving me, I'm sorry if you think I'm useless to this group. I just wanted to get the key, I didn't mean to make you feel like you had to save me after I rushed at the hydra without thinking about how it could still hurt me. I was thoughtless and I'm so sorry, I really am. Just tell me what I can do to make this right, tell me how I can be better, please..."

He looked at me like I had just struck him.

"You think I'm *upset* because you aren't doing enough?" He paced towards me, flipping the scenario because now his approach made me feel like prey. He reached me with a glint of anger in his eyes and cornered me under the boulder.

"I am not *upset* about any of those things, Eight," he bit out. "I don't think that I have to keep saving you, so I'm certainly not *upset* about that. And I never thought that you weren't contributing, so I'm also not *upset* about that either..." He trailed off and shoved his hands through his hair in frustration.

"Then why, B? Why is it like this between us right now?" I pleaded, my voice small and uncertain.

He searched my face, his eyes wide and burning like blue flames.

"I am *upset* Eight because you ran to that hydra, didn't think about it, what could've happened, what *did happen*!" he shouted. "I called to you, tried to get you to stop. We had time to figure out how to get the key out, the hydra was down and it couldn't get back up, but you ran at it without a second thought! I know you're brave, so goddamn brave and didn't want any of us to get hurt trying to get that key, but *you got hurt, Eight*!" He stopped for a moment to catch his breath. "And I almost lost you. I thought I was about to watch you die because you were willing to run straight into harm's way to protect us," he rasped, his voice thick with emotion.

"I didn't mean to B, I wasn't thinking, I know I wasn't but I saw the opportunity and I took it. I wanted it to stop before anyone else got hurt or killed," I explained.

"I get it! But *you* almost got killed..." He stepped closer to me until our faces were a few inches apart.

"But I didn't and thank you for how damn smart you were and stopping Sintra!" I cried.

"If Sintra hadn't honored their mistake, though, you would be dead. I know we promised each other that one of us would live, see this to the end for Rain, but I wasn't ready, Eight. I wasn't ready to watch you die in front of me. Seeing you, the way you looked...the blood... I felt like I was dying with you." He shook his head. "I couldn't stand it and I was *so mad* that you didn't just wait. We're a team and we work with each other! That's how we get through these tribulations. *Together.*" I could feel his hot breath against my face.

"And how would we have done that together, huh?!" I shouted back, anger bubbling up inside me. "Would we have talked about it and you would have made sure that it was you that ended up in danger? That you were the one who took all the risks so you didn't have to be the one to live without me if things went south, B?"

His eyebrows drew together. "That's not what—"

"Right, that's not what you said, but that's what you meant. I'm not *delicate*, B. I don't need you to tell me that I can't take risks, that they're only yours to carry! You don't get to make the choice to leave me because you think it's easier for me to live without you than it is the other way around!"

"I don't think you're delicate, Eight! I never said I thought that. I saw you almost drown in a river and pull yourself out! I saw you walk out of a goddamn fire relatively unscathed while our friend *died*. You think I consider you *delicate*?" His face was a mix of shock and rage. "You are the bravest person I know and I've told you that before. You are worthy of survival yet you threw yourself recklessly towards your death!" I could see his jaw clenching as he braced his hands against the boulder on either side of me.

"Would you have let me go get the key from the hydra if I'd asked to?" I demanded.

He opened his mouth to respond, then closed it with a snap.

"Would you have let me be the one or would you have insisted that you go? Would you have risked your survival instead? Would you have left me to take care of Rain alone?"

"You'd still have Lily," he mumbled.

"Answer the question, B," I demanded.

"I would've wanted to go, Eight. I would've wanted to prevent any harm coming to you—" he tried.

"And you would have possibly left me alone, but it's not okay if I almost do the same for you?" I sighed and closed my eyes momentarily. "B, you aren't only a protector in this group. I can also protect you sometimes, so can Lily and even Rain protects us. I don't know what world we live in outside of this place, but you don't have to be only one thing here. You *aren't* just one thing.

"You're also a nurturer. You care for Rain in a way that I don't always know how to. Like earlier today, you were the only one able to calm him down, the only one who distracts him with games and carries him when he can't keep going on his own. We don't need to pretend we only have one role here, we can accept that we are both nurturers and protectors in our own right. You don't have to take on one responsibility and decide it's only yours to bear. Allow me to have some of it too. Let me protect you sometimes."

"It's not that, I know I can...I just..." he trailed off.

I waited a moment to see if he'd offer up his thoughts unprompted. "You can be honest with me, B. You've never shied away from holding my darkest and lightest parts, I'll do the same for you without judgment," I said when he remained silent instead.

He closed his eyes and swallowed hard. "I can't be a disappointment."

I furrowed my brows in confusion. "B, you're never that..."

"I can be, Eight. I'm a disappointment every time I fail to help someone. I'm a disappointment for snapping at Harley and getting him hurt. I'm a disappointment because I didn't get to patch things up with him the way I wanted before he died. I'm a disappointment anytime I don't protect you or Lily or Rain. I can't be that. I don't know why, but it feels like the worst thing I could possibly be, I can't allow it."

My eyes searched his. "Please, don't ever think that about yourself. You're *not*. You made a mistake, but mistakes are human, and that doesn't make the totality of you a disappointment."

He let out a frustrated groan and leaned forward to rest his forehead on mine. "I know, Eight. I hear you and understand. But I want you to know that I can't always help it. I can't always stop the fear of disappointing you, myself, *anyone*. Because truly, I'm selfish for you and I need to prove I'm worthy. I can't stop thinking about you, about how much I want you, how much I need you, how desperately I want to leave this place whole *with you*. In one moment I thought I would never get that, never get any more of you. Your smirk when you're being a smartass, your laugh, the way you wrap yourself around me when we kiss, the soft spots you have for all of us, how you also care for Rain.

"In one moment, I thought all of that was gone and I was *so furious* at myself I wanted to find a way to murder Sintra, to shake apart the After to find you again. I would do anything for you, Eight. I would walk through these tribulations again if this is the only time we could have together, I would drown in the river if you asked me to, I would try to kill Sintra for you. I would let myself die if that meant you got to go home. I would wait for you for an eternity in the After, just to see your smile again."

My breathing hitched and my eyes welled. I felt like such an idiot for thinking he had been angry at me for my uselessness, afraid I had become a burden to him, afraid his feelings for me had changed as a result.

I hadn't realized how tormented he was by the thought of letting me down and hated how I had made him feel with my reckless pursuit of the key.

"B, I need you too, I want you too," I brushed my nose against his. "You're not the only one who feels like they can't do this without the other. You're not the only one who would feel lost if they were left behind. So, please. If you want to care for me, care for that part of me too. Protect the part of me that would be devastated by losing you. You can't pick which parts of me to leave whole and which parts of me are okay to leave shattered."

"I know, Eight. I don't want to leave you either," he said, his deep voice cracking slightly.

"Then don't and I won't leave you," I whispered.

I felt him nod and then his hands were in my hair and his lips were on mine. This time, his kiss didn't start gently, not like the achingly slow ones we'd previously shared that crescendoed into intense passion. His kiss was desperate and the force of it pushed me back against the boulder.

I could feel every part of his body pressed against mine, but I reached under his coat and twisted his shirt in my hands, trying to pull him even closer. His hands cradled my neck as he continued his ravaging kisses.

I turned away after a few moments, out of breath and slightly dizzy with the intoxication of being with him like this.

He dipped his head and trailed kisses along my throat, my pulse, until a breathy moan escaped me.

B froze. "I want to hear that again," he whispered into my skin and traced a finger down the side of my neck.

Exquisite shivers raced along my arms and back. He kissed my neck before lightly scraping his teeth against my skin. "B..." I moaned.

"Yes, Eight?" He toyed with me, lightly gripping my chin and pulling so I turned to face him, then slowly kissed my lips again, taking complete control over me.

"Please," I said.

He deepened the kiss instantly, forcing my mouth open with his tongue. I grabbed him around the neck, held onto him, wanting the moment to continue forever.

His hands were under my coat now, under my shirt, all over me, touching, feeling, exploring. I was at his mercy and relished every minute of it. Just when I felt I was drowning, he would pull away and let me catch my breath, before his lips returned to mine.

Several minutes passed, then he whispered on my lips, "say it again."

I pulled back and looked into his eyes, their soft blue hungry, waiting for permission to devour me completely.

I could feel my body humming with desire. *"Please."*

He reached down and grabbed the backs of my legs to lift me up gently, taking care that my head remained below the boulder's overhang. I wrapped my legs around him in response and he knelt on the ground before lowering me to lay on my back. We undressed each other quickly, eager to feel our skin against the other's. We didn't feel the cold around us as, without words and using only our lips and hands and bodies, we moved together and created a song of our own. One that we would've known in any realm or any time but could only sing here and now, only together.

He worshipped me, wrung every bit of pleasure from me, treated my body with a veneration I hoped to always remember.

This place, the Between, was so wrong, so *unnatural*. I had detested it and resented having to endure it from the moment I had arrived.

But during this time together with B, I felt only love and completeness.

We both had given the other our heart, to hold for safekeeping, in the hopes that one day, when we left the Between, we'd find each other again and recognize the part of ourselves that we'd been missing.

Chapter Twenty-Five

We laid on our sides, pressed against each other and with our coats draped over our legs for warmth. We twined our hands together and stared softly into each other's eyes. Neither of us wanted to leave this bubble we had created together. This was one of the rare moments in the Between that felt simple, like we could have been experiencing this closeness anywhere and could ignore death always hovering close by.

B let go of my hand and slowly lifted my left wrist. Meeting my eyes with his, B pulled my hand to his lips, turning it over to expose the delicate skin on my wrist where he planted a gentle kiss. My stomach fluttered at the sensation.

"I like it when you do that," I said with a sly smile.

"Oh? Do you?" he murmured.

I laughed loudly at that. "Yes, B, and don't pretend to be innocent," I teased.

"Oh, Eight, if there's anything I won't do is pretend I'm innocent after what we just did together," he said with a leering grin.

My breath caught and I could feel a warm, red glow spread across my face.

"Am I making you blush, Eight?" he cooed and kissed my wrist again.

I closed my eyes and hummed noncommittally, focused on his warm lips moving across the skin of my lower arm, then my upper arm, then my shoulder. He paused long enough to nudge me onto my back as he followed to cover me with his body. With easier access now he nipped at my neck and I moaned appreciatively.

"If you keep at this we'll never make it back to Lily or Rain, B," I said breathlessly. He trailed his soft lips up to mine and shifted to embrace me in his arms.

He broke the kiss and whispered, "is it so wrong for us to live in this moment a little longer?"

I opened my eyes to take in his handsome face and felt a sharp pang of longing. I couldn't imagine a time or a life without B, I couldn't imagine what it would do to me if he wasn't mine in the next life, whether that was in the Before or the After. How was I supposed to be without him after this?

"What if we don't belong to each other in the Before?" I asked as I turned my head to hide the tears threatening to break free.

B put his hand on my cheek and turned me to face him. For a moment we just stared at each other, so close we were exchanging breaths. "I wish I could answer that question. And at the same time, I'm glad I can't. I feel like here and now it doesn't matter. I truly believe that, whether our minds will or not, our souls will remember each other. And I feel certain that a part of me, no matter what life, what place, separated or together, will always belong to you."

Tears coursed down my cheeks and he gently wiped them away. "I think so too, but I'm scared. It took me a while to warm up to everyone here and I think I'm probably lonely in the Before. It doesn't seem like I'm much of a people person."

"I think you're being a bit harsh on yourself," he said, stroking my cheek.

"Easy for you to say," my voice quivered. "Everyone liked you from the beginning here and in your final memory you were surrounded by people. I'm sure you have a lot of people waiting for you in the Before.

I was running alone through a crosswalk." Saying it out loud made me feel so pathetic. I wasn't fishing for sympathy, but it bothered me that I didn't know if I had any meaningful connections in the Before. What if the relationships I'd formed in the Between with Harley and Lily and Rain...and B...were much more meaningful than anything I had in the Before and, in a cruel twist of fate, I wouldn't remember them?

"Just because people were surrounding me doesn't mean they were important to me."

"Okay," I said, even though I didn't really agree. B was so naturally disarming, if he was anything like he was in the Between in his life in the Before, I could only imagine he had people fighting to be close to him.

"And Lily didn't like me from the beginning, and I don't think she likes me now."

I tensed, not realizing he had caught on to how she felt about him, how she avoided him. If Lily hadn't told me B's appearance was similar to that of her abuser, I wasn't sure I would've noticed her responses to him myself. B was so good at reading people, though, and now, I realized, it must have bothered him that Lily kept him at a distance

I searched for something to say, something comforting yet vague enough not to betray my friend's secret. Instead what came out was, "uhm, well, I don't think...maybe it's..."

B put me out of my misery. "You don't have to explain, Eight," he said with a smile. "I'm just trying to make a point that sometimes people don't like others for things we did or didn't do. I'm not above that. Maybe people who we thought were our friends in the Before never really were. I don't know, but I don't think we can make any assumptions about ourselves based on our final moment or about how we've navigated this place."

I let out a slow breath, knowing he was right.

"I mean, look how fast you charmed me," he winked.

I laughed. "I'm not sure we can say fast...I lost track of counting the days sometime ago. But, it's interesting, isn't it? Finding each other here. What an odd place to start having feelings for someone, when you don't even know yourself."

"Maybe you know yourself better here than you did in the Before," he offered.

"Well, I guess you'll have to come find me and give me your full assessment if we get back," I said and rubbed my nose against his.

"*When* we get back."

"God, you're such an optimist."

He bit my lip playfully. "Don't underestimate the power of suggestion."

I rolled my eyes, licking my lip where his teeth had just been. "I think you could use a pinch of cynicism in your life."

"Well, if that's what I need then I'm lucky in multiple ways that I have you."

At that, I reached up and linked my arms behind his head to pull him down to me for a kiss. He coiled a length of my hair around his hand and his tongue played lightly along my lips.

I pulled away suddenly so I could grab his hand. I flipped it over and set a gentle kiss on his wrist, wishing I could make it permanent somehow so that he would always remember how he made me feel. But instead I decided to tell him, feeling emboldened by what we had shared with each other.

"I hope wherever I end up next, my walls are down like they are with you here. I hope I never feel afraid to let other people in like I did when I first arrived in the Between. I don't know how you did it, B, but you've made me feel safe in a hellscape."

The look of devotion in his eyes as he sighed nearly undid me but before I could fall apart, his lips were on mine once again. I ran my hands through his ebony locks, sighing into his mouth. His sweet kiss turned more intense and our bodies moved gently against each other. Just as we were about to lose ourselves, I heard Lily's voice calling out in panic, carrying through the stillness around us.

"B? Eight? Where are you? It's Rain! I need help!"

B and I froze and stared at each other before breaking apart and sitting up quickly. *Shit.* We had left Lily—alone and injured—with Rain for who knows how long.

My stomach roiled with fear as B and I raced to throw our clothes back on. I hopped on one foot as I pulled my boot over the heel of the other and pitched forward, narrowly avoiding bashing my head on the boulder when B reached out to catch me.

"I scouted some landmarks on the way, I know how to get back," I said as we linked hands and ran as quickly as we could toward where we had left Lily and Rain to make camp. The fog slowed us down more than we liked, but I was able to pick out most of the landmarks. We went in the wrong direction just once but quickly reversed course and arrived back at camp to find Lily sitting on her sleeping bag, a sleeping Rain at her side.

B and I stopped short, flooded with relief but unsure what was going on.

"You two get it all sorted out?" she whispered quietly.

I looked up at B, who returned my confused expression.

"Yeah, sure...Lily, what happened?" I asked as I sat down next to her.

She frowned as she looked at me. "What do you mean?"

"We heard you yelling. Didn't you call for help?" I tried to be calm but the worry came through in my voice.

"No...I didn't. I've just been sitting here making sure Rain stays asleep. After his episode today I wanted to make sure he got as much as possible." She looked from me to B and back again questioningly but didn't ask what

I was talking about. "Did you two get it out of your system?" she asked instead.

I felt like a deer in the headlights.

"Don't worry, no one could hear you two...make up. Anyways, I'm going to bed. Sleep well," she said as she shimmied down into her sleeping bag.

I turned my embarrassed gaze to B, who covered his mouth to stifle a laugh but I could tell he had also been caught off guard by Lily's comment.

I stood, walked over to him, and bumped my hip into his. "Not funny at all," I growled under my breath. I rubbed my hands across my face as if I could erase the feeling of mortification. "You heard her call for us too, though, right?" I whispered.

B tucked a strand of hair behind my ear and pressed a kiss to my forehead. "Maybe we're just tired. We did have a long and rather *exhausting* day."

"Both of us imagined the same voice though?" I asked, too unnerved to acknowledge his innuendo.

He scanned the opaque fog around us, then lifted my chin up, and kissed me lightly. "I think we shouldn't make anything of it tonight. Let me start the watch. Try to get some sleep, I'll wake you if anything feels off."

I didn't question him, but I wasn't sure how he would determine what felt *off* when everything about this forock did.

We laid our sleeping bags out and I curled up close to B while he sat up on watch. Somehow, even amidst the dense fog that settled around us like an eerie blanket, I managed to set aside my anxious thoughts and focus on the feeling of B next to me instead. I replayed our time alone under the rock, taking my mind off of the seed of panic that had tried to put down roots in my stomach. Resisting the lure of borrowing tomorrow's problems now, I let myself drift asleep to the memory of warm kisses, soft hands, and sounds of love.

The fog was still present when we woke, but had thickened and reduced visibility so that it was easy to become disoriented as we made our way across the forest landscape over the next several days. I think we generally managed to walk in a consistent direction, but occasionally we passed landmarks that I would have sworn we'd seen before. I wouldn't put it past Sintra to let us wander around in one giant circle to make us disheartened and unsure ahead of the next tribulation—or just for the sake of their own amusement.

We tried to make the best of our circumstances, not knowing what we were walking towards yet again. B and Rain managed to come up with a new game. One of them closed their eyes and spun in a circle while the other hid amongst the fog. They would have a minute to find the other person before they lost and it was the other's turn to hide. I didn't like either of them being out of sight, but B insisted he was keeping Rain close and that he didn't stray far himself. He thought it was better to keep Rain distracted so he didn't pick up on the unease he, Lily, and I felt. For my part, the unease took the form of an even stronger sensation of being watched than I had felt before, as if multiple entities had eyes on us. Occasionally, I thought I saw someone at a distance out of the corner of my eye but when I turned to bring them into focus, they were gone. Or my mind was playing tricks on me and they hadn't been there in the first place.

Or maybe it was Sintra in the fog, taking their revenge by plucking at my frayed nerves after being outsmarted in the previous tribulation.

B and Rain were particularly invested in their dirt game, one night shouting good-naturedly as they accused each other of cheating, so I plopped down next to where Lily sat gently massaging her sling-bound arm.

"Hey, do you ever feel like you...see things...in the fog?" I asked, at least half-worried she'd say no and look at me like I was insane.

Lily whipped her absent-minded gaze from Rain and B to look down at her sleeping bag zipper and started worrying the tab with the fingers of her free hand. I ducked my head to look into her face and could see her eyes had widened.

"I...yes...I do see things in the fog," she said quietly.

"What do you see?"

She compressed her lips in a firm line and looked like she wasn't going to speak any further.

"I can tell you what I see first if you want," I offered hesitantly.

She looked at me, her eyes still wide and nodded.

"It almost looks like a person. I think Sintra might be out there toying with us, trying to intimidate us, make us feel nervous after what happened at the last tribulation," I explained, trying to rationalize what I had been seeing.

Lily returned her gaze to her sleeping bag, and this time slowly pulled the zipper up and down its track.

"I think I see a person too, but I'm not sure what or who it is. Maybe it's Sintra, but..." She trailed off, and an icy feeling trickled along my spine.

"What?" I needed her to finish where she was going with her thought.

She shook her head. "Something I remember from the Before. A legend, one about a creature that could imitate people or animals. You weren't supposed to acknowledge it, not supposed to name it or it would come for you. I haven't been able to shake the thought of that legend over the last few days we've been walking." She turned her head back to Rain and B, as if to make sure the creature she spoke of wasn't prowling up behind them.

"It could be Sintra though," she offered when she saw me nervously picking at my fingers.

"Or it could be our minds, disoriented from the fog," I said, the weight of anxiety making my chest ache.

"Yes, it could be," she said distantly.

I looked at the fog, trying to convince myself we had seen Sintra sneaking around, although that might have meant the next tribulation would start soon and that didn't exactly ease my anxiety.

I laid down on my side facing Lily and pulled my knees to my chest so I was curled up in the fetal position.

"I hope Rain hasn't noticed," Lily said as she looked over at him. She gave the sleeping bag zipper a break and began running her fingers through the silky strands of her hair.

"He's pretty observant, but B also has him distracted during the day. If it is Sintra, I doubt they want to scare him. They have an odd fascination with Rain."

Lily's eyebrows knit together. "I've noticed that too. I wonder what the draw is...Maybe Rain reminds them of someone."

I scoffed at that idea. "I'm not sure who they would've known that would be like Rain. Besides another kid in another one of their fucked-up tribulations. It's not like Sintra really takes the time to get to know us, though. We're just shuttled through the Between like cattle to slaughter."

Lily turned her head to look at me. "You can't pretend to know all the ins and outs, all the ways this place works, Eight. Maybe Sintra was mortal once. Or Sintra could've been...made here."

I shook my head. "If Sintra was ever mortal then they wouldn't treat us like this. They don't have any humanity in them."

"Towards Rain, Sintra has some semblance of humanity."

I resisted the thought that anything could be human-like about the stone being, but memories tugged at my mind. How their mask had slipped to reveal rage when B forced their hand when I was dying after the hydra attack, that weird look after they gave me the new boots for Rain. There was something under Sintra's smooth surface, something they couldn't quite hide.

"I'm sure if something happened to Rain, they wouldn't do anything to stop it. They aren't trying *not* to put him in harm's way. I don't think that counts as humanity. Part of being human is suffering, and I don't even think they know what suffering is."

"Or maybe all Sintra knows is suffering."

Lily's devil's advocate role had started to annoy me. "Sounds like Sintra's problem, then, but they won't get any sympathy from me."

Lily stared at me for a moment before she replied. "All I'm trying to say, Eight, is that maybe there's more to their story than we know."

I took a deep breath and let it out, trying to let the prickly feeling of anger release with my exhale. "You could be right, Lily, but I'll never care enough to ask."

It felt like weeks passed while we wandered through the fog-shrouded forest. B and Rain played their hiding game most days during our walks and I grew increasingly more nervous about the shapes I thought I saw appear in the fog. I was back to having a hard time sleeping at night, even with B beside me. Sometimes I would drift off for a bit only to startle awake in a cold sweat and with my heart racing as I tried to shake off the sensation that someone had been hovering over me while I slept.

I realized one day that the forest was no longer completely silent. Sometimes we'd hear a branch crack, or the whisper of the leaves brushing against each other, but there was no wind to stir them or little animals whose weight would make the branches creak. Even more unsettling, I'd think I'd see a tree move just out of the corner of my eye and whip my head towards it, only to see it standing still. It occurred to me I might have been losing my mind.

The only time I felt a little more at ease was when B and I would hold hands while walking. We would drift a little bit behind Rain and Lily so we could have a moment to ourselves. Lily understood what we were doing and generously allowed us the uninterrupted alone time. We never fell too far behind, though, adhering to an unspoken rule that we all stay close together. I insisted B and Rain give up their hiding game; not being able to see them for any length of time made me feel like I was choking with fear. Whenever Rain wanted to walk with B, Lily and I would hold hands as we walked, both of us growing steadily more alarmed by the figures we were certain we saw darting through our foggy surroundings. We all felt the increasing *wrongness* in the air, and we were all on edge, but we kept walking. We had to reach the next tribulation.

Chapter Twenty-Six

O n watch one night, I was exhausted from walking on little sleep, but occasionally I stood up to shake out my arms and legs or jog in place for a minute to keep myself alert. I kept my eye on the fog dancing around, watching tendrils of it slide slowly up through the branches of nearby trees to disappear into the dense canopy high above.

When it was B's turn to take over, I started nudging him awake knowing he slept hard like Harley had.

"Hey, B," I said as I gave him a couple of light shoves. "I'm going to go to the bathroom, okay? Time to wake up to take watch."

He momentarily opened a bleary eye to me and nodded, then turned over onto his stomach. Well, he was slightly awake at least.

I found a tree a handful of paces away where I could maintain a modicum of decency while I emptied my bladder. I gave myself a couple of minutes to dry off before pulling my pants up again and returning to where my friends slept.

B looked like he had drifted back to sleep, while Lily slept on her side her right arm stretched out towards Rain. Except Rain wasn't in his sleeping bag.

Chills of fear shot through me.

"Rain?" I called, wondering if he had slipped away to use the restroom too.

Please, *please*, let that be it.

I nudged B sharply with my foot until he sat up. "What is it? Is it my turn?"

"I don't know where Rain is. I went to the bathroom and came back and now he's gone. I'm sure he's okay, but I'm kinda freaking out," I said as I pulled on his arm to get him up.

"It's okay, we'll find him," he said as he shoved his sleeping bag down his legs and stood. He took my cold hands in his and chafed them as he swiveled his head looking for Rain.

"Lil, I can't find Rain, can you get up, please?" I called out.

She sat up quickly and twisted her head around looking for Rain as well. "What, weren't you on watch? What do you mean you can't find him? Rain? Rain! Where are you?"

Guilt pierced my stomach. "I was awake the whole time! I went to the bathroom and when I came back he was gone. It was less than five minutes tops," I explained.

She nodded and scrambled out of her sleeping bag.

I dug through my pack and grabbed out the lantern. We hadn't had to use one since the puzzle tribulation and I tried not to think about the manticorpions. I hoped there wasn't anything in this forest that would be attracted to the light.

"Lily, do you still have what I gave you in the canyon?" B turned to her, breaking his stare-off into the fog.

"Yes," she breathed.

"Bring it, just in case. We each will."

I looked at both of them in confusion. They dug through their packs and at the same time pulled out long stones. Wait—they were *spikes*, stone spikes with squared-off bottoms and sharp points. I realized they must've each grabbed one from the hydra when both the beast and I had been incapacitated. B also grabbed out his lantern but Lily left hers, opting to carry the spike instead with her free hand.

B handed me a spike. "I took one for you too. I didn't want us to be caught without weapons again."

"Yes, very smart. Now, let's find Rain." I was too on edge to be thoroughly appreciative.

I started to walk away but turned back on second thought to give him a quick kiss. "Thank you for thinking of me too," I said.

"Always."

After quickly ensuring we each knew how to look for landmarks so we could find our way back to the camp, the three of us split up to find Rain. It had been fewer than ten minutes since I passed a sleeping Rain on my way to the bathroom but I couldn't find him immediately outside the perimeter of our camp.

"Rain!" I screamed through the forest, holding up my lantern. It helped a little bit, but most of the light was dispersed by the fog.

My friends' voices echoed around me as they called for him as well, and I could see B's lantern glowing faintly in the misty distance.

My attention was captured by a rustling sound about thirty feet away. The hair on the back of my neck stood up. *What could be making that sound when there was no brush in this forest?*

"Rain?" I called as I walked cautiously toward the noise. I held the sharp stone spike in front of me protectively, in case it wasn't Rain I encountered.

Suddenly the sound was to my right and I spun to see the shape of a person disappear through the fog as quickly as I'd seen it.

"Rain, please! If you're hiding, please come out! This isn't time for a game and we're all worried about you!" I called into the forest, hearing a branch crack above me.

Turning back, I crept toward where I had first heard the rustling sound. I reassured myself his silence was because he was afraid, too panicked to speak after getting lost in the forest.

The rustling sound stopped and so did I, but then I heard a scraping, dragging sound to my left.

And that's when I saw it.

Something from a nightmare.

"RAIN!" I screamed loudly, hoping that the others could hear me. "HELP! I FOUND HIM, HELP!"

My scream stopped the creature. It stood upright like a human on impossibly long legs that made it at least nine or ten feet tall. It was pale and emaciated, and its arms ended in claws that were wrapped around an unconscious Rain's ankles. Large golden eyes stared at me from a head that vaguely reminded me of a deer's, but huge, with boney protrusions growing out the top of it. Below a concave nose was a small, rounded and lipless mouth, almost the size and shape of a quarter.

I felt my heart stop when it tilted its head to stare at me with malevolent curiosity.

Giving myself a mental shake, I lifted the sharp spike in my hand as I stared back. I could hear running footsteps and hoped B and Lily would be with me in a moment.

"Well, aren't you the ugliest fucking thing I've seen?" I spat at the creature, and bared my teeth, stalling until they could reach me but willing to fight it on my own for Rain if I had to.

Thankfully, B and Lily arrived at my side just then, breathing heavily from their run. I turned and saw they had their spikes ready even as they stared at the thing in horror. Lily's face was pale, as if this was the exact being she was afraid she'd see in this forest.

Before any of us could act, a grating voice came out of the fog, followed by Sintra in their indigo robes.

"Welcome, mortals. Now you four find yourself in your fifth tribulation," they said.

"What did you do to Rain?!" I demanded of them, afraid to break eye contact with the creature holding him in front of us.

"He lives, mortals. Do not fear for him yet."

B growled. "Where's the key?"

Sintra chuckled. "I have it."

My eyebrows pinched together. "What? Are you part of the tribulation, then? Do we have to kill you to get the key?"

Sintra glared at me, having picked up on the note of hope in my voice. "No. You can have the key after you have killed this creature." With a hard stare at B, they continued. "Like a petty lawyer, I'm now forced to clarify that if you lose your life before or after retrieving the key, your death will be permanent. I will be here to give the key to you...if you survive." Sintra's smile was a taunt. They winked in my direction and then vanished in a burst of gold.

Lily, B, and I swept our gazes back to the monster—a fog walker, I decided—and saw it eyeing us with calculation. Like it was a carnivore and was trying to decide if trading in the smaller meal in its clutches for three larger ones would be worth it. Or if it had enough room for all four of us.

"Let's surround it, similar to how we did the hydra. Maybe it won't know which of us to go after and that'll buy us some time to figure out how to kill it," I said quietly, having no idea if the fog walker could understand me.

"Same strategy?" Lily questioned, unsure if my plan was a good idea.

"Why reinvent the wheel?" I gritted my teeth.

"I stay in front, you both go to the sides. I'll grab Rain if you can distract it long enough," B said.

B and I set our lanterns to the ground and we all readied the spikes in our hands. Lily and I slowly stepped out and around the creature while B approached it head on. The fog walker pivoted back and forth, watching each of us warily. Not ready to let go of its meal, its sickly white hands still gripped Rain's ankles. Nausea rolled in my stomach at the thought of what this thing could have done to him if I hadn't come across it when I did.

When we reached our positions, we all paused for a second and in that moment the fog walker's formerly small mouth expanded wide, until it somehow took up half the thing's face and revealed three concentric rings of elongated fang-like teeth jutting from gums. The teeth were all angled slightly outward and had little hooks at the end so that any prey it bit into wouldn't be able to get away. Like a giant lamprey, but apparently one with a taste for warm-blooded humans instead of fish.

The creature tipped its head back and let out a screech that sounded like a jet engine and squealing hogs and the grinding of the earth during a quake, all rolled into one godawful sound, dropping hold of Rain's ankles with the effort.

B lurched forward and slashed at the creature with his stone spike and made to grab Rain's arm to pull him to safety. The fog walker sprang at B and slashed with its yellowed claws. I heard fabric tear and saw long gouges across his chest well with blood. B cried out in pain and stumbled backwards but before the creature could press its advantage and strike again, Lily lunged at it and sunk her spike into its left shoulder at the same time I lunged and dragged my spike across its side.

The fog walker whipped its head at Lily and bellowed in rage, then spun to me, saliva flying out of its mouth. In my peripheral vision, I saw Lily pull her spike free, then raise her hand over her head and bring it down toward the creature's back in a forceful stabbing motion.

It must have felt her movement because the monster crouched and twisted at the same time so that the spike sunk into its shoulder a second time. With another angry howl, it sprang to the side and in one leap landed on the trunk of a nearby tree. Moving like a four-legged spider, it scrabbled up the tree and disappeared into its fog-cloaked canopy. I thought it was likely licking its wounds, taking a moment to recover before it came back to pick us off.

"Rain!" I shouted, running over to him at the same time Lily did.

"I got him! Go check on B!" Lily urged as she turned her wide gaze to Rain and began shaking him to a groggy consciousness.

I dashed over to where B knelt on the ground and dropped to my knees beside him, fog eddying around us.

"B, are you okay? Is it deep? Please tell me you're okay!" I was panicked and on the verge of becoming hysterical at the blood soaking his shirt.

"I'm fine, I think," he said, lifting up his shirt to assess the damage.

Blood dripped from the gouges the fog walker had inflicted down his abdomen.

"Shit," I murmured.

"You have many assets, but comfort when someone is injured isn't one of them, Eight," B retorted, his eyes tracing the wounds.

"Don't look if you're going to pass out," I warned, the metallic scent of his blood in my nostrils.

"I'll be fine," he said, but I noticed the hand holding up his shirt had started trembling.

I heard a branch break above us.

"We need to get up, now. Everyone on their feet!" I directed. I wasn't sure where that thing had gone but I was certain it would want revenge.

And we needed it to return so that we could kill it and be done with this tribulation.

Lily had gotten Rain to his feet and I could see a wet stain on his pants and smell the pungent scent of urine as I approached him. He must have been so terrified when the fog walker grabbed him from the camp site that he fainted before he could even cry out to alert us.

"Are you okay, Rain?" I asked him.

"I... think...so," he said in a small voice, his body quivering with fear.

"Okay, good. Back-to-back, all of us," I commanded, trying to rally us together the way I'd seen B do. He was becoming pale, the sight of his injuries or shock starting to take its toll on him. He was going to need all his energy to stay on his feet, so I would lead the charge this time. I would hold us together so that B didn't have to. I owed him that, at the very least.

We stood in a loose square, our backs to each other and facing outward. "We keep our eyes out for it, in our surroundings or above us. We have no idea where it could appear next. If you see anything, say so. We have to kill it in order to get out of here. Together, okay?" Everyone murmured their agreement.

After just a few minutes of unbearable anticipation, we heard a scurrying noise in the tree above us. I looked up quickly, trying to pick up where it had come from. I heard the same sound again to my right, and then a branch breaking on the ground through the fog in front of me.

Oh god, were there multiple monsters out there in the fog? Wouldn't that break the rules Sintra had set up? Or was the forest itself an ally to the fog walker, somehow throwing out sounds to confuse and disorient us?

I could hear Rain crying behind me, but couldn't shift my focus to comfort him. I couldn't risk missing a sound that would tell me where the creature was, couldn't risk letting it sneak up on us while I was distracted.

"I think I saw the shape of a human in front of me, but it disappeared into the fog again," Lily's voice trembled.

"Keep watching, we can't split up to go look, it's too dangerous. We need it to come to us," I said, feigning confidence to reassure her and the others that our standing there was a good strategy. "Wait it out, hopefully it'll grow impatient and make a move for us again."

"Okay," she replied in a small voice.

The fog continued to dance gracefully around us, keeping the creature's location hidden. Then a voice drifted out of the murk.

"Hey, where are you four? Please help me. I'm trapped and alone. You left me to die."

Bile surged up my throat, as fear gripped me. I grabbed one of B's hands with my hand that wasn't holding the spike, terrified to my core at what I was hearing.

"Why did you kill me, Eight? You are so horrible. You are the most horrible person I've ever met."

I knew, in my rational brain, that what I heard wasn't real, that Don wasn't out there in the fog calling to me. But the part of me that felt guilt at the way I had left Don behind writhed in pain. I clenched my jaw and shook my head. *No.* This wasn't real.

"Why'd you leave me to die, Lil? Did you even try to help me? Or did you just want to make me suffer in the last moments of my life? Is that it? Is that what you wanted? I guess that's all you're good at, huh? Causing pain."

"Lily, don't listen to it. That's not Harley," I said, trying to keep my voice from cracking. "Harley's gone, you know that." The voice had come from almost directly overhead this time. I stared upwards, afraid the fog walker would drop on us from above.

"Were you glad when I was gone, B? So you could take every last bit of my things? Didn't even care that it was mine and I'd just died? Didn't even miss

me? I bet you were happy, just waiting for me to keel over dead for you. You even almost killed me yourself. I hope you feel guilty for the rest of eternity. It's your fault I'm gone."

I heard B inhaling deeply through his nose, but he didn't rise to the bait.

More skittering in the branches had me looking up again. Something liquid dripped through the fog and onto my cheek.

I furiously wiped the sticky, metallic smelling substance away, gagging at what I was sure was blood-tinged saliva from the fog walker drooling over its intended meal.

Rain whimpered. "Make it stop, I want it to stop, please."

"It's going to be okay, Rain. Just cover your ears, please." I was desperately trying not to vomit.

"Mom? Are you coming back, Mom? I miss you so much, please don't leave me. I need you."

A chill ran down my spine.

No.

Lily gasped and broke into sobs behind me.

"Lily, no! It's not him Lily, it's *not*. Please don't listen, it's not real," I tried.

Her response was a wail of anguish.

"Did you even love me, Mom? Did you even try to save me? Did you even try to fight him? You didn't care about me. You just left me on the floor alone and afraid. You left me to die."

"SHUT UP!" I screamed into the fog around us as I heard Lily breaking apart, loud sobs tearing through her.

"My baby, please come home. I miss you so much baby, your family misses you. Come home to us, please."

"NO! I'm not a baby! Stop it! Stop calling me that!" Rain yelled.

I glanced down and behind me and saw him pulling at his brown curls, his face contorted in anger while tears spilled from his eyes.

"Rain," I said sternly, "plug your ears, *now*." I couldn't afford for him to become aggravated, for him to run off. It would be the death of us all.

His tears kept coming and under the sound of Lily's keening I could hear him mumbling, "not a baby, I'm not—"

"NOW!" I commanded and saw him stick his fingers in his ears. Before I had the chance to even momentarily feel relief that he had listened, another voice drifted through the fog.

"So this is how you disappoint us again. You should have known what would happen at that restaurant. Now what are we supposed to do? How can you let us down like this?"

I felt B tense up and squeeze my hand. *A disappointment.* Whose voice was that? I knew it was a trick but I wanted to strangle whoever could've made B feel like that.

"You're just going to hide up there and taunt us all night?" I shouted into the misty abyss above me.

As if in response, the fog thinned out around us to reveal more trees in the near distance. Then the sound of running steps filled my ears and I swung my head around just in time to see the fog walker grab Lily by the arms and start to pull her away from us.

"NO!" I screamed and flung my hands out as I turned, trying to stab the creature with my stone spike. The fog walker ran then, dragging Lily with it. B broke into a run after them and I grabbed Rain.

"Rain, stay here, cover your ears and don't look. Got it? Don't move and don't look!"

I pushed him to sit on the ground in front of me with his back to where the fog walker had taken Lily. He pulled his legs up and wrapped his arms around them. "What's happening, Eight?! Where's Lil? Is she okay?"

A scream tore through the air. I looked to see the fog walker had pinned Lily to a tree in the distance—literally. Its yellow nails were shoved through her shoulders and into the trunk.

"Just don't look, okay?! And cover your ears, Rain, please! Don't make me ask again!" He recognized the urgency in my voice and shoved his head between his knees and stuck his fingers back in his ears before starting to rock back and forth while crying.

B had caught up to the fog walker and had just tried to stab it with his spike. The creature pulled one hand free from Lily's shoulder and turned to smack B away like a pesky fly, throwing him back a handful of feet.

"NO!" I screamed again. I ran toward them, moving as fast as I could to stop what I felt was coming deep in my bones.

No.

Please, no.

Lily screamed and sobbed as she clutched the beast's arm that still pinned her to the tree, pulling at it in an attempt to free herself. Blood poured from the puncture wounds in her shoulders while the fog walker growled, putting its sets of teeth on display an inch from her face.

I ran past B as he started to get up, begging my legs to move faster as I raised my stone spike above my head with both hands.

The fog walker pulled its claws from Lily's shoulder but before she could take a single step it pulled back its arms and then flung them forward to stab with both sets of claws deep into her abdomen.

My savage scream of rage mixed with Lily's scream of pain as I sank the sharpened stone into the back of the fog walker's head.

Chapter Twenty-Seven

The monster slumped to the ground, my spike embedded in its skull and presumably its brain. It dragged Lily to the ground with it, its claws stuck through her. I could see them protruding through Lily's back but it was as if my brain wouldn't process the image. I just stood there and felt my head shake with disbelief.

"Lily, no...Lily!"

B ran over and bent down to gently, so gently, pull Lily up and off of the claws. I sank to the ground and B laid Lily in my arms.

Her eyes fixed in shock, tears slid down Lily's cheeks to mix with the blood that bubbled out of her mouth.

"Lily," I whispered, my voice breaking.

Her eyes tracked to me and slowly she lifted a hand to rest it lightly against my face. It was so cold, like it had been buried in snow before reaching for me.

"I'm sorry," she whispered.

"No, Lily, don't leave! Please don't leave us!" I wailed.

She tried to wipe a tear from my face, but her hand went slack and her eyes took on a distant look.

I leaned down and rested my forehead on hers.

"Will I see him again?" she asked in a whisper only I could hear.

I nodded and felt B's hand come to rest on my back.

"You will, Lil. You will find him one day. You will be together, I know it. That man will never keep you two apart ever again," I said, my voice thick with tears. I stroked my hand through her hair tenderly.

A breath shuddered through her, rattling her body. Her blood was all over me now, but I didn't care. I just held her, held my friend close, not allowing her to leave the Between as alone as she had come into it.

"Take...care of Rain... please," she slurred softly, her eyes beginning to drift shut.

"I promise," I said, feeling like my lungs were closing too.

And then Lily's last breath moved through her and her beautiful light was extinguished. The master of death had blown out her candle and harvested her soul.

I screamed and rocked back and forth, clutching her body to me, while B held his arms around me. I couldn't let go of her, couldn't do anything but hold her body.

Drawn by my screaming, Rain called out, "Eight? B?" as he ran toward us. B jumped up and ran to stop him before he could reach us and see Lily's body.

"Did Eight scream? Where's Lil? What's happening?!"

"Rain, listen. Listen to me." B knelt in front of Rain and raised his hands to cup his face. Before he could say anything, Rain leaned to look around him.

"What happened to Lil? Why is she bleeding?" he cried.

"Rain...Lily is gone. She died."

Rain stared at B in disbelief and jerked his head side to side in denial. But the sorrow on B's face told him it was true and Rain began crying, softly at first then in wracking sobs as B held him to his chest.

"I know it hurts, I know, but imagine Lily is in a better place, Rain. Imagine that one day she'll be waiting for you with open arms. Close your eyes and remember the last time she held you. She will always love you, even if she's not here to tell you that." B's voice was soft, wavering with emotion, but trying to be strong for Rain.

Rain nodded his head against B's shoulder then pulled back to look at him. "I want to see her," Rain said.

"Rain, I won't stop you if that's what you want, but I want you to know that how Lily died wasn't gentle and you won't be able to forget that. It's your choice to see her now or not."

"I want to see her, she's my friend," he said quietly but firmly through his tears. B nodded his head, then stood. He and Rain walked to where I sat still holding Lily.

B stood with his hands on Rain's shoulders as he stared at Lily's body. I looked up. "She will always love you," I cried. He slowly sank to his knees, then leaned over to place his forehead against Lily's chest.

"Mortal, it is time to give her body over." I flinched at the sound of Sintra's voice and back to myself to see I was still holding Lily but now Rain and B sat on either side of me, their hands resting on her body. How long had we been holding our friend, not ready to admit she was gone? How long had Sintra been standing behind us, not daring to speak before now?

I wasn't about to hand Lily over to them. Sintra could burn for an eternity before having Lily's perfect being.

They stepped around to stand in front of us and stood silently for a moment. "Let her know peace," they said as they held the golden key out to me, like a person would hold a carrot out to a wary horse. Like a bribe, and I wanted to turn it down but I knew I couldn't.

I glared at them. "Are you going to tell me that she's crossed the rainbow bridge of bliss?" I asked quietly as rage built inside me. "That she doesn't remember a moment of her murder? Do you feel okay with what you do to us mortals, Sintra? Why do you do this to us?!" I shouted.

Sintra stared at me for a minute, their expression unreadable. "That's a good question, isn't it?" Then a sneering smile crept across their face. "Why does this all happen?" I didn't know what the hell that was supposed to mean, but before I could tell Sintra what I thought of their answering a question with questions, they gestured with their hand and Lily's body dissolved into the most beautiful gold dust I'd seen.

I cried out at the loss of her body's weight against me and took some of the dust into my lungs. I started to get to my feet to tear Sintra apart, but B held onto me while the gold curled around my face, the dust of Lily's essence dancing around us as Sintra disappeared. Rain cried too as he grasped at the air, wanting to capture the gold flakes, wanting to keep Lily with him.

He fell back against my side. "Is Lil going to be happy?" he asked as he held onto me for dear life.

I tried to control the emotion that shook me. "She will be. She will."

B's chest was a warzone. He tried to keep his face neutral while I worked on it, but couldn't stop wincing while I did.

I tried to mimic Lily's movements in stitching, but I knew I was nowhere near as adept. I replicated the water on the wound first and took a flame to the needle, but my stitches were a patchy cluster, further apart in some areas while tight in others, just like they had been on Harley's shirt. I desperately wanted to heal the way I'd seen Lily do it as if doing so would keep her with me somehow. I couldn't erase the image of her rigid body in my arms. I couldn't stop the sadness that made its home in me at the thought that she was never going to make it back to that little boy.

B jumped, startled when I stabbed him with the needle.

"I'm sorry..." I said as I tied off the thread I'd been stitching with.

He wrapped his hand around mine and pulled me against him when a sob wracked through me.

He hummed softly through his own tears. Rain had been watching the forest silently while I tended to B but when he heard me crying again, he nuzzled up to me on B's lap and wept also. The three of us held each other while our tears flowed, B trying to hum us a melody to soothe our aching hearts. Some pains can't be erased, though.

That night I held Rain against my chest as he slept, and B held us both so none of us felt alone. B sang of a beautiful woman who was smart, fierce, and happy. One who found two little boys and cared for them until her last breath. A woman who had found happiness and peace when her life came to an end. A woman whose found family would remember her with great love.

I didn't sleep, though, just laid against B.

"Is all this still worth it?" I whispered.

"Yes, Eight, it is. Don't give up, please. We will make it to the end and know that we made all the horror, the heartache, the pain, worth it. We have to keep going, for each other, for ourselves and for Rain. It's what Lily would've wanted," he said and pressed his lips against my ear.

I nodded, a few tears slipping off my chin to land in Rain's soft curls.

I hoped he was right, I hope this would all be worth it in the end.

Chapter Twenty-Eight

The next morning, we walked back to where we had set up camp to get our packs. We kept the medkit from Lily's pack and B collected the gold key she had been keeping and added it to the three he carried. I continued to carry the first one we had collected after the river crossing and the second from the puzzle tribulation. Rain pulled the grass doll she made him form his pack and kept in his hands at all times, always holding onto or hugging it when we took rest breaks. We stayed in camp for another day, then started walking, hollowed out with grief but hoping to find our way out of the fog.

As the days passed it seemed B's gashes were healing okay, as far as I could tell. If he could retain physical scars from the Between, I'm sure he would, given my horrendous patchwork of stitches, but at least his wounds didn't seem to be growing infected. The skin hadn't puckered and turned red like Harley's had and the area around it didn't feel hot to the touch.

The nights were hard. Neither B nor I got a full night's rest as we took turns keeping watch. Traumatized by having been dragged off by the fog walker, Rain couldn't fall asleep alone so B zipped our three sleeping bags together into one large bag. We slept cuddled up in it, Rain between me and B, so that he felt safe, at least as safe as any of us could feel anymore.

Sometimes when Rain was asleep, B and I would speak in hushed whispers and reach across Rain to hold hands or steal kisses, knowing we wouldn't get time together like we had under the boulder. We had to live with that being the last time we joined until we found a way back to each other after we returned to the Before.

I held onto the hope there would be a way to find B and Rain after we returned. I wanted to know they were safe and happy in their lives. I wanted to see Lily's son and make sure he was protected, away from the man that was so willing to hurt him and his mother.

At night B and Rain would play their dirt game. There was less shouting, not nearly as much poking fun at the other, but it still provided some distraction from their thoughts. One night they offered to teach me the game. I smiled weakly and accepted, not really sure I was actually interested, but knowing that distracting myself from the emptiness I felt would probably be to my benefit.

I didn't understand the game in the slightest and was confused by the symbol language it relied on. Whenever I drew what I thought was the correct answer, they would shake their heads and tell me why using a different symbol would have been a better strategy. After playing with them a couple of times, I declined further invitations to join in, opting instead to watch them enjoy their time together from the sidelines.

"I have no idea how you two managed to create that dirt game, but lucky you did because it saved us at least once so far," I whispered one night to B after Rain had fallen asleep. I didn't know if Rain dreamed in the Between, but his movements had grown increasingly more restless and jerky while he slept. A few times I woke up with bruises on my shin from being kicked.

"We had plenty of time to be creative," B whispered back to me.

"I miss you, B. I miss the moments we used to get together. I feel like they were the only thing that truly brought me joy in this place."

He nuzzled his face into mine. "I'm right here, Eight. I haven't gone anywhere. I know things look different each day, but I'm not leaving your side. I haven't forgotten that one day, when we leave this place, I'll come find you. We'll get all the time we can together and then we'll find each other again in the After."

We kissed softly, careful not to wake Rain and then I fell into a dreamless sleep curled up in B's arms.

One day I noticed a dim purple light seemed to be seeping through a thinner patch of fog ahead of us. My stomach plunged as I immediately suspected it of being a prelude to another tribulation.

"Do you...see that?" I asked weakly.

"Maybe it's the end," B suggested, and the note of longing in his voice echoed my own feelings. I was so tired and heartsore and just wanted to be done with the Between.

"It could be? We finished the last tribulation days and days ago." Despite my trepidation, a spark of hope lit inside me without my permission.

"I want out of here," Rain huffed, twisting around the arm of his grass doll.

"Me too, Rain," I said, squeezing his hand.

"Eight, can I pass through first? Just in case there's something waiting on the other side," B asked. I was nervous about letting him, but I appreciated that he'd asked instead of just taking the risk. I didn't want to let him out of my sight but wanted so badly to get out of this forock.

"Okay," I said.

He pressed a kiss to my lips and tousled Rain's brown curls before he turned and walked into the purplish mist.

I realized I had been holding my breath only when I heard B's voice come from the other side.

"Come here you two," he called softly.

"Ready?" I whispered to Rain.

He looked up at me with his doe eyes and nodded, setting his face in a determined look. "Yeah."

We walked through the fog together.

And I gasped.

On the other side of the mist it was completely clear; no fog blocked our view of our surroundings and the periwinkle sky once again rose above us. And for once, our surroundings weren't all that grim. In front of us was a field of new, muted-yellow and old, silver dandelions covering the ground in a thick carpet.

"It's so beautiful," I whispered, hardly able to speak from the relief coursing through me.

"It is," B said as he gently took my hand and kissed my wrist. It felt like my heart was beating again for the first time in days.

Rain's eyes were wide as he looked around us. "Are these...flowers?" he asked, his little voice quivering with tentative excitement.

"I think so," I answered as I rubbed a hand along his shoulders.

"Can I..." he started to ask, but I already knew what he was asking permission for.

I smiled at him. "Go ahead."

He took off in a run through the tall flowers, not holding back his delight. Seedlings from the old dandelions exploded through the air as he rushed past them, swirling madly for a moment before drifting softly down to the path he was creating through the field. I couldn't help the small laugh that escaped me.

"Well, what are you waiting for, Eight?" B asked, holding out his hand to me.

I smiled up at him and grabbed his hand in mine. We took off after Rain, and I felt the flowers lightly slap my legs while I ran. Dropping my hand, B pulled ahead and teased me about how slowly I was running. I tripped a few times, my foot caught in the thicket of leaves and stems, as I tried to catch up to him and he ran back each time to help me. I laughed, letting the sound fill my empty heart.

We ran like that for a while, playfully chasing after Rain through the field and overjoyed to be out of the gloom of the fog. When we eventually caught up to him, I spun myself in circles and B sat on the ground, blowing at the dandelion fluff, seeing if he could send the seedlings floating around Rain.

I plopped down in the sea of flowers next to B and Rain after I had thoroughly exhausted myself. I was panting, out of breath, and slightly dizzy from turning in circles so many times.

I took my canteen out and drank deeply, passing it to B and Rain who took equally long drinks.

I stretched my legs out in front of me and leaned back to rest on my elbows. Rain collected flowers and bunched them together into a small bouquet in his fist.

"You know something I kind of remember from the Before?" B asked as he plucked a yellowed dandelion.

"What's that?" I smiled at him.

"That if you hold one of these up to your chin and it causes a yellow glow on you, that means you have a crush," he said, wiggling his eyebrows at me.

I threw my head back and laughed. "Isn't that supposed to be buttercups?"

"Cut me some slack, I think any yellow flower will do the trick," he retorted with a wink.

"Okay then, let's see it. Who goes first?" I looked between B and Rain.

"How about Rain first?" B said and leaned forward to hold the flower under Rain's chin.

Rain looked confused. "I don't have a crush on anyone."

"Well I guess we will know that for sure in a second, won't we?" B said, grinning cheekily. There was no yellow glow on Rain's skin, B's highly scientific method of crush detection confirming Rain hadn't been lying.

"Okay, your turn, Eight," B said, tickling my chin gently with the dandelion and making me chuckle softly.

"What do you think? Do I have a crush?" I asked him, raising my eyebrows playfully.

"You know, I definitely see yellow. It's almost up to your cheeks actually," he said, in a mock-solemn voice.

"Oh really?" I made my voice serious also.

"I don't see anything," Rain narrowed his eyes between the two of us.

B shook his head. "How can you not? Practically her entire face has turned yellow."

"Okay, okay, it's your turn now." I snatched the flower from his hand and moved into a seated position. I rubbed the flower lightly against his chin.

"Hmm, I see what you mean. There's a bunch of yellow all over *your* face now. Your eyes are almost glowing yellow too. You definitely have a crush on someone," I widened my eyes at him.

Rain snorted. "You two are so weird," he said and turned back to assembling his bouquet.

B and I grinned at each other and leaned in to share a long kiss.

"Gross..." Rain muttered, causing us to break apart in laughter.

"You know, something *I* remember from the Before is that you can make wishes on the dandelions that have become silver and fluffy," I said.

Rain rolled his eyes. "Everyone knows that, Eight."

"Okay, well then, how about we make some wishes?"

The three of us each picked a puffball dandelion and then paused as we thought about the wishes we'd make. Catching each other's eyes, we knew we were thinking the same thing. One by one, we raised our dandelion up and blew on it to release its seedlings into the field around us as we each whispered the names of our fallen friends and wished for their peace.

I grabbed a fourth dandelion and made a wish for Lily's son. Wherever he was, I wished for him to find peace in the world, to find purpose. I hoped that he could heal from the heartache of losing such a bright soul as his mother. I wished that one day they would meet again in the After and be together, free of fear and pain. I wished for them both to be eternally happy.

We slept in the dandelion field that night. I checked B's stitches before we all bedded down, worried I would find his wounds had turned infected after all but they still looked like they were healing appropriately.

In an odd way, the three of us felt like a little family. When I shut my eyes, I could imagine that B and I were married in the Before and Rain was our child. Maybe we had been meant to find each other in the Between so that we could protect each other like a family would. The thought brought a smile to my lips and a warm, comfortable feeling to my heart.

I kissed Rain on the forehead and B on the lips before settling down to sleep for a couple of hours prior to my watch. I drifted off, my nose full of the earthy scent that dandelions released as they were crushed beneath our sleeping bag.

Chapter Twenty-Nine

"Wake up! Please, both of you wake up." B's voice, low and urgent, came to me as he shook me back to consciousness. A bleak darkness cut through my sleepy, warm contentment. I wanted to hide my face in Rain's curly hair and ignore the horrendous feeling steadily growing in me.

"What is it?" I groaned, keeping my eyes closed, holding Rain to me. I hoped if I didn't open my eyes and look I could ignore what I was sure was happening.

"Sintra," B whispered.

Dread clawed through me at the confirmation. I wasn't ready, I could never feel ready for another tribulation after the last one. It was too soon. I wished it was just another *personal* visit, but I knew deep down that wasn't the case.

I shook my head. "No."

"Yes, your mortal lover speaks the truth. It is time for your final tribulation," Sintra said, their voice carrying more than a hint of wicked joy. I didn't have to look to know they had a twisted grin etched on across their face.

Rain hadn't said anything, but I could feel his body trembling in my arms.

"It's going to be okay, Rain, you still have me and B. We won't let anything happen to you," I said firmly while I stroked his hair gently.

I had to hold back my own tears when I heard him sniffle into the side of the sleeping bag.

Our final tribulation.

The three of us forced ourselves up into a seated position and anxiously looked around for what was coming to maul us. Was it going to be another creature? Another element? How would this one play out?

"What are we supposed to do?" I narrowed my eyes as they rested on Sintra's stony face.

"Your final tribulation will not take place here. Gather your things together, mortals."

I wanted to argue, wanted to resist anything Sintra told us to do but I knew it was futile. Sighing, I stood with B and Rain and unzipped our sleeping bags and stuffed them into our packs. We then ate a bit of light chocolate and swigged some water.

When we were ready, we stood expectantly in front of Sintra as they brought their hands, palms together, in front of them.

"Are you all ready?" they asked.

None of us answered, picking up on the rhetorical nature of their question.

They shot one last glance at Rain, who shrank back from them, then I felt my body being ripped apart, like Sintra had taken a chainsaw and split me in two with it. The smell of burning rubber filled my nostrils as pain so extraordinary it made it difficult to hold onto my consciousness, flashed through me. I fought the darkness that tried to worm its way into my mind, but it was pointless.

The last thing I remember was being whisked away from the tranquil field of flowers into a consuming darkness and my mind slipped away once again, against my will.

I awoke feeling like my body had been pulverized. My head hurt and I kept blinking my eyes hoping my vision would clear up and the pounding would stop. I was lying on my right side and my hip was sore from pressing into cold, hard ground.

I reached across my body with my left arm and with great effort pushed myself up to sit. My eyes were coming into focus and I saw smooth, grey stone stretching out to the horizon ahead of me interrupted only by the small pile of our packs. And Sintra.

They were always watching, always waiting.

"Welcome, mortal. I have been waiting for you to rouse yourself. I should have remembered how much you enjoy your sleep."

"Where are Rain and B?" I growled weakly up at them in reply.

"Your friends are well, mortal," was all they said.

My heart raced in fear and I had to draw deep for the necessary energy to shout at Sintra. "Where are they?!" As weak as I felt, I would find a way to murder Sintra if they had taken B and Rain to the After.

"Do not fret mortal, they remain in the Between with you. Although, the After *is* waiting with bated breath to see who will join their ranks next," Sintra said as they stepped closer to me.

"Simply look behind you," they said as they gestured their head.

I swiveled, feeling rage and panic surge through me. I forced myself to stand on wobbly legs, my body quivering intensely from the abuse of the journey here.

"B! Rain!" I called as I stepped forward toward them, only to fall painfully to my knees.

B and Rain stood handcuffed to separate metal poles staked just a few feet away from the edge of a cliff, their mouths gagged with heavy strips of cloth.

B's eyes were wide with fear as he stared at me. Tears streamed down Rain's face as he pulled uselessly against his handcuffs.

"What did you do to them?! What game are you playing at Sintra?!" I yelled, scrambling to my feet again even as my body shook with the effort.

A slow, malicious smile spread across Sintra's face. "This tribulation is only for you, mortal. Since you defied death, now you must become it. It is rather easy. You choose which of them leaves the Between alive and which gets to join the After."

I froze.

"If you do not pick, all three of you will go to the After. You will not return to the Before," Sintra warned, the smile on their face becoming razor sharp.

"No!" I cried.

I stared at B and Rain, the devastation of dying hopes and dreams built on promises flooding through me.

The promise B and I made to each other to do whatever we could to ensure Rain's survival, and my promise to Lily to take care of Rain.

B and I promising to find each other once we returned to the living.

Choose who lives.

Tears blurred my vision as I haltingly stepped towards the man I had fallen in love with and the little boy who had become like my own. The promises I had made grated against each other in my heart and I faltered.

B strained against his handcuffs, his eyes pleading, asking me for something I couldn't give him. My stomach sank as I accepted the time I had with B was coming to an end. As if in a trance, I forced my feet to carry me to him, shaking my head in denial. Tears streamed down his handsome features.

When I reached him, I stared into his beautiful blue eyes, remembering the conversations we'd had, the thoughts we'd shared, the moments of intimacy between us. I realized I'd changed since arriving in the Between. I'd become more open to friendship and love and I wanted so much to share more of that with B, but I never would. I never could. The two of us were never going to have the chance to build a life together.

We had to part, here and now.

I reached out to trace the curve of his cheek one last time. Knowing Sintra could hear me, I said, "me."

B's eyes widened and he thrashed even harder against his restraint, his wrists turning white from the pressure of the handcuffs digging into them.

With a strength borne of my love for the man in front of me I nodded once, then closed my eyes and walked back to stand in front of Sintra. "Me, I choose me."

"As you wish, mortal," Sintra said, a satisfied smile spreading unrestrained across their face.

"Wait! Let them go first, I want to say goodbye," I said before they could wave their hand and transform me into gold dust.

They paused for a moment, as if weighing whether or not I deserved to say goodbye. "Oh, yes, why not," they decided, condescendingly magnanimous in their victory. They snapped their fingers once and I heard B's and Rain's handcuffs and gags fall away.

I turned and ran back to a stunned B and Rain with a cry. We threw our arms around each other and held on tightly.

"Don't go, Eight! Don't leave me, please! Please!" Rain cried into my stomach.

"I love you so much Rain," I sobbed as I pressed my cheek to his head. "I'm always going to love you, okay? We will see each other again one day, after you live a long life. We will find each other in the After. Be good to your family, make yourself a good life and then come tell me about it. Promise?" My tears soaked his brown curls.

"No, Eight, I need you to come see it with me," he begged.

I shook my head.

"That isn't an option, Rain. I need you to be brave now. Be brave for me, please." I lowered myself to my knees so I could look him in the eye and hoped he could see all the love I had for him in mine. "Will you do that for me?"

He cried harder and wrapped his arms around my shoulders. We stayed that way for a minute and then I felt the slight nod of his head against mine with relief and sorrow. I turned to kiss his cheek and tasted the salt of his tears.

I slowly stood and faced B. The pain in his eyes was a knife in my heart.

"I'm sorry, B," I choked out. "I wanted to find you, I swear, I wanted to make everything we talked about come true and—"

My words were cut off as he held my face and kissed me deeply, fiercely, as if he would never get enough of me. As if this kiss had to last him a lifetime. I surrendered to the force of our love for one another one last time, our tears mingling on our lips.

I felt one of his hands caress lightly down my upper right arm and then down my forearm. I braced myself, knowing he was about to kiss my wrist for the last time.

Instead, I felt metal handcuffs click into place.

Chapter Thirty

M y body grew rigid in disbelief.

"B, what are you doing? What is this?! Stop! Get this off of me!" I yanked against the handcuffs manically, trying to free myself.

I turned to Sintra, who was watching the exchange with wide eyes and a clenched jaw.

"Sintra, do something! It's me you want anyway, you heard me say I want to die! SO KILL ME!"

They shook their head, partly in denial of this demand and partly as if in disbelief at what was happening.

"SINTRA!" I screamed again, desperately.

They whipped their head towards me and snarled, "I cannot intervene once the tribulation has started, mortal."

"You're a liar! You already intervened when you removed the handcuffs in the first place!"

Their gaze turned ice cold and the temperature of the air around us almost seemed to plummet as well. When they spoke, their voice was a deadly whisper. "I did *not* intervene. The choice had already been made."

"But I was the choice! Not B! And now he's going to die!" I screamed.

"It was not an intervention, it was a favor I was granting by allowing—"

"This isn't a favor, *you bitch*! He's going to die—"

"Make no mistake, mortal," they cut me off, and I swore I saw a flicker of fear ghost across their face. "This tribulation will not end until a sacrifice has been made. *You* made a mistake in your weakness for him and now he will die because of it."

My mind reeled as I remembered Sintra's earlier words to me— *"You are a survivor, mortal. Others flock to you for it. Others also die for it."*

No. Oh, god, no.

I threw my gaze to where B held a tearful Rain in a tight hug. As I struggled against my restraints I heard him say quietly, "I'm going to miss you, Rain. Have a good life. Protect Eight one last time for me, okay?"

"B! STOP!" I screamed at him. He straightened and let go of Rain to grab my free hand. Locking eyes with me, he lifted it to his lips and tenderly kissed my wrist.

"B!" My voice cracked.

Holding my hand against his heart, he whispered, "I love you, Eight. Please make sure Rain gets back safe, please find happiness. I'll wait for you, I'll always wait for you."

"No! Please, don't do this! Don't make me be the one to live without you!"

Never taking his eyes from mine, he quickly stepped back and away from me until he reached the very edge of the cliff.

"Come find me when it's your time, Eight," he said and this time his smile was a bright and dazzling gift, just for me.

Then he stepped backward off the cliff and I felt my heart shatter against the background of my screams.

Rain stumbled over to me and we fell to the ground together as I threw my arm out uselessly toward the space where B had just been, wanting to grab onto him and pull him back to us. *To me.*

Rain and I clutched each other, wailing like wounded animals, high-pitched with pain and hysteria. We lay there, gasping for breath through our misery until I felt the handcuff suddenly release and I was free.

In an instant, rage flared through me like lightning, tangling with my despair and giving me the energy to lurch to my feet and swing my body toward Sintra.

I set my sights on them, pointing a finger, as I ate up the ground between us.

Sintra's expression was uneasy. "This is not how it was supposed to happen," they said.

Good, let them be afraid. I hoped retribution was coming for them.

"You evil demon," I seethed, my voice dangerously low as I got closer.

"We are *not* evil. *I* am not evil. We are balance, chance, and opportunity. We do not inflict malice," Sintra said indignantly.

"If you aren't the evil you claim to be, then why is your alleged giving a double-edged sword? You offer death, then suffering, more death and maybe a chance at life," I spit through tears. "He didn't want this, I didn't want this, *we* don't want this. BRING HIM BACK! *NOW!*" I screamed. "GO TO THE FUCKING AFTER AND FIND HIM, SINTRA!"

"No," they said, a flash of pain twisting through their stone features. It was fleeting, gone almost as quickly as it had come, making me wonder if I'd imagined it.

I stepped closer, my fists tight at my side, tears pouring from my eyes. "Fuck. You. Fuck you, Sintra, you fucking MASOCHISTIC STONE CU—"

"Eight, no, please!" Rain shouted as he ran over to throw his arms around my legs in a desperate attempt to hold me back. "Please, I can't lose you too," he begged.

"He is right, mortal. You still want to get the child back safely, correct?" Sintra said quickly, and held the final golden key out to me.

I mashed my teeth together, wanting nothing more than to take a chunk of marble out of them. I wished I had something, anything to bash in their face. I wanted to see them ground into dust and scattered in all directions. But I would keep my promises to B and Lily.

I yanked the key from their hand.

I strode over to our packs and searched with shaking hands until I found the other five keys and added them to the sixth from this last, horrific tribulation in my palm. As I did, I heard a disjointed screech and looked to see a golden door had appeared to Sintra's left. It looked like an ordinary door except for the six locks on it and its gleaming intensity. It hurt to look at it.

"Place the keys in their locks and the door will open to take you back to the Before," Sintra explained.

I turned to where Rain was standing. "You get to go home, Rain. You get to go back to your family," and managed to just cry as I said it and not howl with grief.

Once more he ran to me and threw his arms around me. "Not without you, Eight! I need you! Can you come with me? *Please*?!" he cried.

"Only one can pass through at a time, child," Sintra said quietly.

Rain ignored them. "I can't do this without you, Eight! You *promised* me! Until the end!"

I pulled his arms from around my waist, my heart anguished. "Rain, listen to me. I will always be with you, right here," I said as I tapped his chest where his heart beat. "Don will be with you, and Harley, and Lily...and B. We are all going to be with you forever. And we'll meet again, I know we will. But there are people, your family, who love you and miss you and are waiting for you to return to them. You are so brave, Rain. I know you can do this."

I kissed him on the forehead and walked over to the golden door. I didn't want to let Rain go, but B's sacrifice couldn't be for nothing. My hands were still shaking but I managed to get a key into each lock.

The door flung open to reveal a golden mist thick enough I couldn't see through it. My hair began to drift around my face, as if a breeze blew through the door.

I returned to Rain's side. "Are you ready to go through?"

He shook his head fiercely, his small hands twisting into my shirt. "No, Eight, I don't want to! I'm afraid!"

With a lump in my throat, I nodded and stroked his soft curls. "It's okay to be scared, Rain. I'm scared too," I admitted. "I'll be right here, though. I'll watch you every step of the way."

He stared at the ground, not moving.

"Rain, look at me. Look at me, please." I put my hand under his chin and tilted his face up to mine. "It is time for you to go home."

He stared, searching my face while tears streaked down his. Then in a heavy, resigned voice he whispered, "Okay..."

I turned him around by the shoulders towards the door. I placed a hand against his back and pushed gently. "Don't look back, Rain. No matter how much you want to, don't look back, just keep walking."

I could see his body shaking as he took his first tentative step.

"Now repeat after me. Thank you, fear," I said, my voice thick with tears.

"Thank you, fear," he echoed, his voice hitched with emotion.

"For caring about me," I recited. He took another step.

"For caring about me."

"For protecting me," I continued. He was just two steps away from the door when I saw him hesitate.

"Say it, Rain. Don't look back," I ordered in a voice made steady by sheer will. I pulled my hair out of my face, not wanting to miss the last time I'd get to look at him.

"For protecting me," he cried and stepped forward.

"For keeping me alive," I finished.

He paused on the last step, his shoulders shaking with emotion. I saw his little head turn to the side, as if he was going to look at me one last time but then he caught himself, remembering his promise, and said, "for keeping me alive" as he stepped into the open doorway.

And then he was gone.

I stared at the door, sobbing and bereft. I was alone, everyone I cared about gone. All but Rain taken by the Between and the savage tribulations we had faced. *Who was I without them?*

I became aware of Sintra standing next to me and was suffused with such fury that for a moment I didn't even care about getting back to the Before. All I wanted was to break Sintra as they had tried to break me countless times.

I lunged for them, ready to use my nails like claws, ready to break my teeth on their marble form if it meant I could inflict some pain, if it meant they would suffer even a fraction of what I had suffered.

But before I could, Sintra's cold hands caught me around the throat and they held me at arms' length. I grabbed at them, trying to pull them away from my tightening airway. I didn't care if I died, but I did care if I died before I could hurt Sintra.

They pulled me close until our faces were just a few inches apart and I saw resentment set in their stone features.

"You should have died, mortal. *You.* I will never understand why he coveted you, protected you, *loved you,*" they seethed. Shaking me like a ragdoll, they continued. "Regardless, an exchange was made. You get to go back to your pathetic life. You get to see if you can make anything useful out of it, but know one thing...You do not deserve the second chance you are getting.

"Now, stop wasting effort on trying to harm me. Leave this place. See if you can make his sacrifice worth it," they snarled.

With a last look of contempt, they threw me backwards with such force I tumbled through the golden door.

Chapter Thirty-One

Around me, all was black. I floated, my mind and body separated from each other so that I felt composed of the nothingness surrounding me.

"Come back."

Distantly, I heard a man's voice. It sounded familiar, but I couldn't place it. I kept floating.

Then I heard voices raised in excitement— *"I think she's waking up. I think she's coming back!"*—and mechanical beeps over the sound of a woman crying.

"That's it, you're almost there."

Suddenly, my throat was on fire and it felt like my chest was burning with each breath I took. Around me everything was still black but a tentative hope flickered to life inside me.

I heard the sound of pacing, shoes squeaking against hard flooring, and voices murmuring.

I pulled in a breath and forced my heavy eyelids open.

"Diana!" a man shouted, and rushed to where I lay in a bed, then grabbed my hand and squeezed it hard. I startled back, not entirely sure what was happening.

"Give her a second, Aspen! You're going to scare her. She just woke up for heaven's sake!" A woman reprimanded the man holding my hand.

I looked around and saw I was in a room. There was a woman with grey hair in a bun standing next to the tall, brunette man who had my hand in his. Memories rushed in. "Aspen? Mom?" I croaked, my throat raw. I reached my free hand toward my mother but felt a slight tug on my arm.

I looked down and saw cords sticking out of me at the same time I realized there was a tube inserted into my nose.

"Am I in a hospital?" I asked, panic tingling through me.

"Yes, Di, you were hit by a car when you went for a run. You've been in a coma. We didn't know if you were going to...*make it*," my brother said, his voice cracking with emotion.

I didn't know what to say. I vaguely remembered going for a run, remembered seeing a crosswalk sign indicating eight seconds and knowing I had time to get across the street safely before the pedestrian light ended.

"I...was...?" I was too confused to articulate the question I wanted to ask.

"You've been here for a while, Di. You almost died on us a few times," Aspen choked out. "We didn't know if you'd pull through. They had to give you compressions and once you almost drowned in your own saliva. They kept trying to suction it, but it was like you were underwater. It kept coming and we thought..." he trailed off.

I must've looked horrified by this news because Mom grabbed Aspen's arm tightly. "Stop, Aspen. She needs time. Stop dumping all this on her right now."

I closed my eyes, trying to take it all in, trying to make sense of what they were saying. I must have slipped into sleep when I did because the next time I opened them they were wearing different clothes and Mom was sitting next to me and Aspen stood near the foot of my bed.

"Mom?" I whispered my voice raspy from disuse.

She leaned over and brushed my hair back from my face, looking at me tenderly through her tears. "Oh my girl, you're awake. The doctors said to let you sleep, how do you feel?"

Blinking myself more awake, I sat up against some pillows. "Um, a little disoriented, I think. I'm in the hospital, right? I was in a coma?"

She picked up one of my hands and held it between hers. "That's right, but the doctor said you're well on the road to recovery now that you're awake." She paused and I saw tears in her eyes. "I've missed you so much, honey. Can I hug you, please?"

I nodded. "Of course, Mom," I said and was enveloped in her familiar scent, like flowers in spring, as she carefully put her arms around me.

A painful sob bubbled up through me as it hit me that I felt safe.

She looked at me, wiping tears off my cheeks even though hers were falling equally as hard.

"I love you," she said with a smile made all the more beautiful considering she must have been driving herself sick with worry if I had almost died a couple of times.

"I love you too," I replied, grabbing her hand with my good one—my other arm was in a cast. I looked up at Aspen and said, "I love you both."

Just then a nurse passed by the room's open doorway. When I turned to watch her, my gaze fell on a distraught man with salt and pepper hair in the corner of my room. *My father.*

I could feel my face fall.

"Dad..."

"Diana," was all he said at first as he stood. Dark bags pillowed under his eyes providing visual evidence of his worry.

"I...I'm so sorry, kiddo," he said.

Mom pulled her head back into her shoulders, looking like she had eaten something sour as Dad stepped closer to my bed. This must have been a fun room while I was out. "I was so scared and I'm just...so sorry," Dad said, his eyes watering.

"For which thing exactly?"

"I'm sorry for hurting you, for losing contact with you, I'm sorry for it all," he said as he maintained a hesitant distance from my bed.

I looked to Mom and Aspen and then back to him. "What about them? I know they didn't almost die like I did, but did you ever apologize to them while I was apparently fighting for my life? Or are your apologies only good for people having near-death experiences?"

I didn't know what had me feeling so angry and testy, but I couldn't bring myself to be kind to him just then. I didn't feel remorse for what he had been through like I did for Mom and Aspen.

"I...I'm sorry though," he tried again.

"Well, thanks, but I think I just want to be with Mom and Aspen right now. Maybe we can talk later," I said.

"But..."

"Leave us, Cane," Mom said sternly as she pointed at the door.

"I...but...Jean..." his voice trailed off.

"*Now*. That wasn't a request," Aspen said for my sake. Clearly they had all had enough of each other from their days spent waiting by my bed.

Maybe Dad and I would patch things up sometime down the road, but at that moment all I wanted was to be with Mom and Aspen. I wanted to hear their voices and wanted to listen to their stories. I wanted all the gossip I missed from my mom's book club, the medical drama from Aspen's work. I wanted to relish the things I had taken for granted before the accident.

After Dad left, they asked what I remembered from being in a coma, if I had heard them talking to me over all the days they had sat vigil in my room. I tried but couldn't recall anything other than the vague memories of my run before the accident that landed me in the hospital. It almost felt like there was a misty dark wall blocking off part of my memory. I only knew that I had been in a dreamless stasis while they had fretted for my survival.

It turned out I had been in intensive care for a month. I was bothered that I had nearly died and had nothing to show for it. I couldn't explain it, but the blank void of the weeks I had lain in my hospital bed felt like unbearably precious time I wanted back but would never get. I felt something similar to grief but had to force myself not to focus on it. Instead, I tried to think about how having another chance was a blessing. I wasn't religious and didn't feel any closer to knowing what happened to us when we died, even if I had almost died, but I would take another chance at life. I would not squander it with the trivial bullshit I had spent my time worrying about before my accident.

I would make it worth it.

Two days after I woke up the second time, I was moved out of the intensive care unit and onto a floor where I didn't need such close monitoring. I was making relatively good progress, according to my medical team and Aspen and they were hoping I'd be released in a week or so.

"Hey, look what I found in the cafeteria for you!" Aspen came in with a wild smile one day, while I stared at the tiny TV screen across from my bed, drooling on my hospital gown from boredom.

"I'm sure it's not as good as other places, but I thought maybe it would perk you up. One of the bakers here made strawberry shortcake today. I know it's your favorite, so I thought I'd snag you a piece," he said with a wink before maneuvering the hospital bed's table to a position in front of me.

They had removed the tube from my nose when I left intensive care, so I could eat on my own. I found food difficult, though, as if my taste buds had been altered by not using them for a month. Everything had a metallic zing to it, probably from whatever medications they were still giving me.

I looked at the strawberry shortcake and felt a churning in my stomach. I probably ate it weekly before my accident. Maybe I had eaten it too much because now I had absolutely no desire to taste the sweet dessert.

"Thanks Aspen, I'm not super hungry, but maybe I'll save it for later," I explained.

"Sure, Di," he said.

A nurse in dusty-rose scrubs walked into the room just then and started checking my vitals on the machine next to my bed. *What a nice color*, I thought.

"Can I help you order any food?" she asked me kindly.

"I can help her, don't worry. The number for room service is on the menu," my brother said politely. *Way too politely for him.*

She nodded briefly and walked back out, her tasks completed.

"Wow, such manners you have magically developed," I said with a wink at him. It was either that or he was hitting on her; it could go either way with him.

Aspen sighed, rubbing a hand down his face.

"I wasn't exactly...well-liked by the staff in the ICU when you were there," he mumbled.

I smirked at him. "I couldn't imagine why."

He looked out the window for a second before turning his gaze back to me, his face flushing red. "Apparently a bunch of nurses went out of their way to avoid being assigned to you while on shift because of me," he admitted.

"Aspen!" I slapped his arm with my good one, my mouth hanging open in shock.

"Look, I know! I couldn't help it! Sometimes your doctor made stupid decisions and I couldn't keep my mouth shut!" He rolled his eyes at himself.

I didn't stop the laughter that burbled out of me.

Aspen grinned. "Anything for you, little sis."

I shook my head, smiling at him. I felt so much love from my little family. I knew that things were rocky at the moment, that I had a lot of recovery ahead of me that I couldn't avoid, but I still felt thankful.

I laid back in bed, sighing. I watched the TV absentmindedly, appreciating the people that I was lucky enough to have in my life.

I fell asleep after a while. I had warm dreams of love and family. Dreams of reuniting with Aspen, Mom, and even Dad, and making soft wishes in a field of dandelions to always remain together. Until the end.

Chapter Thirty-Two

Three months later

I sat on a park bench, appreciating a slow moment before the start of a hectic day at my new job. After long days spent on applications, interview coaching from Mom and Aspen, a professional spruce-up of my réumé courtesy of my brother's wallet, I was now a curatorial assistant at a local museum. I had given Hayley my notice just after I was released from the hospital and I'd been pleasantly surprised by how understanding she was about my leaving.

My life had nearly come to an end and, with the gift of hindsight, I realized how discontented I had been with it before the accident. I was putting myself first now, reprioritizing and organizing my life. Some day in the future, when I was an old woman, I wanted to be able to look back at this second life and know I had made something of it.

I looked down at the news article I was reading on my phone. Some company that used to work with Miles Sharpe was auctioning off his microphones, trying to raise funds to support a cure for childhood cancer. Apparently Miles had been very actively involved in the pediatric cancer community. He had visited children's hospitals regularly when he toured in a new city and directed a steady stream of money to fund cancer research.

A waste of a human.

That's what I had thought about him before my accident. I had been annoyed that I had to coordinate his meetup with Hayley for some cooking promo.

I could be such an absolute asshole sometimes. I had no idea this artist had such a propensity for charity. But even if he hadn't, why had I felt the need to judge someone I didn't know the first thing about? Someone out there was heartbroken, someone who knew him, not as a celebrity, but as a person.

His fans mourned for weeks when his passing was announced. He'd been out at a restaurant with friends, celebrating his thirty-sixth birthday when he'd gone into anaphylactic shock because fish sauce had accidentally been used in his meal. Miles had been in intensive care for weeks, ultimately dying a month after the incident.

He'd only been four years older than me.

"That's so sad," I said out loud before I could stop myself, not remembering I was in public and sharing a bench with a stranger.

"Hmm?" the woman next to me questioned as she turned away from watching a few children playing on the grass in front of us.

"Oh, sorry, I was just reading something about that Miles Sharpe artist. Apparently he did a lot of charity work when he was alive. I just didn't realize," I explained while watching the kids try to bounce an inflatable ball off each other.

The woman looked at me, her brown curls bobbing around her face.

"Very sad, yes," she said and then paused. "My son likes his music. It's all he's been listening to lately, he says—" she stopped and cleared her throat.

"He says what?" I asked, instantly curious for some reason.

She shook her head and took a deep breath. "He says it makes him feel less alone. His, Miles', music, that is. I think it must be because he's just been through a lot and this person has been on the news non-stop. He must feel some type of connection to him. I don't know..." She breathed out a long exhale. "He just seems more at ease when his music is on."

I nodded. "I can see that. He had a great voice," I said. "I like to listen to his music too when I need comfort." I didn't tell her the extent to which I had been listening to Miles Sharpe lately, and didn't feel like getting into the details of the past several months. But I had often turned to his songs when I felt all the messy emotions—anger, sadness, resentment—during my recovery. There was something about listening to his music that felt meaningful. Maybe I felt connected to it because we had been in a coma at the same time, both of us adrift in darkness. For a reason I didn't fully understand, Miles' music—his voice—spoke to a deeper part of me and softened my anxious thoughts.

I had never met Miles, but I could understand why her son felt soothed by him because I did too.

The woman offered me a soft smile, then grew more serious. "My son almost died a few months ago. He had leukemia as a child and we thought it was gone. I was going to bed one night and checked on him before turning the hall lights off and found he wasn't breathing. I rushed him to the hospital where they told me he was no longer in remission." A tear slipped down her face. "He was on machines and unresponsive for a month, but then he came back. My baby," her voice cracked, "he came back to me and now he's cleared again. My baby is in remission again."

A tear slipped down my own face. "Can I hug you?"

Surprised, she paused for a moment but then nodded and turned toward me so that I could embrace her, a stranger who had been through something earth-shattering.

She leaned back, breaking the hug. "I'm so sorry," she said, vigorously wiping away her tears. "I don't usually cry like this, it's just been...hard.

I'm not the same anymore and neither is he." She lifted her chin towards a boy who stood about fifty feet from us.

I could see he was pale and gaunt, and had patchy brown hair standing up around his head.

"It's usually curly like mine, but it's just starting to grow back in. Drives him crazy how spikey it is." She waved to him.

I smiled between them both. "You look so much alike."

The boy waved to his mother then turned his doe eyes to me. He scrunched his face up, confusion clouding his expression before he looked questioningly back at his mom.

"Thank you." Her eyes glistened as she talked. "He'll always be my baby, even though he hates when I call him that. He thinks he's too grown up to be called a *baby*." She shrugged and was pensive for a moment.

"I don't think a child will ever get tired of hearing how much you love them, how much you care about them. Keep telling him that, keep showing how much you love him because there are plenty of parents who don't and leave a wound behind," I said quietly, allowing the realization I had made in therapy to surface to this stranger.

She looked at me, her soft features not showing pity for me, but sadness. "You're right, thanks for the advice."

I nodded reassuringly, thankful she didn't probe me for more. Even though I had so much to get through, so much to learn about myself still, I was slowly piecing together who I was and why it had felt so natural to push people away before my accident. I knew my missed connection with my father was a root cause of it, but the anxiety of almost dying meant rummaging through my past traumas had become unavoidable. I was constantly plagued with nightmares of drowning, being on fire, covered in insects, or falling off a cliff. Most nights I woke up gasping, but my therapist assured me this was a normal way to process my near-death experience and with the right tools, I could overcome them.

I also had dreams in which I could see no faces, but was surrounded by a family. Not my actual family, but one that felt almost as familiar nonetheless, like there was a connection I was missing out on.

In a way, those dreams haunted me the most, because I realized a month after I woke up that I didn't really have anyone in my life that I felt remotely as close to, other than Mom and Aspen. So not only had I been purposeless before the accident, but also friendless.

I realized more than anything that I didn't just need to find meaning, but I also craved companionship. Some forged bond to help me get through the dark and difficult parts of life. Someone, or someones, I could lean on when life was hard, but who could also lean on me when they were mucking through the shit in life.

"I think God or an angel was protecting him, making sure he came home to me," the woman on the bench whispered softly, jolting me from my own thoughts.

I grabbed her hand and gave it a squeeze. Another tear streaked down my face, over my cheek and off my jaw, kissing the skin on my wrist when it landed.

"Someone must have been," I said in agreement, letting go of her hand. "But he's lucky to have you looking out for him as a mother."

She smiled at me. "Thank you for listening to a stranger ramble about her kid."

"Anytime. What you're going through is difficult. I'm told it only helps to talk about it."

She laughed softly. "Well, if you ever want your turn, let me know. I owe you one."

"I might actually take you up on that. Maybe we could grab coffee sometime?" I offered tentatively.

"I'd love that," she said, digging her phone out of her pocket.

After we exchanged numbers and I said my goodbye, I looked down at my first possible new friend's contact. *Ruth.*

I felt my lips quirk up as I walked away from the park. I let a feeling of immense gratitude wash over me. I was thankful, for me, for the boy in the park I didn't know, for Ruth who got him back, for all of it. Somehow, we were all lucky enough to get another chance.

Epilogue

An old woman found herself in a place that was both familiar and foreign. The air around her had a thick purple hue to it, which brought forward a maelstrom of feelings—devastation, hope, loss, but also enduring love.

The woman's face was wrinkled, the passage of time written on her skin. What couldn't be seen on her skin was the sense of peace, of readiness, she felt permeated her. She was prepared to pass into whatever was next knowing she had accomplished everything she had set out to do in her life. She was ready to discover what came next after her mortal experience.

She hadn't been prepared to be greeted by a stone statue that smiled at her tentatively. Golden cracks running across the statue's skin gleamed familiarly, even as the statue looked...uncomfortable...with the old woman's presence.

Now memories flooded the woman's mind and she noted that the statue looked exactly as they had the last time they met, although they no longer wore the indigo robes she recalled from before. Now, they wore a shimmering gold fabric that drew out the amber etchings in their skin and the honey color of their eyes.

"Hello, Eight," they spoke carefully, offering a slight smile.

The old woman didn't smile, just peered at the marble statue she hadn't seen for a lifetime. The ire of her youth had faded remarkably, her readiness to move to a new beginning making this moment bittersweet.

"Sintra," she said. "I see you changed your outfit."

Sintra looked her up and down. The woman's hands rose to touch the wrinkles on her face self-consciously in response.

"It has been awhile, mortal," they said. "And many things have changed about me since we last met," they stated cryptically. Then, almost as an afterthought they added, "you can choose which age you'd like to appear in your next home, do not fret."

The old woman stared, trying to reconcile this...pleasant...Sintra with the one she now remembered fully.

"Are you ready?" Sintra held out a hand to her.

She waited a moment as more memories emerged, some awful, some beautiful.

A question burned through her and she couldn't resist asking. "Why didn't you want me to have a second chance?"

Sintra looked thoughtful for a moment. "You had everything I wanted and could never have."

The answer was simple and too difficult for the woman to wrap her mind around. "That's *it*? Why you constantly had it out for me...you were *jealous*?"

Sintra's face was open and honest in a way the woman had not seen before. "Love without condition is *everything* and knowing that desiring it seems so simple to you is proof enough that you have never felt what it is like to desperately try to earn someone's affection. To want someone to love you entirely and completely for *you*, not to love you for the purpose of fulfilling an agenda."

Almost imperceptibly, the woman's heart squeezed in pity for Sintra. For a moment.

But then she took Sintra's still-outstretched hand, looked into their eyes and said more for her own benefit than for theirs, "I did do it, you know. I made it worth it."

A genuine smile lit Sintra's face. "Good, Diana. Now, shall we go? There's someone who's been waiting a long time to see you."

The woman smiled as a last memory bloomed in her mind and everything erupted into a brilliant, gold light.

Acknowledgements

Between was a rollercoaster of emotions for me as a first-time writer. I wish I could say I went into it with a definite plan for each chapter, but it didn't end up happening that way. Most nights I sat at my computer trying to fit in as many hours of writing as I possibly could while letting whatever I was feeling in the moment flow out. I found it extremely difficult to put my computer away and try to get some sleep before work the next day. I couldn't wait until weekends when I could type away, unrestrained for hours on end. I absolutely fell in love with my characters and I would laugh with them, feel their anxiety, and cry when one of them died. Regardless, I kept going though puffy eyes and a tear-stained keyboard.

I'm so thankful for my family, especially my mom Nola, my dad Scott, family friend Debbie, and my aunt Jan, who kept me actively engaged in the writing process and read every chapter immediately after I finished it. Their feedback, encouragement, and reactions were instrumental in keeping the story going for me. I would also like to thank my sister Andrea, who read and helped me complete some initial edits of *Between*, gave crucial feedback that enhanced character arcs, and helped me stay active on social media. I'm appreciative of my sister Tiffany for giving me feedback and taking time to read my book regardless of her busy hours at work and her first pregnancy. A huge thanks to my husband, Luke, whom I love and appreciate for helping me dream about writing a book, encouraging me to finish once I started, and sharing ideas that strengthened the plot. Also, thank you for literally letting me take one of your recurring nightmares and turn it into a tribulation. I apologize for making it worse by adding a hydra.

I'm also so very thankful to Christene, my editor at CSK Editing Services, for polishing my novel and taking it to the next level. I appreciate all the hours and love you poured into my book. There's absolutely no way I could've made it this far without you! I owe you dinner—but also have you in mind for a BMW if I ever win the lottery.

Another huge thanks to my friends Madigan, Bianca, Annie, Jared, and Carrie for being my first few test readers outside of my family.

I want to extend another thanks to J.E Larson of the *Valdor Series*, a fellow author from Alaska, for being willing to answer all my questions about the process of writing a book. I cannot thank you enough, J.E Larson! Your patience and willingness to lend a hand to a stranger was incredibly kind. I encourage anyone reading this to pick up her series and show it some well-deserved love too if you haven't already.

Writing a book was an enormous undertaking and completely humbling. I have only ever been on the reading side, but this idea came to me a decade ago in college. I dismissed it, figuring I'd never be able to string together enough details to write a whole book. I was also extremely worried about pacing a story too slowly or too quickly. I'm not under any delusion that I did it perfectly, but at the end of the day, I'm proud. I absolutely lived and breathed this book and I still can't believe I finished it. Maybe one day I'll wrap my mind around it fully!

Within the content of this book, a triggering topic of discussion is domestic violence. This is unfortunately common throughout the world, and where I live in Alaska, domestic violence is a public health crisis. According to the Alaska Judicial Council in 2020, 48% of women experienced intimate partner violence in their lifetime. Additionally, the indigenous population—the heart of our country—is disproportionately affected by domestic violence. According to the National Institute of Justice Journal in 2016, 84.3% of Alaskan Native and American Indian women experienced any amount of violence in their lifetime, while 55.5% experienced physical violence by an intimate partner. That means a devastating four out of every five American Indian or Alaskan Native women have experienced violence to any degree and over half have experienced partnership violence. The horrific experience and outcomes of interpartner violence is what I wanted to call attention to through Lily's story.

If you or anyone you know is experiencing domestic violence, please contact help at 1(800)799-7233. Also, there are many local women and children's shelters available throughout the U.S. In the Anchorage area, The Clare House, AWAIC, and others have helped a lot of women find safe places for themselves, family members, friends, or children.

If you are questioning whether you are in a physically, emotionally, or mentally abusive relationship, please confide in someone you trust or call the hotline. Do not let anyone dull your light because I promise you, *you* are worth it.

About the Author

Photo by: Mary Lila Webb

Cayenne Sirois is new to writing, but very much enjoys the craft. She's an avid reader of science fiction, fantasy, and romance of all types. Outside of writing, she works as a clinical dietitian and specializes in neonatal intensive care. She's a huge tea drinker, loves cats and dogs equally, and dreams of adventure and travel when she's not working. She currently lives in Anchorage, Alaska, but her first true home was Tucson, Arizona. She moved to Alaska shortly after graduating from the University of Arizona with a degree in dietetics and nutrition. Also, if you were wondering, yes—she was named after the pepper.